Graham P

CERBERUS

A WORLD GONE TO THE DOGS

AUSTIN MACAULEY PUBLISHERS™

LONDON • CAMBRIDGE • NEW YORK • SHARJAH

A CIP catalogue record for this title is available from the British Library.

ISBN 9781035835140 (Paperback)
ISBN 9781035835157 (ePub e-book)

www.austinmacauley.co.uk

First Published 2024
Austin Macauley Publishers Ltd®
1 Canada Square
Canary Wharf
London
E14 5AA

Graham Pryor studied American Studies and English at the University of Hull. Subsequently, he pursued a career in information management, leaving his childhood home in Hythe, Kent, for the north-east of Scotland, where he has lived and worked for the past forty years. *Cerberus* is his fifteenth novel and, he says, his favourite.

Hi Pamela
If you don't enjoy this book, Monty will want to know why!

To PETA, HSI and every other organisation that strives to ameliorate the consequences for animals of sharing this planet with humans.

Graham

Dogs are best.

Thanks to Austin Macauley for their continued confidence in my writing.

Table of Contents

"Dogs do speak, but only to those who know how to listen."

Orhan Pamuk, author.

"As long as there are human beings about, there is never going to be any peace for any individual upon this earth (or anywhere else they might escape to)."

Charles Bukowski, author.

Part 1
Awakening

1. The Grey Man

Clover stopped suddenly, fully arrested by her thoughts, the wind-blown sand taking the opportunity to wind slithering coils around her legs. "Hey," she exclaimed, "look at what we're doing. We're taking ourselves for a walk." She turned and looked back along the deserted beach, seeing how far they'd come, even while the whorls of sand were quickly eradicating the steps she and her companion had left behind. That they were alone and free had hit her for probably the first time, the emptiness of the long beach reminding her of the space they had put between themselves and their previous existence.

The long-legged Airedale terrier stared at her with an air of mild condescension. "But we are creatures of habit, you know that. And it will take time to get used to being without restraint, to set our own routines." He shook sand from his nose. "Just enjoy it, Clover. Doesn't it feel good to be free of the leash?" Monty shook himself again and took off in a wild rush of pleasure, his stiff tail upright and his head high, dashing in a circle around his friend and sending the loose sand flying in drifts, until his head whirled and his long tongue hung loose from his mouth. Exhilaration!

When he was ready, they plodded on again in silence, but Monty was aware that Clover's silence was a busy one. "What is it?" he asked at last, his words thick and sibilant in his untrained throat.

She was fretting about the cockapoos. "I don't think they'll ever come around," she whined. "They so miss being petted, it's like it's in their DNA. You heard them, Monty, they said it's not natural to be independent of humans."

"That's exactly the trouble with cockapoos," observed Monty. "They aren't natural. They've been synthesised, an unnatural splicing of breeds to meet human requirements. Every wolf gene cut out. I can't stand 'em, ingratiating little buggers, they've got the please disease."

"So what should we do about them?"

"Leave them be. Natural selection will deal with the problem. Anyway, we've bigger conundrums to deal with than the reluctant cockapoos."

"We have?" He had Clover's full attention. She had sensed all morning that he had been struggling with a big question, but she hadn't dared to ask.

"What is really bothering me," he said after a long pause, during which he meticulously licked grains of sand from his nose, "what seems to me to be the thing we should properly understand in all this strange business, is why the grey man has done it in the first place."

"It being the…"

"The emancipation, of course. Us, being able to speak like this, given control over ourselves, the ability to speculate and be responsible for our freedom, having no masters or mistresses, no insistence on obedience, no slavish subservience to their rules."

16

"You make that last bit sound so terrible, Monty. But I quite liked being petted, and having a good vigorous brush when my fur got itchy. Now, that was a delight."

"But it was for their benefit, Clover. You were their toy."

"If you say so."

"I know it's not easy, but you'll adapt. Adaptation comes naturally to us; we've been doing it for thousands of years."

"It seems to me that that's what the grey man has done to us, only far more rapidly." Clover stopped momentarily to examine the skeleton of a gull, her train of thought only suspended while she analysed the scent it held. "We're a bit like the cockapoos, actually. He has deliberately adapted the way we are."

"That's what I was saying," replied Monty. "But what was his purpose in making us more conscious?" It was a question he could not fathom. The grey man had explained only that he was here to perform an extinction, the eradication of the human species.

There was, of course, not just one grey man but several thousand, and Monty and Clover had unknowingly encountered a number of them, but always individually, leaving them to believe they were all one and the same. When looking back at their first encounter, the day when everything changed, the dogs remembered only words and gestures and nothing of the technology that had been applied to them, for at that time it was beyond their comprehension. But as they awoke from tumultuous dreams to find they had been gifted speech and logic, their sense of wonder for a while banished all critical thought, and they behaved with typical canine expediency, responding to the alien with grateful eyes and wagging tails. It was only later, when the seed of logic matured in their hot-wired brains, that they demanded their emancipator explain what really had happened, and what had been done to them.

"But it was never properly explained," growled Monty. "Whether it was going to be just us, the canids, or if other species were to be awakened, as the grey man called it. All we heard about was what he had in mind for the human population. It sounded frighteningly cold-blooded too. I don't know if that was deliberate, so that we didn't get all sentimental about them—you know, spell it out from the start; but it worked for me. How about you, Clover?"

"I found it too fantastic to believe," she replied. "They were so powerful, our human companions. I mean, we could show our teeth and snarl to express our opposition to something they wanted from us, but it was rare that we could overcome an adult human entirely. They had weapons, and because they had the opposing finger and thumb thingy I would always feel at a disadvantage. Baz, my police dog friend, even he admitted to feeling at a handicap. He could bring someone down, but if they had a knife or a gun, the outcome was never guaranteed to go in his favour. Then there were the subtle ways they had to maintain control; the withholding of meals if we misbehaved, being shut in the garden when it was raining, or chained to a dog kennel for punishment. The whole culture we lived in was characterised by the human dominance of all life-forms on the planet."

"There you go," snapped Monty. "You've just admitted it, you were their toy, their plaything. You've described the way it was to a T."

Clover growled with irritation. "All right, yet they could be benevolent—not always, I admit, but at least in my home with my last owner. I know he loved me."

"I'm not going to argue with you. The Labrador in you is still too full of empathy. Thank Shuck your collie half has seized this new way of being, otherwise I might have to give you a regular rousting."

"Stop!"

"Look, I didn't—"

"No, I mean wait. And quiet. There are humans up ahead. See, there in the dunes. I thought I heard voices a way back."

Monty flattened himself to the sand and lowered his tail. Clover too stretched out, her nose on her paws and her ears drawn close to her head. She might be a cross, but her ways of stealth were all collie.

It was a group of three children playing on the slopes, two boys and what looked to be little more than a toddler. They had found a sheet of rigid plastic in the line of detritus at the high tide line and were using it to take turns sledging down the dunes' sharp gradient to the beach.

"They haven't noticed us," whispered Monty. "More importantly, they haven't heard us. Let's just get up and wander over to the marram banks where they won't see us getting away. But in any case, if they do spot us, there's nothing odd about seeing a couple of dogs on the beach."

"We can't just leave," argued Clover, whose senses were keener than Monty's. "Can't you hear it, that painful bleating noise? Someone over there needs help."

Monty cocked his head to one side and listened. After a while, he coughed and agreed, "Sounds like a damned cockapoo. A young 'un by the silly racket it's making. We'll have to go over and read them kids the riot act."

"Really? But I thought you said we shouldn't expose ourselves, I mean our new faculties, to humans. At least, not until we know there are more of us than them."

"Come on," said Monty, "I'm not that daft."

The pair of dogs trotted up the beach, quite nonchalantly, as if they were intent on discovering choice things to nibble amongst the seaweed and plastic rubbish which had been deposited onshore by the eternal waves. Finding a decomposing gannet carcass, Monty emphasised his indifference to what was going on nearby by lifting his leg and anointing the deceased bird with a hot yellow jet of pee.

"I wish I could do that," complained Clover.

"Silly bitch," snorted Monty, "you're not going to start all that gender nonsense are you, like the humans?"

The puppy that could now be very clearly heard had a string tied around its neck, and was being dragged behind the makeshift sledge at speed, as it hurtled down the dune face. Its little legs were a blur and at midpoint it tumbled, to be dragged the rest of the way on its back. When it refused to stand and climb back up the slope, it was given a hearty whack with a kelp stalk, which made it even more reluctant to comply.

"What did I tell you?" whispered Monty. "And you talk of benevolence." He stood up tall on his paws, he was tall for his breed anyway, and sprang through the marram clumps, surprising the children who were busying arguing over whose turn it was next to ride the sledge.

"Ooh," chirruped the toddler, its face alight with glee, "a doggie."

"Quick," said the oldest child, pointing at Monty, "grab it. We can get it to pull the sledge." He then noticed Clover creeping low to the ground. "There's another! With two of them pulling we can all get a ride home." He made a lunge for Monty, who sidestepped out of reach.

Clover, her collie persona fully to the fore, rushed forward and nipped the boy sharply on his ankle, making him scream and collapse onto the sand. "Fucking thing," he yelled, grasping handfuls of sand, which he flung, uselessly, at the two dogs. He still had the string that secured the puppy wound around his wrist, causing it to mewl and squeak from increased strangulation as the string was jerked. But the other boy and the toddler just stood and laughed at their friend's pain and, when he heard, a fight ensued between all three, an interval in which Monty ran forward to bite through the string and free the infant cockapoo.

It was not so easily done and the boy raised his fist at Monty, reaching out with his other hand to grab the puppy. That was the moment for Clover to deploy her disparaged teeth-and-gums tactic, and she crouched ready to spring at the child, her entire array of fangs bared and her bright pink gums exposed as she emitted a fearsome growl. Instantly, the boy dropped the puppy and stepped back, allowing Monty to sever the string and pull his new charge away, only to see the second boy creeping toward Clover, brandishing a long stick.

Monty barked to warn her and she turned to dodge the blow that fell, clipping her rear. Enraged, Clover now spun at the boy with a roar, in her anger shouting out, "Hit me again and I'll rip your throat out!"

Whether it was her threat or simply the surprise of hearing a dog talk, the effect was immediate, all three children rushing away over the dune's edge and down to the beach, wailing in terror.

With the rescued puppy doing its best to keep up, the two friends took the trail along the top of the dunes, aiming to cross the narrow moorland track that would take them home.

"Imagine," remarked Monty, "those kids when they grow up. What beasts they'll be."

"They won't," Clover said firmly.

"Oh, come on. Surely you don't…"

"No. Look down there." Clover pointed with her snout.

Down on the beach the three children stood unmoving in the late afternoon gloaming, their arms linking them together, watching transfixed while the tall grey man approached them with a steady step. He carried a long pole with what at that distance resembled an old-fashioned lantern at its tip. As he drew close to the trio the lamp brightened, enveloping them in its glow. Then suddenly and silently the light was extinguished, leaving only the grey man standing motionless on the sand.

2. Community

"I don't really want to go into the house anymore," confided Clover. "It feels alien, somehow. Funny that, I thought I was so happy there before."

"Well, no-one's making you," growled Monty.

"But I cannot sleep without my squeaker."

"Is the door locked?"

"Well, it wasn't, because my master lay there after the…the…"

"Yes, all right. I'll go in. Where did you leave it?"

There was no sign of her master's corpse, only a shallow deposit of orange dust on the doormat and a smell like scorched metal. At least, that's how Monty would have described it, and he'd been a blacksmith's dog, so he should know.

"Once we've completed your precious retrieval we must get shot of this little bugger," said Monty. "I don't want him dribbling on me all night when we bed down. Besides, he hasn't been awakened yet, he'll latch on to us as his masters." Nonetheless, the gruff Airedale nuzzled the puppy and gently licked its nose. "I suppose it'll be hungry. There's some of that rabbit left in the barn. But first, let me go and find your squeaker."

Monty climbed over the step into the kitchen and disappeared, silently muttering, "Bloody squeaker, what a wuss."

Clover's master had lived alone and the house had always seemed unnaturally quiet to Monty, whose owner the blacksmith lived perpetually in a world of loud noise and heat. The solitary man had always welcomed Monty's visits, however, and provided him with water to drink on a warm day. There was a bowl of water on the kitchen floor now and he lapped at it gratefully, shuddering when he found he'd taken up a drowned moth on his tongue.

Up the carpeted stairs, having failed to find Clover's plaything in the living areas, his tread silent as he climbed, Monty was reassured by the familiar silence. There were no renegade dogs in the house, he was sure, not even the local lunatic. He knew very well the scent of mad Red, the setter who'd gone crazy after being awakened and tried to force himself on every bitch, in heat or not, that lived in the village. The last Monty had heard was that Red had been given a beating by the boxer twins two streets away, and subsequently made himself scarce. He felt sorry for Red, despite his ugly behaviour; the poor creature had never been allowed to run off-lead. It was no wonder he went nuts when given his freedom. Yet Monty also harboured a strain of jealousy that tempered his sympathy. Red was an entire male, while Monty had long ago lost his wherewithal to the vet's scalpel. *Fat chance I could ever run amuck,* he grumbled to himself.

Then Monty heard a soft ticking noise. Surely that couldn't be the red setter, not here, not hiding away in Clover's house. She'd always spurned his attentions and repelled him with a vicious enthusiasm. No, Red would always hurry past this house. Then he heard the voices; he counted the presence of three individuals in the main bedroom, speaking in a tongue that was unfamiliar to him. He crept along the landing, reaching the bedroom door just as a long grey foot stepped through it. Monty froze, hearing a torrent of alien syllables flung at him. The voice sounded irritated, but the grey man always sounded like that, it was just his way.

Then the grey man touched a metal rod to the space between Monty's shoulders and instantly he heard a voice reassuring him. He heard but did not hear, not aurally at least, words developing in his head rather than entering through his ears. "Stay calm, we mean you no harm. Are you lost, or seeking shelter?"

Monty shook his head and the image of Clover's squeaker, the green rubber bone that she loved to play with, entered his thoughts.

"You seek this?" A second grey man came to the doorway, making Monty flinch. He had the squeaker in his hand, and in the other was a shiny device comprising five silver balls joined by a cat's cradle of spines. He pressed the device against the squeaker and it emitted a series of clicks. "What is this?" asked the first man, the words resolving in his brain, as before. "We cannot define it."

"It's a toy," answered Monty.

All three grey men in the room started speaking rapidly at that, and Monty heard through the metal rod the first man declaring in a sceptical tone that the concept of toy would require further analysis.

"Don't worry," interjected Monty. "It is a harmless plaything." He leant forward and took the squeaker in his mouth, crushing it with his teeth so that the embedded whistle gave a shrill squeal. Instantly, the three grey men leapt over the bed and pressed themselves against the far wall. "Hey," called out Monty, suppressing a chuckle, "it won't hurt you." But of course, without the rod on his back they could not understand him.

The three grey men watched him for a long breath until he dropped the squeaker and, seeing it inert, they stepped out from the wall. The first grey man touched the rod to the space between Monty's shoulders once more and asked, "Is this what you came for?" He prodded gingerly at the squeaker with his toe. "Is that all you want?"

"It's what I was seeking," agreed Monty. "But while I'm here, there is something else."

The grey man put his head on one side in question mode *(like a dog,* thought Monty). "Well," explained Monty, "you have mentioned that you're here to exterminate the humans, but I'm curious why you feel compelled to do what seems to me a terrible thing. Furthermore, and curiouser still, is why have you done this to us, the canids?"

The first grey man sat on the floor, his long sinuous legs angled like those of a grasshopper ready to spring. His mouth moved but, with the rod touching his back, Monty felt the translated words coalesce inside his head. "The answer to your first question is simple. The human race had become too dangerous. We are aware that the means for interstellar flight have been developed here on Earth, almost to the point of application. But we cannot allow this bellicose and destructive species to infect space beyond your own star system, hence our intervention. Our mission has been endorsed by the seventeen cosmic nations; I assure you it is not our decision alone." He referred to the two other grey men, who were seated on the bed, and they nodded agreement.

If a dog can look shocked, Monty may have been the first to show the expression. The grey man barely took breath before continuing.

"In explaining your awakening, I should tell you that we are awakening all of the Canidae, not merely your own species. You must tell me if that is unwelcome."

Hell, thought Monty, shivering. *All the Canidae. Wolves I can take, but foxes, jackals, dingoes, and…and…and…all those others.*

"Is that a problem?" The voice was full of concern.

"I don't know. Let me think about it." Was it a problem? Monty wasn't sure. In fact, there was another matter that now hung its shadow over him.

"You see, we thought the traits we saw were universal. We were encouraged by this." The grey man beckoned to another of the three to pass him a square black box with a screen, which Monty recognised as being similar to one his master had often stared at. The grey man placed his hand across it and the screen flared with light *(Hmm,* noted Monty, *three fingers but no opposing thumb. Yet still an advanced species.*). Monty watched carefully as a short video played. It was an advertisement for a dog rescue organisation. Subtitles were played at the bottom of the screen but Monty, unlike Clover, could not yet read. He could, though, understand the soundtrack, a man's voice explaining that *A dog is the best friend a man could ever have, totally loyal, intelligent and courageous. A selfless, loving companion.* The grey man spoke over the rest of the promotion: "We did further research and confirmed these claims; we also found that you are social

27

creatures, you do not possess such negative inclinations as cruelty or spite, which are found in humans, and that you live harmoniously in packs with a leading pair."

Monty listened proudly, but still unnerved by the man's reference to the Canidae.

"The seventeen were concerned that by eliminating the humans we would leave a hazardous void in Earth's pyramid of fauna, and we were searching for a way to fill it. You are that way. We assumed that the traits we have just seen expressed are owned not just by your species but are common to all the Canidae. However, your reaction suggests otherwise. Please tell me we have not erred; it would be a very significant error and a difficult one to reverse."

"I cannot tell you either way at present," answered Monty, his thoughts in a whirl.

"If you have other questions, we will do our best to answer them. We realise this must feel very strange for you."

Strange? Thought Monty. *It's more than strange.* He shook his head to clear his mind, a powerful shake that travelled down his body all the way to his hind quarters, finishing with a wriggle at the end of his tail. In doing so, he dislodged the grey man's rod and broke the connection between them, so that the grey man did not hear him declare that he had a head full of questions.

What the grey man with the rod heard was a low rumble from Monty's throat, which served only to disconcert him, and he sat back upon the edge of the bed. Taking that to signal their conversation was over, Monty snatched the squeaker from the floor and turned back to the stairs, his descent to the ground floor slow and thoughtful, his mind in a turmoil.

"But Clover, forget the damned squeaker for just a moment." Monty's unease was showing as irritation. "Look, tell me, what does the word Canidae mean to you?"

Clover was still distracted by the return of her toy and only half listened to her friend. "Is it something to do with food? Food comes in cans, we do know that."

Monty sighed. "It has nothing to do with food. But listen, if you had asked me that same question yesterday I might have suggested the same silly answer." Annoyed at his own testiness, he stuck his nose into the box of Markies that Clover had retrieved from a local store, and sat for a while, crunching the biscuits noisily. Then, as if inspired, he said, "The Canidae is the biological family of dogs. Not just dogs like us but all related species, such as wolves, coyotes, foxes and jackals. In fact, there are thirty-four species of canids." He stopped to see if Clover was listening.

"But how do you know all that?" she asked, her eyes wide.

"That's what is bothering me. The grey man—and, by the way, there is more than one grey man—he spoke to me in your house and used the word Canidae, a word I had never heard before. As soon as he said it all knowledge about canids flooded into my brain. It was just like when you bite into one of those cartons on the rack in the store, and the milk floods into your throat, sudden and unstoppable. Only this was knowledge that rushed in."

"Oh vet!" cursed Clover. "That sounds gruesome."

"It was okay," said Monty, "but what I want to know is, was that human knowledge that I gained or has the grey man filled me with his own, alien thoughts—and can they be trusted?" He prodded Clover with his nose. "Like you too," he continued. "How did you know to use the word gruesome so meaningfully just now? Is it something your master would have used repeatedly that stuck in your head? And that's another thing," he growled, "why are we speaking in our masters' language and not the language of the grey men?"

She shook her head and busied herself burying the squeaker in the straw at the back of the barn. "I think we should go and talk to Tiny," she said, having satisfied herself the toy was safely concealed. "Tiny was the first hereabouts to be wakened—and he was given that special tag to hang on his collar." It was a brave proposal by Clover, who had always felt terribly nervous in Tiny's presence, a little discomfited by his wise self-assurance but more seriously unsettled by his age, which she rather unfairly regarded with morbid attention. "There's a certain whiff of the dead about him," she had once remarked to Monty, who had immediately declared her feelings to be nonsense, "a silly collie prescience you need to put to the back of your pretty skull. Tiny is a most congenial fellow."

Tiny was an old great Dane who'd taken up residence in a rickety black fisherman's shed down by the estuary. He'd been there ever since his master passed away, surviving on rabbits caught on the river bank and by scavenging at the back door of the local hotel. At sixteen, he was well past the ten year lifespan that was typical for his breed, and he was revered for it amongst the region's canine community, who regarded him as a sage and a reliable source of advice. But Tiny's notoriety had commenced long before he had many years to his name. As a young dog, two boys had cut off his tail with scissors, a despicable act but not one that was without worse repercussions. For Tiny's friend Joel, a powerful German shepherd dog, or GSD, on seeing the evil perpetrators fleeing

30

their crime, gave chase, tossed one into the river and brought down the second, incautiously tearing out his wicked throat.

For that, poor loyal Joel was summarily despatched to the vet to be euthanised; and locally awarded honours amongst the canine community that were not far short of sanctification. Forever after, whenever the first fiendish boy (who, regrettably, had survived his ducking) found himself unable to avoid walking past a dog, he would be met with bared fangs and a ferocious roar.

It was a disapprobation that he would never escape since, moving to another town, he would find that, through the medium of twilight barking, the nature of his guilt had been passed from dog to dog across the country. Thus was Tiny's name also shared between each canine community, as one who had survived human cruelty and been revenged through the selfless loyalty of another. Subsequently, many a dog suffering at the hands of a human being would curse his tormentor with an imprecation that drew on the authority of the ghost of Joel.

When the two friends reached his shelter on the riverbank, the cockapoo puppy stumbling along behind them, Tiny was gnawing his way through a pack of frozen cooked chicken that he'd thawed in the afternoon sun. "There's something not quite right about it," he warned, tossing them the pack, "but I don't think it's poisoned."

"Oh no," exclaimed Clover, who'd been reading the label on the outside of the pack, "it has been spoiled with what it calls Cajun seasoning. But you're right, it's not exactly poison." She gave Tiny a penetrating stare to check that he had not been upset by the food.

"Ah," muttered Tiny, "my eyes, I didn't see that, my eyes aren't so good in this light."

There was, in fact, no light except for the glimmer from a gibbous moon which, suspended in a cloudless sky, reflected in the still water of the tidal river.

"So," said Tiny enquiringly, "what brings you here, my friends?"

"I think Clover has just given you an example of the question we have brought you," explained Monty. "She said the meat had been spoiled by the addition of Cajun seasoning."

"Indeed," agreed Tiny, bemused.

"But neither you nor I—nor indeed Clover—were confounded by the term Cajun. In fact, I know—Shuck knows how—that Cajun seasoning is a mix of spices and herbs. Now, how is that?"

"That is what we came to ask you," confirmed Clover. "How do we know all these things, and why?"

"You'd do better to ask them," said Tiny, looking up. Across the black sky, tiny crimson darts streaked soundlessly down towards the eastern horizon.

"Shooting stars?" said Monty, incredulously. "I've only recently come to speak a human language. I think talking to stars is a bit beyond me, just yet."

"It's more of them," growled Tiny. "The newcomers. They're going east. There are other lands there that are teeming with homo sapiens. Those red lights in the sky are their reinforcements, arriving in flying craft from farther away than I can imagine."

He stood and shook himself, turned around three times and sat down in the grass at the entrance to his shelter. "Hey," he murmured, "I still enjoy that little ritual, so I'm still dog." Tiny laughed, showing his broken teeth. "But let's sit and talk," he said, "once we've fed the little one you have brought with you."

So while the puppy slurped its way through a tray of salmon and peas terrine the three dogs sat together to—in Tiny's words—"share what we know about the current situation."

"So," began Monty, "I think we all know why the grey men are here—and note I said 'men', for we all now know there are more than one, many more according to Tiny."

"And we all know," picked up Clover, "from Monty's recent encounter, that we, as a species—"

"Family of species," corrected Monty.

"Family of species," continued Clover, grudgingly, "have been selected to take over as the dominant group."

"Most conscious group, I would say," interjected Tiny, "dominant sounds a bit too much like a human expression."

"All that we can agree to know," said Monty, "but it raises further questions. It appears to me that the knowledge we are gaining is human knowledge. I've not experienced otherworldly thoughts entering my head, have you? Is that because we'd find it more easy to understand human than grey man knowledge, or what? But having been given language and the gift of utterance, one has to ask, what was the grey man's purpose? I know I was told it was so that we would fill some kind of gap in the diversity ecosystem, but that only gives a partial answer. What, by Shuck, are we meant to do now?"

"I think I have the beginnings of an answer for you, Monty." Tiny sat up and stretched. "I believe we have been given the human's tongue and knowledge—don't ask me how the grey men took hold of all that knowledge—so that we would be able to understand the humans better and communicate with them with ease, should some of them survive or if they were to return somehow."

"So does that mean the humans are likely to come back?" Clover was torn between anxiety and delight.

"No. They're dead."

"But can come back?"

"We'd have to ask the grey men about that, but I understand extermination to be a matter of some finality."

"My master," said Monty, "used poison to exterminate the rats that infested his forge. He warned me not to touch it. But there were rats again a month or so later. Consequently, he used the exterminate word so vehemently and often that I came to learn its meaning. It doesn't seem to mean final—at least it didn't for rats."

"We'll just have to leave the question of extermination open for now," said Tiny. "But here is my theory: we have been armed—and I do mean armed—with human language and knowledge, so that we can be their equals were there to be any resurgence of homo sapiens, from whatever quarter. In fact, it's my opinion that dogs have been selected to keep the humans from returning, like Cerberus, who stopped the dead escaping from Hades."

"So humans can come back from the dead!" Clover was on her feet, her eyes wide open with fear.

"Cerberus—it's just a story," explained Tiny. "Like the tale of Tiangou, the flying dog who eats the sun."

"So we're the guardians of Earth," growled Monty.

34

"Guardian is a role that we are used to performing." Tiny lay down. "Listen, I'm tired, let's leave any further questions until the morning. You're welcome to curl up here with me."

The cockapoo puppy was already asleep, nestled against Clover, who had curled up with her tail around her, and seemed ready to sleep without the comfort of her squeaker.

"Look there," observed Monty, approvingly. "Now that's a question for tomorrow; what shall we do with the young 'un?"

3. Tiny's Disc

It wasn't only the cockapoo puppy that had not been awakened, and the answer to what should be done with that wee soul was quickly decided over a breakfast of recently caught rabbit and kelp stalks, the latter having been hastily gathered by Monty from the beach. The puppy would best be left, resolved Tiny, with the huddle of grieving cockapoos which had set up home together in a pet goods store, where they derived some level of comfort from being close to the kinds of toys and treats their owners had lavished upon them—not to mention, observed Monty, the large bags of kibble left on the shelves.

But, to repeat, it wasn't just the cockapoo puppy who'd not met the grey man.

The three friends' attention was drawn to other local groups of unawakened canids by the somewhat eldritch and circuitous development that derived initially from the disc that hung at Tiny's collar. I say eldritch with purpose, for Clover, who was of a particularly sensitive nature and already a little agitated by being in Tiny's presence, found the eerie quality of this innocuous-looking device enough to keep her hackles raised for most of the time she was in close proximity to it.

Clover's unease began when Tiny, without warning, appeared to choke on a rabbit bone and sat bolt upright, his mouth open, swallowing hard, his eyes closed and his ears cocked, as if he was fully focused on listening to something the others could not hear. His breathing too had slowed, indicating perhaps that he was concerned the wheezing in his lungs might obscure some secret message he was receiving. Could it be he'd had the call, was Clover's first thought. After all, he was an old dog, well past his natural end, and things had been pretty stressful of late; maybe he'd been told it was his time to go meet with Black Shuck and the spectral hounds of the afterworld.

But there was nothing ailing Tiny, and in a moment or two he yawned, shook his head and relaxed. "Well, that is good news," he announced to his two companions. "From Indonesia. They've freed the outstanding captives from the last remaining dog meat farm."

"And who is Indonesia?" asked Monty. "Is it a he or she? It sounds like an illness."

"Neither," answered Tiny, "it's another land in our world, far in the east, close to where the grey men were flying last night."

"Oh, come on, you're pulling my tail," retorted Monty; "how on earth can you know that?"

"It's the disc he has on his collar," announced Clover. "I heard it just now, a tinny, shivering sort of sound, the sort of noise you might expect an ant to make when speaking. Or a ghost."

Monty was not going to contradict her. He remembered how she had once complained of not being able to sleep because of the sound coming from the electronic pulse in her master's digital watch.

"Clover is correct," confirmed Tiny. "I didn't notice it at first, it was hanging there where I used to have my old home disk; but I think this device was used during my awakening, only the grey man must have forgotten to remove it. From time to time, I receive new knowledge through it; it also lets me know when there are grey men nearby."

"And are there any at the moment?" demanded Monty. "Because if there are there will also be humans, since humans are their business, and humans are a potential threat to us."

"Not presently," answered Tiny, "but there was a burst of activity in the night. It woke me. I think it was coming from Willow Croft."

Clover, who was still feeling jittery, suddenly sprang into the air, as a shiny black nose, followed by a smooth black and white head with amber eyes, was thrust around the entrance to Tiny's shelter.

"Is that bit of kelp going spare," said a soft voice, "only I'm always partial to a piece of kelp, and besides, we haven't been fed this morning."

"We? Are there more of you scroungers out there?" growled Monty in his fiercest voice.

"Not just here," replied the stranger. "The others were too upset to leave, but I'd not been there long and I'd not grown too fond of the place."

"There, the place? Do please explain." Typically calm Tiny was not in the least bit troubled by the newcomer's having appeared so unexpectedly. There was something of the beagle about him, and Tiny knew beagles to be of a companionable nature.

"Willow Croft. The grey man came in the night."

Willow Croft was a place that engendered mixed feelings amongst the dogs of the town. First of all, it was somewhere they all hoped they would never experience, but at the same time they knew it could one day prove a haven of last resort, an escape from the vet's needle and an early death. But being sent to Willow Croft would mean that some enormity had befallen—a master's demise perhaps, a rescue from cruelty, or having been found away from home with no collar and disc—any manner of life's vicissitudes that might result in being taken to the local dogs' home.

Monty remembered how, as a young dog, he and his friends from the small industrial estate would slip away from their artisanal masters, while they daily laboured in their workshops, and creep through the shadows of the water meadow until they reached the chain link fence that marked the boundary of Willow Croft. Only the bravest pup would take the dare to approach the imposing entrance gate and raid the bins that had been left out for collection. Hackles would have already been raised by the barks and howls coming from the low brick buildings that housed the dozens of lost or abandoned creatures they occasionally saw being exercised in a grassy enclosure. For there would always be the fear that they could be spotted by one of the humans who worked there, someone who might run out and catch an adventurous pup, another captive bound for incarceration. But if you came back from the bins unscathed, with something tasty in your mouth, then you were a hero, and you could strut at the head of the pack with your tail held aloft as you all headed home, granted the lead in ritual marking with a pee jetted at selected trees and gateposts just like a pack leader.

Yet, despite this frisson of fear experienced by the adventurous pups, the town's dogs were also aware that Willow Croft was a place not of punishment but of refuge and kindness. It was in no way to be compared with the House of Hell in the next valley, which few cared to mention, and then always in an undertone. Not a single adventurous young dog of sound mind would seek to explore there, not for all the steak in the butcher's shop, and all puppies sucking at their mother's teat would be told, *Stay away, it is a place of misery and awful death.* But on the other paw Willow Croft, yes, sometimes a bogeyman, but always essentially benign, a place where unhappiness might go but where it would in time be bettered.

"Hmm, Willow Croft. I hadn't considered it before, but it is what the humans themselves would call an enigma, a place where human endeavour was ruled by kindness." Tiny rolled his eyes. "Not a lot of enigmas in this part of the world."

The new black and white patchwork dog put down the kelp he was chewing. "We've always heard it spoken of as Willow Croft, not Enigma, but you're right, they did treat us kindly, even the vet. I didn't like being kept in a pen, that wasn't natural, but it was warm and dry, with regular meals, and we were taken for walks twice a day. We even got cuddles and belly rubs from the humans who looked after us."

The three other dogs gave growls of disbelief and sighs of pleasure at this. Then the newcomer spoke on.

"That's why they're so distressed this morning—I mean, some of them were already head cases, emotionally damaged I would say—and when they found that the humans were being disappeared right before their eyes, well, there was a right tumultuous caterwauling. I suppose they felt they'd been abandoned all over again. It was distressing to hear, even for a cynic like yours truly."

"And Yours Truly, what name do you go by, if you're not too cynical to have a name?"

"Me? I'm Loki. Loki by name and Loki by nature, as my mistress used to say. My master passed and my mistress said I was far too noisy for her to bear any longer, hence my stay at Willow Croft. My short stay, as it happened." Loki took their absorption in his story as an opportunity to snatch the last stick of kelp and, looking around to see if he'd been noticed, spotted the cockapoo puppy, who was dozing in a corner. "Hey, Minny," he called, "Mummy's been looking all over for you."

The puppy, of course, did not understand any more of what he said than the name he called, but at that she became fully awake and sprang delightedly across the floor to plant her wet tongue on his nose.

"You know this infant, obviously," remarked Monty. "Do you think if we delivered her to her mother that might calm things a little up at the Croft?"

"It would help," agreed Loki. "Damn kids. They were only supposed to be walking her down the lane and back while their parents completed the adoption. The humans at the Croft were furious when all they found at the end of the lane was her tiny cotton slip-lead. I thought that at ten weeks she was too young to be rehomed in the first place, but there was a lack of space."

"That's our morning, then," decided Tiny. "Perhaps we can sort the others out when we get there."

They left without further ado and crossed the water meadow in single file, Tiny testing every significant tuft of grass for evidence of newcomers and freshly marking the limits of his assumed domain. Then through the little industrial area where Monty's owner had kept his noisy business.

Smoke reached their powerful noses long before they saw any fire, which was when Monty ran ahead and barked excitedly in front of the broad stone building that spread between two side streets.

"It's his master's workplace," whispered Clover to Tiny. "The human still used a real forge with burning fire as well as his electrical equipment. I imagine that, left unattended, it may have set light to something else."

"I've been wondering about things like that," admitted Tiny. "Like the cows up at the farm, and the milking machines; how will they be getting on with no-one to milk them?"

"They'd have to quickly round up some hungry calves," suggested Clover. "If the sheepdogs are still there, they'll help them out with that."

"I think I'll check later, all the same," decided Tiny. "Come on, we'll need to help Monty get past this."

The fire was past its height, the roof having caved in, probably during the night, and flames flickered rather than raged amongst the wreckage of the workshop.

"At least, I know he wasn't in there," remarked Monty, disconsolately. "He wasn't a bad sort, treated me like a pal, although of course, I was also his possession."

"Now you're your own dog." Loki planted his cheerful nose close to Monty's ear. "It's to be celebrated—all of us. Free dogs, not pets." He looked up into the sky and gave a whooping howl. "Dignity!" he cried.

That little episode of theatre broke Monty's focus on his old home and the five dogs trotted on through the town. It was uncannily quiet. No traffic, no doors opening and closing, none of the familiar hubbub of human occupation. All the shop windows stared blankly and unlit upon the street, like mausoleums, but without cadavers resting within. Only the corpse of human endeavour lay behind those vacant panes.

"What do you suppose the grey men have done with their bodies?" wondered Clover to Tiny. She was more relaxed to be walking alongside him than when confronting him in his hide; he seemed less ancient when on the move. "I mean, weren't there billions of them at the last count?"

"From what I've witnessed," answered Tiny, "it's not a matter of bodies. It's not as if they're shot like a rabbit and lay there bleeding with a hole in their head. There's no anguish, no visible pain. They simply cease to be."

"Like not being born, you mean?"

"Maybe. I don't think they've been sent to the human equivalent of Black Shuck to be judged, but the grey men have somehow made them nothing. That's what they wanted, not to have the human threat exist in any way, alive or dead."

"I wouldn't want to be made nothing," shivered Clover. "I'd rather take my chances and meet Black Shuck."

Tiny laughed. "You'd have nothing to fear from Black Shuck, Clover. No fear there. Buck up, lady, get on and—as our new friend urges—celebrate your freedom."

Clover was yet to feel entirely comfortable with this unexpected freedom, and mention of cows and sheepdogs had stirred in her an old longing. She'd never been a working dog but she'd always yearned to learn the tricks of herding and now, with no master to organise her day, she wanted to be useful and applying her innate skills.

A growing clamour from the end of the street drew the attention of the group. There was a fight going on outside a shop, a lot of yipping and yelping and a scuffling of well-manicured claws.

"Goodness, how are they going to survive if they can't live harmoniously amongst such a splendid environment?" Tiny was genuinely perplexed.

"Bred for humans, they behave like humans," observed Monty, sardonically. He glared contemptuously at the two cockapoos who were brawling over a large rawhide bone.

Not hearing the travellers approach, the two cockapoos' first realisation that they had company was when Loki grabbed the rawhide in his jaws and with a jaunty growl declared, "That's a nice piece, I believe it's mine, chaps. Ta!"

The two smaller dogs shrank back, tails between their legs when Tiny strode up, roaring, "How are you lot going to manage when all this is gone?" He nodded at the open shop front, where stacks of dog food lined the shelves. "There's enough kibble here to sustain all the nation's strays for at least a year. Why are you fighting over a manky piece of donkey hide?"

The two young dogs gave a squeal and dashed inside the shop, leaving Loki to enjoy his sequestered prize. He had only moments to sink his teeth into the tough hide before a very blonde and large golden doodle sauntered out the shop door and, towering over Loki, demanded, "It's not yours. You're a thief. Give it up."

The stolid beagle cross continued chewing, glancing sideways momentarily only to mutter "possession is ownership, chum, back off".

It was clear how this was going to develop and Tiny stepped between them just as the doodle barked, "I'll fight you for it."

Clover's uncertainty about Tiny evaporated at that moment as he stood tall on his long legs, stiffened the stump of his tail, and snapped, "You will do no such thing." He slammed the wedge of his big black head into the doodle's neck, sending him lurching sideways. "You big curly-haired fool," snarled the great Dane, "you look like a sheep and now you're acting like a sheep, following the same old combative human ways. Are you in charge of this lot?" Tiny glared at the cluster of doodles who had come to the door to watch the confrontation, jostling there noisily.

The golden doodle recovered his composure and approached Tiny to rub noses, signalling his submission. "I'm Bunny," he declared, ignoring Loki's snigger of derision, "and indeed I'm doing my best to keep order here. We've had a bit of trouble with a pack of lurchers who've been round trying to kidnap a couple of our bitches. There was a huge beast with them that only had to look at my gang for them to roll over and submit to anything. I thought I'd have to fight them off too—in fact some of my cockapoos are coming to the conclusion we'll have to grant them feeding rights."

"Strays?"

"I suspect that to be the case."

"Well, they've as much right to this stuff as you, and as strays they are better prepared than you to looking after themselves. When do you expect them back?"

"At twilight barking."

"Well…" Tiny looked around at his friends. "There's no need for you to be aggressive with all and sundry just because a bunch of street bums have come the heavy with you." He sniffed at an empty box in the gutter, then took a long and unhurried pee before continuing. "The world has changed, and us with it. There are new ways of being, my friend. Still, if you can get that lot of poos to calm down before twilight, we'll be back to help you. Right Monty?"

Grudgingly, Monty barked a short assent.

"Good. Only we have other business to attend to today. But I promise we'll be back."

The doodle gave a tentative wag of his tail and Tiny nodded to his companions. "Shall we?" he prompted, and with everyone giving ritual whole-body shakes to recognise the matter had been concluded, they all set off once more.

"Where did he get that expression from—Tiny, just now?" Clover whispered to Monty. "You know, 'come the heavy'."

"Shuck knows," growled Monty.

"Cool, ain't he? Old grandpa Tiny." Loki had been listening in, his filched rawhide aslant in his jaws.

"It'll be hot for you, mongrel, if he hears you call him grandpa," quipped Monty. "He could whip you any time."

"Listen," muttered Loki through his teeth, "don't refer to me like that. I'm no bitsa. My mother was a proud springer and my pa the best hare-catching beagle you could hope to meet. I may be mixed race but my consequent morphology could beat yours hands down, Airedale."

"Oh, I can't bear all this," squealed Clover. "All this bravado and throwing words around that I'm sure none of us

46

properly understand just yet. It was so much simpler before; with a full range of barks, howls and growls we got on well enough."

"Clover, the world has changed. Tiny has made that point but moments ago." Monty knew his friend was troubled, but either she adapted or she'd suffer forever.

"Here Clover, have a chew on this." Loki thrust the hide bone at her but she shook her head, yet waving her plume of a tail in gratitude.

"Come on, you three, Minny wants to go home." Tiny had turned at the end of the street. "Look, up there."

They all looked up the hill to where the Willow Croft buildings sprawled between dark willow stands and decaying bales of long harvested straw.

"Home indeed," muttered Loki. "For some."

4. Pack

It was as Monty remembered from his puppyhood, the grass long and bleached by the sun, rolling like breaking waves against the chain-link fence, the waste bins overflowing at the gate, and the clamour of frightened dogs in the low kennel buildings that was carried in spasms across the still morning air. But it was different, that sound, less abrasive, not as apprehensive, not quite the remembered sound of dogs in two states of mind, on the one hand feeling safe at last and yet fearful of what next. Instead, the sounds that reached Monty this morning were stained with sadness, low howls of loss and bewilderment rather than fearful expectation.

"Poor souls," remarked Clover. "It must feel to them just the same as when you are first taken from your mother and siblings. They've lost their protectors just when they were feeling safe, possibly for the first time."

"Come on, Minny, let's find your mum." Monty was not given to sentiment and brusquely nudged the young cockapoo through the open gate. She'd shown no inclination to join the cockapoos in the pet store and quite eagerly scrambled into the compound grounds. "Looks like Loki was correct;" Monty felt he had to show his acceptance of the new dog, that gesture toward Clover with the rawhide had been a winning move.

"Hope so," said Clover. "I think this lot will need some serious cheering up." She waited for Tiny with a question that had been bothering her all the way up the hill.

"Tiny, can you tell, are there any of the grey men here? I'm really not in the mood to meet one of them. I still haven't made up my mind about them and what they're really doing here, and my senses tell me not to trust them."

Obligingly, Tiny stopped and seemed to be listening, his eyes closed, his head first cocked this way, and then that. Clover could hear his pulse quieten, and a brittle tingling coming from his disc that set her whiskers aprickle, but she was not aware of whatever it was he was listening for. Eventually, he gave a short growl and opened his eyes. "No, not here, Clover," he reported, "not in the dogs home, but not very far away. Why, do you think they mean to harm us?"

"I just don't know," she explained. "I just have a feeling."

"There's nothing to be gained from worrying about something that you don't know; doing that can only lead to paranoia." Tiny stumbled over that last word and growled. "I didn't know that word until a moment ago," he confessed. "But paranoia sounded just right. Look, Clover, I'm as bewildered as you, but I'm of a mind to be like our new friend Loki and just decide to enjoy it all. I don't sense anything bad about the way we have been awakened."

Clover felt reassured by the big old dog, who she found herself warming to by the hour. "Come on," she urged, "the others have already gone in."

They found Monty in a pen whose door had been taken off its hinges. A large cockapoo bitch lay on a quilted bed with three of her young busy at her teats. They all looked too grown to be suckling; perhaps the mother was ensuring they were fed now the shelter staff had gone.

"Bet you can't tell which one is Minny," challenged Monty. "But I have to say Loki was spot on, and it's good to have reunited the poor mite with its mother."

Clover stepped into the pen and tentatively rubbed noses with the nursing bitch, who sat unmoving and hesitant. She leant back sharply when Tiny's shadow filled the doorway but recovered when he crossed to her and volunteered his rump for her to sniff.

"I had five," said the bitch, whose name was Rani. She nuzzled her puppies. "Two had been adopted and we were all expecting to go to new homes within days, me included." She gulped. "Then those creatures came with their strange lamps and our carers were all gone."

She caught sight of Loki in the corridor. "He didn't care, not that one," she gave a sneeze of contempt. "When the pens were opened, he ran up and down shouting that we'd been liberated. Of course, he'd only been here a short while, so why should he care? Came from a good home, apparently."

"Complaining about me again?" Loki stuck his head out from beneath Tiny's long front legs. "No wonder I left. But I brought your Minny back, so what's bugging you now?" He crawled out from under Tiny and unceremoniously nudged Rani's neck. "Look girl, the world's ours now, you haven't got to worry any more about where you'll live, who is going to give you a bed or feed you. There are no rules anymore, for Shuck's sake. Enjoy!"

Rani stretched her neck and yawned. "I didn't mean to be unkind," she offered in apology. "It's just we've felt rather alone since some of the other dogs decided to leave, they seemed to have been bitten by the same adventure bug as you."

"How many of you are here now?" Tiny had the beginning of an idea.

"I think fewer than twenty, only I do not count well. I could tell you their names, though. It's about half the number that were here before—"

With a short bark and a wink, Tiny encouraged Loki away from any further confrontation and asked him to guide him in exploring the shelter, which was arranged into several blocks of pens, or stalls. It had been a modern facility and the accommodation was well furnished with soft bedding, even with automatic water dispensers provided in each pen. Tiny looked carefully into several pens, where dogs lay curled on rugs and beds, most of them staring back sullenly at the big black intruder.

"But this is luxury compared with where I sleep," laughed Tiny.

There were store rooms in one block where sacks of kibble and trays of wet dogfood were piled high.

"They'd just had a delivery the day before the grey men arrived," explained Loki. "Looks impressive doesn't it?"

"And I am impressed," admitted Tiny. "In fact, all this gives me an idea. Look, can you go round the occupied pens and get everyone who's still here to come to Rani's. Something I have in mind they might like."

There were fifteen rescue dogs that assembled in the corridor outside Rani's pen, quite an assortment of breeds but predominantly staffies, with a peppering of black mongrels.

They all looked downcast and ready to run at the slightest provocation.

As they shuffled and panted nervously in each other's faces, the boldest of the group, a shaggy black dog with retriever in his mix, spoke up belligerently. "OK, what is this? Don't say someone actually wants to rehome us?" It was obvious bravado and Tiny didn't rise to the sarcasm in the dog's awkward new voice.

"My friend, there is no someone. All you have is yourselves—and us. But I have a proposition that you might find appealing."

All fifteen quieted. Proposition sounded like a tempting word, even if it was unfamiliar to them. But what could this old Dane have for them?

Tiny had their attention, and he moved to stand in front of them. "Acting on the advice of your fellow rescue, young Loki here, this morning we returned Rani's Minny to her mother. It is the first time I have ever seen inside this shelter but, having had a quick look around, I would say that those of you who stay here have been quite fortunate."

There were some barks of agreement but mostly silent disgruntlement at that.

"Now, I know that many of you are disappointed that there are no humans left to look after you, but really, the grey men who have taken them have done you a favour. Surely no dog with any pride would not relish the opportunity to be free, to look after himself, not to have to care whether he was coveted or not by a human, but to be himself."

Still, there was only limited enthusiasm from the assembled dogs.

"Well," said Tiny, with a flourish of a tail that was not there, "let's resolve your problem in the way that canids always have done. If you need to feel safe and cared for, you are invited to join our pack."

"So, we're a pack now, are we?" mumbled Monty to himself.

"With your agreement," continued Tiny, "we'll make this place our base. It is comfortable and secure. At the top of a hill, we can see all around—and if anyone is approaching. As a member of the pack you'll have everyone looking out for you. And we can forage and hunt together—the human supplies won't last for ever. We can keep each other company, we can keep each other warm. This is a good place and we can make the most of it."

The shaggy black dog raised his head: "If we're joining your pack I suppose you are the pack leader," he said resentfully.

"It's my idea, and I am the eldest," Tiny answered. "I claim leader rights for the moment, until—"

They waited, anticipating a momentous statement. It came as a statement of the obvious.

"A pack needs a breeding pair to lead it. When such a pair has been identified, I shall relinquish the role. In any case, I am very old and I sense that Black Shuck will soon be issuing a call for me to face him."

"We don't know you, some may have heard of you, but many of us are not from hereabouts. Why should we trust what you say?" The spaniel who now spoke trembled at her own temerity.

"Because he has the disc," shouted Clover, she too surprised by her boldness. "He talks through it with the grey men. He could kill you all with one of their lamps if he wanted, but he won't. Like the grey men he wants you all to be set free from your fears."

There was much muttering and growling after that, and skittering up and down the corridor as agitated dogs tried to calm their thoughts with fatigue. One or two tried to creep closer to Tiny, to catch a better view of the magical disc that hung from his collar. Eventually, it was the staffies who concluded the affair, coming forward as a vigorously bonded group and declaring their allegiance to the pack.

"Always count on a Staffordshire terrier to be family-minded," whispered Monty to Clover. "They've probably already decided who'll be the breeding pair."

"Don't be disgusting," she hissed. "You do come out with some wicked thoughts."

"And how about you?" scoffed Monty. "I think Tiny is going to want some answers from you. He hasn't really got a grey man's lamp, has he, back at the river?"

Clover wouldn't answer, and when she saw Tiny looking at her she rolled onto her back next to Rani, and pretended to wash the puppies with her long tongue.

Tiny, meantime, had selected Loki as the one to organise everything. "You know these dogs and they know you. I'm taking that as a recommendation. Please ensure that everyone has a cell for themselves or with a friend, and ask them if there's anything they want to know or a problem to be settled. Let's meet mid-afternoon for a pack conversation, and to see who wants to join us at twilight when we go to meet the strays."

"You know," he said to Clover when he went back to detach her from Rani's kids, "this talking business is extremely weird. The weirdest thing too is that I'm using such words as weird and business, and understanding them. And by the way, I forgive you for that creative intervention, since it worked; and by coincidence there really is some kind of conversation taking place right now with the grey men. Or, more correctly, between them."

Clover licked Tiny's face in a gesture of contrition, and followed him as he went to find a cell of his own in which to rest. Without a further word between them they lay down together and Clover, who a day before would have shrunk at the thought, went straight to sleep, pressed into the curve of his flank.

5. Garth

Tiny didn't sleep, but the warmth from Clover's body relaxed him, and he drifted into a restorative trance. He rarely slept nowadays but would slip into a comfortable daydream, a serial dream in which he'd meet his friend Joel, who would recount his audience with Black Shuck in terms both terrible and glorious.

He was enjoying the feeling of being wholly relaxed, deep in his reverie, when Clover gave a start, crying, "Who, who is it?" Her head was lifted and her eyes wide, all alert.

"Who?" prompted Tiny, sleepily.

"I heard voices," whispered Clover. "Strange, tinny voices, right next to my ear, although they were also far away and completely unintelligible. There," she jerked her head, her ears pricked; "there they are again. I wasn't dreaming."

Tiny felt the infinitesimal vibration coming from the grey men's disc. "Was it this?" he asked. "You mean you can hear it yourself? Actual voices? You said before it was a noise, like ants I think."

"Actual voices, but they make no sense."

"It's the grey men. They are close. I think they are having a spot of bother."

"Perhaps the humans are putting up a fight."

"Not humans. Canids—I mean dogs."

"I thought the grey men meant no harm to us."

"They don't." Tiny was certain on that point; the disc told him so. "But I think we should investigate."

"We?" spluttered Clover. "I told you I find them rather scary."

"But you're a brave collie, one who can outrun the wind and see off the bad-tempered ram when it acts obstreperous. You have nothing to fear but your new-found imagination. Listen, if you are hearing voices from my disc then that could indicate that, like me, you will be able to understand the words of the grey men—without their metal wand, I mean."

"Tiny, I'm only half border collie. I've never had to face an angry ram, much as I'd dearly like to try."

"Oh but you have. I heard you, you were dreaming, a short while ago. You had brought in a large flock up on the west moor, I heard you argue with a ram that refused to budge."

Clover's long jaw hung open in bewilderment and embarrassment.

"But we must go," urged Tiny. "I'm not receiving any information, just a very powerful suggestion of trouble. Someone needs our assistance; I'm convinced of that."

Clover hesitated, thoroughly disconcerted by the apparent invasion of her dreams by her heartfelt longing to be a working dog. She was doubly thrown off-kilter by the realisation that she could hear the grey men speaking through Tiny's disc, not that she could understand their language.

"Clover, move. Please." Tiny was through the door and, her mind made up, Clover shot after him.

They stopped only momentarily to speak with Monty, asking him to look after the pack and to sustain morale while they were gone.

"But where…?" He felt isolated, stuck in charge of a group of dogs he didn't know.

They gave him no answer, just an assertion that they were on a mission of mercy, then they were gone.

"Never mind mate," said a voice, and Monty found Loki's wet nose in his ear. "I know these buggers; we shan't have any trouble. Don't know about them two, however." He nodded towards the fleeing Tiny and Clover. "D'you think they're aiming to be the breeding pair, old grandpa and the sleeky collie? He's still got his nuts, ain't he?"

Monty just gave a shake of his ears. "I just hope he remembers his appointment with Bunny and the strays," he growled.

With his nose in the air, seeming to follow a scent although it was something else that drew him, Tiny's course took them uphill at first, along the ridge where pheasants stalked in the long grass—one of Loki's favourite weekend haunts before he was lodged in the shelter. The birds cackled noisily as the two dogs raced past, their sudden explosion into flight adding urgency to the eight paws that thudded past them along the track.

Soon, panting with long tongues, the pair found themselves overlooking a darkly shadowed valley, the hillsides dense with mature trees. There was a single road down there, its dusty surface winding up the steep rise to a cluster of buildings where a hollow had been gouged out of the hillside.

Tiny stopped and inclined his head to one side, and Clover heard again that strange metallic vibration coming from his disc; but no distinguishable words were apparent.

"That's the place," said Tiny. "That's where we are needed."

Clover stepped back a pace or two. "You know what that place is, don't you?" she asked in a quavering tone.

"I did once, I'm sure, but my memory can be quite patchy at times."

"That," she gulped, "is the House of Hell, the place where humans torture dogs and drive them mad. No-one comes out of there alive."

"I remember it now," said Tiny, "I'd remembered it wrong to start with. In my mind, I placed it a couple of valleys away." He shivered. "Stories about that place used to give me nightmares when I was young. Dogs running around with two heads, blowing great clouds of smoke out of their mouths, stuff like that. Once when I was out rabbiting with Joel we came across a beagle who reckoned he'd escaped from that place. An unlikely story, but he was wearing a wire muzzle with some strange device fixed on the end, which suggested he could have been telling the truth. We managed to bite through the straps and free him, but the poor devil was completely off his head, he kept crying that all the air had gone out of the world and we were doomed. I invited him home with me but he ran off, howling at anything that moved, birds, rabbits, even the leaves on the trees. Never saw him again."

Clover gave a low growl. "The grey men will be keen to eliminate all the humans over there, then, if that's what they do to our kin. I'd be happy to help them. By Shuck, just show me one of them and I'll tear them to shreds."

Tiny started off down the hillside, Clover rushing ahead with a low gait. "Best leave the tearing to the grey men," remarked Tiny. "We're in charge now, but that doesn't mean we have to behave like the humans when they ran the world. The grey men made that very clear to me. They also said there's plenty for everyone, there's no need to fight over anything."

At the valley bottom, they walked out of the woods onto the dirt road that led up to the laboratory, a heavy silence pressing down upon the still air.

"Watch out!" cried Clover, and Tiny sprang back to the trees. He immediately peered out and up the road, where a trio of noisy beagles emerged, coming fast around the bend.

"It's okay," he reassured her, "they have only one head each." He laughed. "Looks like escapees."

The clamour made by the beagles broke the suspension that the two had felt since emerging onto the road, the three escapees boisterous in their gleeful bid for freedom.

Suddenly aware of Clover and Tiny, all three beagles set to howling, a typical beagle reaction to an unexpected encounter, meant to convey a challenging expression of 'I see you, identify yourselves'. Only, considering the place from which they'd fled, Clover and Tony both wondered if all three were somehow off their heads—and potentially dangerous.

They stood together staunchly in the middle of the road and waited, the beagles running and tumbling incautiously toward them.

"I smell you, I smell you," called one. "I smell the earth and the river, I smell blood and fire." The dog held its nose high, catching a seam of scent on the breeze, and faltering.

"No," cried another, "you are mistaken. What you smell is the fox in the wood. These strangers' scent is of milk and honeycomb. They are here to bestow luxury upon us after our brush with Hell."

"Then I am glad to be in error," replied the first, its mouth open and drooling.

"Wait!" barked the third beagle. "You have both misunderstood the situation, for I scent death. Is this not Black Shuck come to receive us? Look at his livery, black as the raven, his stance as fateful as the Stygian crypt. See too, he brings his handmaiden from the spectral horde."

The first two beagles came to a stop, their tails low and still, their ears flat, and all three stood in a line across the road, sniffing and peering, their unruly excitement despatched by a sudden attack of gravity.

Tiny raised himself up and walked steadily forward. This could be a dangerous situation. They weren't rabid, he knew that, but there was definitely something not right about this three. He stopped about a lunge's distance from the wide-eyed trio.

"I always thought you beagles had a supersense when it came to smell. Yet you can't tell the scent of a redeemer." He spoke slowly and in a moderate tone. "You do understand me, don't you?" he checked. "I am Tiny, and this is my domain that you are passing into. It is not the place that humans referred to as the rainbow bridge. Come, try me."

Clover tensed, ready to spring to his defence when the third beagle advanced and, with its tail wagging once more, proceeded to sniff forensically under Tiny's stump of a tail. After a long moment, it turned to its companions and declared, "Indeed this gargantuan is no threat to us. It smells comfortable."

At that, the other two also advanced to test Tiny's aromatic flag, and as they came near the great Dane was able to see the scars that gave evidence to the dogs' origins. One had lost an eye, with the socket stitched closed, the fur on the crown of its head had been shaved away and blood oozed from some puncture holes. The third beagle, the one who had declared him to be Black Shuck, wore a helmet of grey wires that was attached to a lump in its neck. At close sight of the third dog, Tiny stepped sideways and gave a deep growl, so that it might not come too near. All along its upper jaw he'd spied a row of angry-looking pustules, sores that followed too regular a pattern. How sick was this dog? Tiny didn't want to find out.

"You are from the place up there, the place we know as the House of Hell?" It seemed obvious, but he wanted to have it confirmed, for both himself and Clover to be prepared.

"Yes," said one dog. "There is nothing else up there, thank Shuck."

"And where might you be going?" asked Tiny.

"We seek Black Shuck," replied the beagle. "For eternity, we have been preserved on the edge of hell. Now our torment is at an end and we are destined to be welcomed to the realm of the black dog over the rainbow. This gift of speech was sent us as a sign that we are to achieve great things there. It is our time."

"Listen," commanded Tiny, "I come in the form of Black Shuck as his emissary and to guide you where it is safest to conduct your journey." He turned and surveyed the road down the valley. "Follow this road until it bends close to the river. Do not continue where a new road begins and takes you to the town. The town is not a safe place. Instead, from that point keep to the river bank, and when the river turns from grey to white like curdling cream, jump without hesitation or fear into its waters. The river will take you from there to Black Shuck. Now, if you are ready…"

The three beagles listened intently, unquestioning, and when he had finished all three broke into joyous exclamations.

"We thank you, dark messenger of Shuck," cried one. "We are ready." And they took off at speed, no longer rolling around across the road but with purpose, like the dogs they were born to be, fleet of foot and deadly in pursuit of prey.

When they were out of sight around the next bend, Tiny called to Clover. "The air here smells bad, come, we must go up."

They trotted together up the hill, silent until they reached a look-out point over the valley.

"Was that not a wrong thing to do?" asked Clover. "What, have you inherited some human attributes along with your human tongue?" She looked sidelong at Tiny, wondering if she had always been right to be circumspect in his presence.

Tiny turned his gaze from the valley and looked at her quizzically.

"I mean, you've sent them to Butcher's weir, haven't you? They won't survive that without a miracle."

"Those poor beasts were already dead," announced Tiny. "Or near to it. Did you not see the infection on that last one? I couldn't let them go into the town—everyone would be dead before long."

"But—" Clover was nonplussed.

"Over the years, I've heard quite a lot about what they do up there, the humans," explained Tiny. "At least, one of those beagles has been deliberately contaminated, and by now his companions will have likely been infected with whatever abomination the humans had concocted."

Clover shivered and immediately felt unclean herself.

"Hopefully, we didn't come into close proximity for long enough to get ill." He paused and stretched. "But those three beagles, they're happy now, they're on the path to Black Shuck's realm. Drowning in the weir will be quick and, I'm sure, far less unpleasant than what they've endured in the House of Hell."

Wickhurst research station was an imposing old grey stone building, originally a country house built for one of the hunting and shooting fraternity. To those who were not well-disposed towards Wickhurst, its tradition of blood sports made it a natural home for its subsequent owners, a research subsidiary of a global pharmaceutical company, which almost exclusively comprised vivisectionists and associated animal experimenters. The original building had been added to by single storey prefabricated buildings, where the victims of the unholy practices allegedly undertaken in the name of science were kennelled. At the end of a dirt road and set into the hillside, with a dense border of forest, the seclusion of Wickhurst had also contributed to its selection by the parent company. With the nearest housing over two miles away and uninvited visitors limited to the more intrepid rambler, there was little likelihood that the squeals of anguish that came from Wickhurst's subjects would reach many offended ears. Protest groups too were easily dissuaded from coming close;

there were tall iron gates at the entrance to the courtyard and festoons of barbed wire in the immediate periphery of the woods.

Clover and Tiny were not troubled by those tall iron gates, both of which now leant, crumpled and at an angle, from their broken top hinges. A motor car with much of its front end buckled and a forward wheel missing, lay on its side halfway through the gateway. There was no driver visible in the car or nearby.

As they inched forward past the wreck they heard the sound of an engine running and Tiny urged caution; but the car that had been abandoned in front of the building's main entrance, with its engine left running and two doors wide open, had indeed been relinquished, and apparently in haste.

"I would say that someone's been trying to escape," observed Clover.

"I wonder if there are any more inside," conjectured Tiny, "only I'm sure your splendid ears will have heard what I am hearing."

The double door at the entrance to the Wickhurst building had also been left wide open. It was dark in the reception foyer but the two dogs could see a long, murky hallway that led off into the distance, at the end of which there was a small rectangle of light. From that narrowing distance came a loud banging and muffled shouts. Something was visible, moving jerkily across the white rectangle, and over the desperate shouting they could hear the roar of some terrible beast.

"I think this is what I could hear at the shelter," confided Tiny to Clover. "Through the grey man's disc."

At that moment, a lone grey man appeared silently from the stairs behind the reception desk, approached the dogs without greeting and touched Tiny with his rod.

"Do not go there," bloomed the words in Tiny's head. "It is a canid, one we have freed, although we cannot calm it. We have spoken to it kindly but it decided we must be more of the manner of men who have harmed it. It responds to us with savagery."

"Then we must go and talk to it," replied Tiny. "I assume it has been fully awakened."

"It is dangerous," said the grey man. "Two other Derin are with it and are being threatened. There is a human too. But we do not want to unmake the canid."

Tiny quickly explained the situation to Clover. "Come on," he pressed, "we've come this far, let's not go back because of a load of growling and snarling. We've heard the like plenty of times."

They set off together, walking in step. "That grey man," remarked Tiny, "he told me what they are called—their species I mean. He said Derin, or something near enough."

"I'm still going to call them the grey men," thought Clover, aloud. "They come in the clouds and move like shadows."

Drawing closer to the source of the commotion they could see that the corridor ended with a glazed door, which stood open. Beyond, was a brightly lit passage, all painted white. Just inside the main corridor, this side of the white passageway, was another door; it was closed and a grey man stood with his back to it. He held out his rod in front of him like a weapon, pointing it at a large animal that had half-emerged from the brightly lit white walkway, where it lunged and snarled with tremendous wet fangs. Occasionally, its roars fashioned into human words, but to Clover and Tiny they were indistinguishable cries of anger. A second grey man stood just beyond this great dog, for dog it truly was; he held a long pole bearing the familiar lantern device, which flared occasionally with a seeming impatience to brighten.

There was more for the two dogs to take in, for all the while the great mastiff roared and leapt there came screams and shouts of panic from behind the closed door, and occasional bouts of banging. But every time the grey man reached for the doorknob the furious dog leapt and roared even louder.

Tiny edged forward along the wall until his nose was close to the flank of the grey man who guarded the closed door. Seeing the great Dane approach he turned his rod and touched Tiny's back.

"I don't think he really means to hurt me," the words percolated through Tiny's mind. "He wants what is in the room behind me, but I cannot allow that. If he kills the human, he will himself be destroyed. We have awakened him—indeed all of you—for life, not death."

"There's a human alive in there?" exclaimed Tiny.

"It is, we believe, the human who tormented this poor creature," said the grey man. "We have been wanting to unmake him, but we cannot enter the room with this great beast attempting to go in."

He turned his rod back to the mastiff, who had edged forward and now took a bite at it. There was a sharp crackle and the grey man raised his hands to his ears, the mastiff too seeming to recoil with a shock.

"Wait!" called Clover, darting between them. She amazed herself with her self-assurance as, "You cannot beat them," she said to the dazed beast. "You must stop. Stop and let them extinguish the human. Is that not what you want?"

The mastiff, recovering, showed her his fangs and the slavering pink of his gums. He stamped his front feet and growled. In return, Clover pulled back her lips and narrowed her eyes, looking the complete ill-tempered collie, her single white marking like a flash of lightning from her head to her nose.

"If you don't let them, they will have to unmake you too." She thought how apt a term it was to describe what the grey men were doing. "Now, wouldn't that be a shame when you have just been given a fresh chance at life?"

The mastiff attempted to stare her down, but Clover simply stood her ground by imagining him as a recalcitrant ram. She wasn't going to be intimidated. *I'm not going to be scared by a dog with floppy pink pig's ears,* she determined. They remained head to head for what seemed minutes but it was probably only seconds before he spoke.

"In that room is the human who made me a monster. My blood is no longer my blood, my ears used to belong to a porcine, and I have this infernal device inserted to my brain. Back there"—he swung his head to indicate the brightly lit passage—"you will discover many wretched souls whose lives have been blighted through modifications to their anatomies, and their senses burned through the application of chemicals. But I, I have been robbed of my soul by this device you see on my head."

Clover broke her concentration to glance up at the top of his head. What looked like the top of a bottle sprouted a few centimetres at the centre of his skull, where a circle of fur had been shaved away. Its surface was shiny like glass, but not glass, and wires coiled around its base. Bile rose in her throat at the sight of it.

"With this thing, I am no longer myself but the slave of whoever owns the voice that commands," said the mastiff.

"Listen," insisted Clover. "I am not commanding you; I am explaining to you. The human who did this will cease to exist if you let them through that door. Isn't that enough for you? If instead you go in there and kill him he will cease to exist, it's true, but you will always know that you behaved like a human, tearing him to pieces and doing it purely for revenge. Let the grey men deal with this and you can come to believe that all of this has been a nothing, a bad dream. Just think, you have been awakened from a long and troubled sleep and now there is a new world for you out there."

Where am I getting all this from? she worried, and saw Tiny watching her attentively. Then she felt the tingle from his disc, just a metre away, and caught the grey man turning his head toward Tiny with a look of great portent on his strange sinuous face. At precisely that moment, she also thought she glimpsed a thin shaft of light, no more than a thread, and narrower than a whisker, flicker between Tiny's disc and the device atop the mastiff's head.

The huge beast cast his baleful eyes at the grey man who wielded the rod, and at the door behind him, then wordlessly he sat on his haunches and licked his nose. It was a standard canine signal and without hesitation Tiny joined Clover, speaking right into the mastiff's face. "Don't laugh, but I'm Tiny. Some human's joke. But we all have our burden to bear. So, who are you?"

69

The great mastiff licked his lips and, with a tremendous shake of his head, seemed suddenly to relax, his powerful bulk perceptively decreasing in front of their eyes. "I am Garth," he replied in a quiet voice. "Actually, I am Noble Holmegarth of Aquitaine—or so I was registered at the Kennel Club. But Garth is a fine enough name for me."

Clover went forward and braved the mastiff's formidable jaws, giving him a sniff of friendly greeting.

"I have not always been captive here," continued Garth. "From puppyhood, I was owned by a wealthy human, a professional gambler. But on a night when luck had deserted him I was offered as a stake in a game with the owner of this hellhole, and the dice fell against me."

"Oh Shuck!" exclaimed Clover. "How long ago?"

"Six winters have passed since I was brought here," answered Garth. "At first, I was treated like the house dog. I could guard, I could see off the squirrels, stuff like that. But then they began to take an interest in the possibilities of working with a dog that was much larger than the usual contingent of beagles. I had fortitude and intelligence, as well as strength, and that intrigued them. A new challenge, I suppose."

Clover wasn't sure she wanted to hear how that challenge was explored, and happily the mastiff's attention was suddenly diverted as the grey men opened the door that they had been defending. The dogs saw only a flash of a white lab coat as the one human in the room backed away from the door. Then the grey men were out of sight, the door closed and, in an intense silence there grew a brilliant light that framed the outline of the door. It strengthened for an instant then was completely gone, the door opening once more onto darkness, the shuttered room devoid of all human life.

One of the grey men stopped and placed the tip of his rod on Garth's shoulder, while the one who carried the lantern slipped silently away into the white-painted passage, where were located the unfortunate beagle pens.

"Your ordeal is over," said the grey man to Garth. "Do not torment yourself with anger and regret." He turned to Clover and Tiny, as if to garner their approval of his instruction, although neither could hear his words in a language they knew. Then, to Garth again, "It is what you will have been hoping, we know, but we shall not repair you. Yet the device in your head will no longer be a source of suffering. We have agreed, it will from this day be your signifier, your means of exchange with the seventeen nations we represent. Do not abuse the power it gives you. We shall know if you do. Now, we have work to do."

The grey man touched the end of his rod to the device on Garth's head and all three dogs felt, or imagined they felt, an immediate warming of the atmosphere in the corridor. For Garth, the warming was not confined to the air; his brain surged with light and he felt an infusion of something he could not recognise spread throughout his body. He was used to being injected with all manner of concoctions that would burn, or turn him drowsy, some that made him shake, others that set his teeth on edge and made his eyeballs feel fit to explode. But this time it felt as if he had pulled the whole unsullied sky into his mind, a dreamy floating sensation where he soared above the world, tingling with an inner cleanliness, aware that for the first time in a long age his breath, which had grown foetid and foul, was clear and exceptionally cool.

Garth's legs gave out and he lay down, a different dog to the one who had terrorised the two grey men.

"Are you unwell?" asked Tiny.

"I saw all the stars in the sky," said Garth, rolling onto his side, "and I knew every one of them."

He's either lost his mind or he's on his way to meet Shuck, thought Clover. *Poor wretch.*

But Garth was feeling revived. "Watch," he commanded. "We shall shortly see something truly miraculous, something not of this world."

Garth lay quietly, his face turned to the white walkway, where the three dogs could see the grey men silently opening pen after pen, and encouraging their occupants to come forth. Soon, a sorry line of smallish dogs trailed down the passageway, some blind and finding their way with noses held high, some visibly maimed, with limbs either missing or altered, their bodies patterned with heavy stitches. A damaged cohort of victims, which briefly gathered before Tiny and Clover, hesitating only until Garth stood up and, with a single deep bark, led them back to the building's entrance foyer.

"Come on," insisted Clover to Tiny. "Something truly miraculous, he said."

Arriving in the foyer, it appeared that the two grey men had somehow transported themselves from the pens unseen. Nothing seemed impossible at the present, but as Tiny later remarked, "How would we know it were them?" Yet there were indeed two of them waiting there, and when the last beagle had stumbled out from the corridor, its eager nose tasting the fresh air that came through the front door, one of the men held up a lantern on its pole and a soft yellow light spread over the cluster of hapless dogs.

The second grey man crossed to Garth and with his wand touched the device on the mastiff's head. "These we shall repair, no need for concern," said the man, and proceeded to walk around the border of the light, his wand now held up to the lantern.

Avidly, Clover and Tiny watched from the shadows of the corridor's end, at first seeing nothing and then realising that what they could see was exactly that, a space beneath the lamp that contained nothing but light, no beagles—not a whisker.

As the grey man circled the mantle of light it began to change shape, from a cone with its vertex at the lantern's edge to a hanging bulb, and eventually to a sphere that detached and floated in the air. To the dogs it appeared as an enormous bubble, far greater than anything they'd seen in the boiling effervescence of Butcher's weir. And as the sphere took form the beagles returned, floating now within the sphere, strangely passive and with an absence of their typical chatter. The sphere itself was turning, in the opposite direction to the grey man, who continued his unhurried pace, and as its speed increased it took on the colours of the captive dogs, the spinning globe blooming with white, red and black striations that eventually covered its surface.

"It's all becoming a blur—or my eyes have really had it at last." Tiny shook his head and looked away for a moment. When he looked back, the globe's surface was all colours and no colour at all—at which the grey man stopped walking and the lantern was extinguished, while the globe continued to spin, so fast it seemed stationary. Then the second grey man stepped out from what had served as the sphere's vertical axis, the sphere shimmered once, then a second time, and disappeared, like a bubble, with a pop.

"Where are the dogs? Have they killed them?" Clover felt desperately anxious.

"The grey man does not kill," said Garth with gravity. "The beagles have been taken for repair."

"But where, where are they?"

"A very long way from here." Garth sounded so confident that Clover knew not to ask for any more.

6. The Incomparable Pom

The space in the centre of the foyer retained no sign of what had taken place but moments before. With her keen nose, Clover paced back and forth but could find nothing but clean, if musty, air. The beagles had left no scent.

"We should leave," she said. "Much time has passed."

"I'd like to check first," said Tiny. "Just check that no-one has been left behind."

Garth wouldn't go back to the scene of his torment and said he'd stand guard at the door. It occurred to Clover that it was more likely he wanted to savour his first moments of freedom on his own, for he padded to the open door and plonked himself down with his eyes closed, his forepaws crossed and his nose bobbing in the air.

So Tiny and Clover hurried back down the corridor and through the further door to the white-painted outbuilding, which housed the animal pens.

It had been six weeks since her awakening, yet Clover's ability to read, although remarkable amongst the canids, was still rudimentary. Each pen had a small card fixed to the outside of its door, but Tiny swept past so quickly that Clover, matching his haste, was unable to attempt deciphering the words printed on them.

Every pen that they passed was empty of life; some contained bare plastic beds, some a thin rumpled blanket. The pens were uniformly small, with wire walls and steel sheets for floors. Pieces of human equipment they didn't recognise were suspended over some of the pens. They saw only two drinking bowls. The general atmosphere was one of a contempt for life's comforts, and the two dogs well appreciated the alacrity with which the beagles had fled this place.

"I can't believe that anyone would choose to remain," panted Clover, "but I can sense a presence down at the end."

"Me too," agreed Tiny, and he broke into a run.

The penultimate pen on their right-paw side was open, its door swung at an angle, but it was indeed still occupied. What confronted Tiny and Clover was a large white puffball, something resembling an outsize dandelion clock, a dense woolly thing that filled its pen, leaving it no opportunity to turn round. From time to time, the puffball, having heard their approach, shivered and shook with small grunts and moans.

"I think I know what it might be," whispered Tiny, "although this one is gross."

"Let me look," suggested Clover, standing on her hind legs in order to read the notice on the door. Slowly she made out the letters printed there, although her pronunciation was untutored. "It says…" She licked her nose thoughtfully. "It says 'Xylene—Caution, gloves'."

"That's not what the creature is, it sounds more like an instruction," grumbled Tiny.

"No wait, there's more. 'Accelerated evolution project. Gene splicing 54/XP'."

"That neither," snapped Tiny. "It's human gobbledegook. But I do know what evolution is, and it's not a dog breed."

He craned his neck and sniffed at the puffball. "It is a dog," he confirmed. "Hey! Come on, time to go," he barked at the animal, foraging in its woolly thicket of fur and finding a leg to pull.

"How dare you!" squealed a thin voice. "How dare you insult the great, the magnificent, the incomparable Pom." The puffball shifted in an attempt to turn round.

"It's stuck," declared Tiny.

"I know what I'd do if it was a sheep stuck in a bush," said Clover.

"Well, we can't just walk away now," decided Tiny. "So what would you do?"

Clover reared up again and took hold of the thin little leg and, placing her forepaws on the rim of the pen for leverage, doggedly tugged the creature out from its confinement. It squeaked and uttered cries of complaint, but eventually it fell with almost a bounce onto the wooden walkway.

"My," exclaimed Tiny, "you're a big girl aren't you? I've not seen the likes of you before."

"The likes of what?" demanded Clover.

"This impressive character is, if I'm not mistaken, a Pomeranian, otherwise known to humans as a pom-pom. A dog, yes, a curious one, but as much a dog as you and me, and very much a special kind of dog."

"Undeniably I am, I am the great, the magnificent, the incomparable Pom, the most special kind of dog, as you have acknowledged. I am, let it be known, the last of past multitudes and the first of a whole new race of poms." The dog's pointed fox-like muzzle extended with conceit.

"Well," said Tiny, "you're certainly the largest Pomeranian I have ever encountered. Your kind usually ride around inside a wealthy woman's purse and eat poached calf livers for breakfast. So what has happened to you?"

Clover stood quietly, wholly bemused by this exchange. She'd never met a Pomeranian and didn't know what to expect. She certainly didn't warm to the creature, which waited shivering on the white-painted floor, perhaps hoping its matching hue might make it invisible.

Tiny, sensing Clover's puzzlement, spoke to her quietly. "Pom-poms used to be largish canids, almost the size of a malamute, then over the years the humans bred them smaller and smaller, to be toy dogs. I remember those I've come across as little bigger than Minny from the shelter. But this one's a real monster."

"I hear you, you black fiend," shrieked the Pomeranian. "You need to afford your queen greater respect, or..."

"Shall we put you back in there?" Clover had no time for this impudence. "We have no need for kings and queens, that's human nonsense. So, come with us or stay and starve. Now, we have business elsewhere."

The pom-pom yapped a little and emitted small bleats of disappointment, then stood proudly erect and tottered away down the passage, leading her two rescuers.

When they reached the front entrance, Garth appeared to be snoozing. The pom-pom approached him from behind, with no pretence of stealth, and sniffed him from a distance. She sneezed and Garth jumped up to his full height.

"Oh no, not this over-blown critter," he groaned. "I thought I'd seen the last of her preening and carrying-on.

Didn't care to go with the beagles, I see. Too high and mighty."

"She was stuck," explained Tiny.

"Too fat," laughed Clover.

"How dare you?" squealed the Pomeranian. "I am the first and finest of a new generation of my breed."

"She was a pretty little thing when she arrived," conceded Garth. "Then they hooked her up to all manner of tubes and bottles, weighed out her food regularly, and weighed her too I should add. You could see the changes in her, changes in her manner too. She used to chatter quite amicably at first; I learnt her name was Pom. Later on she couldn't bring herself even to acknowledge my presence—and I'm not someone who's easily overlooked. What was the most peculiar thing is that they even groomed her—daily—when the rest of us never ever saw a brush or comb. They were fattening her up for something special, that was clear."

"Perhaps pom-poms are good to eat," suggested Clover. "Tiny, weren't you saying yesterday that you knew of someone called Indonesia, who had a dog meat farm?"

"My guess is she was being developed to be a model for a new breed type. The humans made a lot of money from specialist breeding."

While they chewed over the circumstances of the Pomeranian, Pom was standing outside the front door, trying not to listen to what she considered vulgarities. But, "Oh look, the moon!" she yelped, "It's been so long since I saw the enchanting moon."

Her observation stirred Tiny, who was deep in thought, trying to work out what had been intended for Pom. "Friends, we must return to Willow Croft. We made a promise to the cockapoos."

It was late afternoon and the pallid face of the moon had begun its rise in the north-west of the sky.

Neither Tiny nor Clover made a point of inviting them, but Garth and the Pomeranian followed as the valiant pair trotted from the building, feeling mightily relieved to have escaped its menacing presence.

Once away from the road and into the wood Garth pushed his way to the front of the group. "What's this promise you are intent on keeping?" he asked Tiny, who gave a series of short answers as he puffed his way up the steep valley side, explaining about the dispute between the strays and the cockapoos.

"A problem with strays?" repeated Garth. "Unlikely, I would have thought. Perhaps the cockapoos are the problem. Do you know, it's thought there are 200 million stray dogs worldwide. And wherever you might find them they are highly organised, either into loose social groups or close-knit packs. All very well-ordered and sensible. It's what gave the grey men such encouragement."

Tiny stopped, a paw raised in anticipation of his next step. "How do you know all that?" he demanded, sharply. "This is very particular knowledge you are revealing. Have you been talking to the grey men?"

Garth's broad mouth hung open and his eyes seemed to mist over a little, making him look drugged. But his voice, which initially had been thick and wet but was now marked by its surprisingly bright diction, came without a tremor. "This device," he flicked his eyes upwards to indicate the implant in the top of his skull, "this abhorrence is different since it was touched by the grey man's wand. In fact, I'm not sure it is an abhorrence any more. You see, if I stop thinking about what I'm scenting on the air or in the undergrowth, if I cease wondering which path to tread or where we're going and instead let myself meld into the space in my head, it's as if I am living in what the humans called a library, the place where all knowledge is stored. I first became aware of it when I was waiting for you at the front entrance."

He looked at Tiny, sure that he wouldn't be understood, but Tiny returned his gaze and nodded.

"It's not the same as it was," explained Garth. "There's no voice saying 'do this, eat this garbage, unbolt the cage'—all that kind of nonsense. There's no compulsion, no fear of punishment if I'm slow or can't do it. It's more like I am now the voice; I just draw myself into the inner space, and when I need to understand something, the books that I need—you know what books are, Tiny?—they just fly off the shelves and read themselves to me. It happens very, very fast, quicker than a raindrop falling off a twig."

"Extraordinary," gasped Tiny.

"And what I find rather scary," Garth said in a quiet voice so as not to scare Tiny, "what is far beyond my imagination, is that the room in which the library is held, which—don't forget—is inside my head, is immense. In the far corners, I can see a sky full of stars twinkling, and that's not the end."

"I'm not trying to rubbish what you describe," said Tiny, his own voice now hushed, "but could all this be a consequence of the things that the humans pumped into your veins? I've heard the humans used to do that sort of thing to themselves and, as a result, 'saw' things."

"Who would know but the humans themselves, or otherwise the grey men?" Garth wouldn't conjecture further. "But as soon as you introduced the idea of some tension between strays and cockapoos, the information about the strays' social organisation just arrived unbidden. It seems the occurrence of some kind of dialectic could be the trigger."

"Dialectic?"

"I know, that's a new one to me as well. You know, a disputation is what it is."

"All right," said Tiny, "but we have no time for disputation right now. We have to get back. Let's save our conversation until we have a better opportunity to talk about triggers and libraries and other such marvels. But I must say you are opening up a whole new aspect of this awakening experience, and that was itself already remarkable."

While they were speaking, Clover had been assisting Pom, who had found the steep slope daunting for her little legs, for long unused to tackling anything more than a walk to the grooming chamber. As the collie cross came up she passed an enquiring glance at Tiny.

"It's all right," he said, nodding at Garth, who had forged ahead. "Either the poor bugger has been driven mad or he has been given extraordinary new faculties. I'm sure we shall find out in time."

7. Strays

Monty was feeling agitated. "They didn't even tell me where they were going," he complained to Loki, "let alone how long they'd be." Monty was a dog who liked to know how things stood; uncertainty was anathema to him. He had amazed himself with the positive spirit in which he'd dealt with his awakening, and all that had happened since. But then, although everything was strange, it was at least quantifiable, a situation he could grasp and deal with.

Now though, Tiny and Clover going off like that was shrouded in secrecy, and he had no signals as to what to do next. His master had been a man of signals; he rarely spoke to Monty but made known what he wanted him to do through a vocabulary of hand gestures, facial expressions, whistles and grunts. Such was the level of understanding between dog and master that Monty almost routinely anticipated what the blacksmith expected of him, or what the man was going to do next.

"What's the problem?" asked Loki. "I wouldn't worry about old grandpa Tiny, he's been around a long time, there's not much that's going to trouble him. And the bitch—"

"Her name's Clover!" barked Monty, vehemently.

"And Clover, she's a canny, er, young dog."

"But the cockapoos," interjected Monty. "Tiny promised."

"Well," said Loki, untroubled, and he shrugged the matter off.

"Tiny left me in charge." Monty licked his nose, impatiently. "I don't know what to do now he hasn't come back. He didn't say."

Irritated, Loki put down the giant dog biscuit he was attempting to gnaw and sucked his teeth. "Alright then, so if you're standing in for grandpa while he's off gallivanting, you've got to keep his promise for him. You go and talk to the strays. You've mastered this talking stuff very well, in my opinion. Very masterful, I would say. I don't know why anyone would want to do it, but the phrase *talking the hind leg off a donkey* comes to mind, Shuck knows where from. My head's full of all sorts of stuff like that, perhaps it will make sense in time. Anyway, this afternoon, all I've heard is you explaining to the others how it's going to be in this new pack. Everyone's duties and obligations and such, and all the benefits too. I could tell everyone, well almost everyone, was quite impressed."

Loki's knack with flattery came easily to him, and it had the effect he was hoping for, Monty standing proudly to attention, his tail erect and his ears alert. "If you will take charge here, I'll take the staffies," the inspired Airedale announced. "They are a robust little bunch of soldiers."

"Best not use the word soldiers," suggested Loki. "We're not spoiling for a fight and, as far as I know, the lurchers are not expecting one either."

"They're not expecting me," snapped Monty, striding away to look for the staffies.

84

"Bloody terriers," muttered Loki, "always on the lookout for a good scrap."

Since it was fast approaching twilight barking, Monty set off as soon as he had gathered the staffies together. There were nine of them, and, much to Monty's displeasure, they had been joined by the belligerent shaggy black dog that had spoken up during Tiny's introductory address. "This could be interesting," he commented to Monty, once the likely situation had been explained. "A fight between cockapoos and lurchers, ho! It'll be over before it has begun."

"There is not going to be a fight," insisted Monty to the whole group. "A confrontation maybe, but we are there as mediators, to ensure a peaceful resolution." The staffies' faces were unreadable and he wondered whether they too were in a quarrelsome frame of mind.

The sun was balancing on the edge of the horizon when they crossed the silent ring road and made their way down the main street of the town, their shadows thrown up tall on the walls of the empty buildings. It lent the group a feeling of confidence to see themselves larger than life. In the deep pink sky, a shower of black shapes fell towards the rooftops. "The grey men," someone called.

"It's starlings, idiot, looking for a night-time roost," scoffed the shaggy black dog.

There was a lot of jostling amongst the staffies at that rebuff but before it could develop into an argument Monty called a halt. Large grey shadows were circling in the middle of the next crossroads, four-legged shadows that declared these were not grey men but dogs. One very large individual broke from the group and loped towards them, its eyes red in the setting sun. Its approach set the staffies chattering, while the shaggy black dog scuttled around to the back of the group.

"Well, well, what brings this little band of adventurers abroad at such a time?" asked the tall lurcher. He stood high over Monty and sniffed the back of his ears. "My name is Tak," he ventured, "and it seems I am the current spokesman for that merry gang down there. You are?"

"Monty," answered Monty, wondering if this was the 'huge beast' that Bunny the doodle had mentioned. He didn't look that huge. All the same, with that powerful head poised over him, Monty was wondering if he was going to feel two long jaws of teeth around his neck at any moment. "You can call me Monty," he said bravely. "And this is a small contingent from my pack. We are going—"

"With me," said Tak. "You can be our witness. One should always respect the opinion of a clutch of staffies, straight as a dye they are."

There came a long deep-throated call from a couple of streets away. Not quite a bark, nor a howl, but something in between that soared into the sky. Faint responses could soon be heard coming from streets away.

"Twilight barking," remarked Monty.

"Exactly so," agreed Tak.

"Then we must hurry," said Monty.

"Must we?" asked the lurcher.

"Before it's dark," mumbled Monty, realising his error.

Then they found that they were walking encircled by the strays, about two dozen of them, which were predominantly but not exclusively lurchers. Monty recognised one or two of the others, a bearded collie, a whippet, a jack russell he remembered seeing hanging around the door of the butcher's shop on a number of occasions.

Beyond the crossroads Monty recognised the row of shops that included the pet store, beyond which he fancied he could make out the ruined blacksmith's premises. Drawing closer he could discern the lone outline of the golden doodle, Bunny, but it seemed that all the cockapoos had been told to stay indoors. Monty turned to Tak. "Excuse me, but you didn't say what we were being asked to witness," he spoke with no sense of accusation or effrontery, he was doing his diplomatic best for Tiny.

"Ah!" Tak called everyone to a halt. "For our new brothers here," he explained, "I must illuminate." He turned to Monty and his pack. "We are the West End Strays. Before the grey men came and gifted us language, we lived on the street in a community of equals. It was a hard life and yet not such a hard life, for whatever we might have, we shared with each of our brothers. In fact, we did quite well, most of the time. You see, we would seek out food from those places where large numbers of humans would gather to eat, drink and rest; I have subsequently learnt they were called inns, and restaurants and hotels. There was so much food wasted in these places, and what was surplus would be offered to us. But all that is now in the past. The humans have been unmade, as the grey men describe it, and our source of an easy diet is no more."

Tak ceased talking and looked at Monty as if expecting to hear what he should do now that his food source was gone. When nothing was forthcoming, he continued.

"We are a congenial bunch," he asserted. "As I have mentioned, we share what we have when we have something to share. It is a way of ensuring the giver always receives when he has nothing to give. Our practices are no doubt the reason why you have come into town this evening with your little posse."

Some of the strays sniggered at his description of Monty's gang and he quietened them with a snarl of displeasure.

"We saw that cowardly doodle waylay a group of strangers this morning, a group led by a creature resembling Black Shuck. I think you, Monty, might have been among them—a good sighthound never doubts his eyes. We are not dumbfucks, and it was not hard to connect that conversation with your appearance this evening, although I must say it was very brave of you to come without the huge black dog. We have a certain, if undeserved, reputation, and I'm sure he would have been a force to reckon with—but please don't take that as besmirching yourself."

"I have never shirked a stand-off," said Monty stiffly.

"Never mind that," said Tak, "the issue we are here to consider is the plentiful store of food in what the humans called a pet shop, a shop that never belonged to the crowd of genetic idiosyncrasies who currently occupy it and are spoiling the supplies in a most unruly and undisciplined fashion."

Monty already felt his view of the situation was shifting, not least because of Tak's impressive use of language. But after all, everyone knew that lurchers were highly intelligent, and he'd come prepared for an intellectual tit-for-tat.

"So," said Monty, "I think I know what you are going to say next."

"I'm sure you do," laughed Tak. "All that food is not theirs to squander. We mean it to be shared amongst all who need it, for the cockapoos have no more exclusive right to it than us. Perhaps the grey men have said to you what they said to us, that there is plenty for all, and there is no need for any conflict to secure what one must have in order to exist."

"But," Monty held up a paw to gain attention of all the strays, "they said you were trying to abduct some of their females."

At this, the entire pack of strays roared with laughter.

"You must be joking," called one. "I'd rather mount a stinking vixen than a cockapoo bitch. Give us some credit!"

"That was a ploy by the doodle to gain your sympathy," said Tak. "No, all we did was to approach them and suggest we help them organise the supplies so that they last longest, and that we had rights to a share. Sadly, the cockapoos, who are all grieving over the loss of their humans, went into meltdown over that, and the big golden doodle, who's loving it being their self-appointed champion, started to become aggressive."

"He's down there now, Bunny's down there at this moment. Let's go and talk." Monty pressed forward through the ring of strays and took the lead with Tak beside him. He whispered out of the side of his mouth, "What is meltdown, Tak? I got the sense of what you were saying, but the specific meaning of it, what is that?"

"No idea," replied Tak. "I'm the same as you. In fact, it's all like that at the moment, words and thoughts coming out of my mouth, usually feeling as if they match the context, but often I wonder, Shuck knows, what on earth was that? There's something about this business of being awakened that hasn't yet been explained. Those grey men, I'm still thinking they have some secret motive other than what they've told us."

"I agree," muttered Monty. "They're not exactly malevolent, but by Shuck they're secretive."

Bunny stood his ground as the combined force of strays and the group from Willow Croft padded down towards him. *He may be a bit precious,* thought Monty, *but he's no coward.*

"Greetings," offered Tak, stooping for a ritual sniff of Bunny's undercarriage. "We come accompanied by the noble Monty. We need to talk and I'll come straight to the point."

Bunny seemed not to hear him, or at least he pretended so, and looked over the heads of the gathered dogs. *Looking for Tiny,* thought Monty.

Ignoring Bunny's diffidence, Tak explained, as he had to Monty, how the strays had survived prior to awakening, and how they had as much right to enjoy the provisions kept in the pet shop as the cockapoos. He made the offer of the strays acting as quartermaster, in exchange for access to whatever supplies they needed, on an equal basis. A supreme diplomat, he chose not to mention the alleged abductions, not wishing to embarrass Bunny into further opposition.

Bunny listened without speaking, but stood with his eyes on Monty and, when Tak had finished, the doodle said, accusingly, "You were here this morning, with the big black fellow."

"Yes," agreed Monty. "He apologises, he's been delayed. But you may remember, when he was here earlier he said that these chaps have as much right to this store of food as do you. Now I've been listening to Tak and what he says makes sense to me. May I take a look inside?"

Without waiting for an answer, Monty strode over the pavement and into the shop. Nervous cockapoo faces shrunk into the shadows as he marched in. They looked more nervous still when he roared his displeasure, seeing many sacks of kibble torn open and their contents strewn across the floor amongst urine-soaked mats and dog toys that had been pulled from their hooks. He didn't look for long but sprang back to the street.

Monty walked up close until he was whisker to whisker with the golden doodle. "Some mess," he said. "A disaster in the making. Look, this supply of food won't last forever, and it will last even less time if you leave it to the rabble in there." He turned back to Tak, "They need to separate living quarters from the food store. Can you do that? If the supplies are properly organised and rationed fairly, they'll last much longer. It'll give this lot plenty of time to work out how they're going to feed themselves once it's all gone."

Without hesitation, Tak stepped towards the shop door and Bunny lunged forward with a menacing growl that caused Tak to show his teeth in retaliation.

"No," came a deep voice. "We don't do that anymore." Tiny swiftly moved out of the shadows and grasped Bunny by the thick fur at the back of his neck until his growl subsided.

"I overheard what my comrade Monty said just now," he declared. "It makes absolute sense. With the humans gone, we are free to take control of our lives, but if we are to survive we have to organise. Some of us will fare very well in the country, running wild, foraging and catching prey, but the wee canids you have living in that squalor, which I can smell from here, are town dogs, and will need to learn a very different method of survival."

"As for you," he turned to Tak and the strays, "it seems to me that you were as much slaves to the humans as any of us, even while you appeared to live an unconstrained life, for you were depending on them for your sustenance. As another of my comrades remarked this morning, now you're your own dogs and it's a condition to be celebrated. Go on, sort out this place, but it won't be a forever home. You have speed and intelligence, and a knack for surviving on your wits. You need to look beyond these sacks of kibble and trays of processed meat."

Tak looked humbled, which had not been Tiny's intention. Why hadn't he thought of that, why had he not sought a new strategy to match their changed situation?

"Thank you, Monty," said Tiny, drawing his friend aside. "We were delayed, but it was a useful delay. I'll explain later. Is that large lurcher the leader of the strays?"

"That's Tak. He referred to himself as their current spokesman."

"My friend," said Tiny, padding over to Tak, "since you are the leader here, can you sort out this situation without there being further dispute? It seems you have set out a fair solution. Don't worry, I'll deal with the golden doodle."

"In truth, I'm not their leader," admitted Tak. "I merely speak on their behalf, having quickly mastered the human tongue." His tone was apologetic; he was still feeling sore about his lack of vision. "Netta was our leader until a week ago, and a fine one. Someone put broken glass in a pot of stewed meat that she'd scavenged from a hotel and she bled to death. I am not of her capacity to lead. We strays are in any case a fairly loose association; we don't seek masters. But I will deal with the situation here."

He called to the bearded collie: "Jake, can you please go and speak to that rabble in there, calm them down, explain what we're going to do for them." He turned back to Tiny.

"His friendly face isn't going to scare them," he explained, "unlike mine. Jake's an affable lad, wouldn't say boo to a sheep." He laughed and Tiny nodded. The great Dane's own thoughts were being distracted by the activity that he could sense coming from his special disc, a conversation, some transmission originating with the grey men that was not meant for him, and a response from someone somewhere nearby. The minute words flashed back and forth, and for once he couldn't make them out. It puzzled and worried him that there could be other grey man mysteries afoot in his home town from which he was being excluded.

Then the minute chattering ceased and the disc, which had grown very warm, cooled.

"Are you all right," asked Monty, seeing Tiny grown stiff and uncommunicative.

"Just looking for my new friend," replied Tiny. "Someone Clover and I rescued this afternoon. I thought he was just behind me in the run down from Willow Croft."

No-one had taken any account of the shaggy black dog, who had hung back when Monty took the lead into the town centre. Could he have been the only one among them who found the empty buildings in the town centre unnaturally dark and intimidating? Probably not, but it was he alone who found reassurance in the unbroken pattern of red, amber and green, the traffic lights that continued to shed a semblance of normality upon the last crossroads. So it was that he was the first to spy the thing that shambled down the street from the dark beyond, the powerfully built beast bearing an egg that glowed in the middle of its skull, with unnatural floppy pink ears and great teeth that reflected red, amber and green in its cavernous mouth. And if that wasn't enough to scare the whiskers off an innocent snout, then regard those baleful eyes which boiled with wrath.

They took account of the shaggy black dog now, as suddenly he rushed out of the shadows with a loud yelp and pressed himself against Tiny. "It's coming," he cried, "ready yourselves. It's the hellhound come to take us."

With an assortment of yips, barks and whines, everyone turned and looked back up the road from whence the unwilling emissary had run. In the deepening twilight, with barely a glimmer in the sky, a large creature shambled carelessly towards them.

"It could be the hellhound, you know," observed Tak. "It looks like a mastiff, so it fits the description. But that thing on its head, I've never heard that mentioned before. Anyway, it's a dog not another alien, and I'll go to greet it."

"No need," said Tiny, quickly stopping the lurcher. "This is Garth, the friend I have been waiting for."

The small crowd of dogs parted and shuffled back to let Garth through, and he approached and rubbed noses with Tiny.

"What, am I that scary?" he jested, then out of pure mischief threw a huge bark at the shaggy black dog, who ran in frenzied circles on the pavement until Garth stopped him with a heavy paw placed on his back. "My apologies," he roared, "I'm such a bad lad. No offence."

"We're almost finished here," explained Tiny, "thanks to my friend Monty and Tak. But I'd like you to help, Garth. The golden doodle standing by that shop door, we need to extricate him from a difficult situation, give him something fresh to absorb him. He's had to concede defeat and I want him to avoid losing face, if you know what that means."

"Of course, of course, I do," said Garth. "I need to tell you about that, how I know what so much means. I've been talking…"

"Later Garth, we can talk later. But can you just go over and invite him back to Willow Croft, persuade him to join us for a meal, suggest we could use someone like him up at the shelter. He's a bit self-important, but I think you've made enough of an impression to convince him it's in his best interests to accept. He's wasting his talents here with the silly cockapoos."

Tiny was as eager to hear what Garth wanted to tell him, as was Garth keen to explain his delayed arrival. But Tiny had guessed at least part of the story and wanted to hear the rest in comfort and in company. Observing the strays and the dogs from Willow Croft, and marking the restless way they wore their new freedom, he could see a troubled future; he also had the seed of a solution.

8. A Queen and a Hero

"Ever since that grey man touched my implant with his wand—I refer to it as a wand very pointedly, because it does all feel like magic—well, ever since then my head has been full of a great cacophony of sound." Garth looked around the assembled company to ensure that everyone was listening.

The dogs from Willow Croft who'd accompanied Monty had all returned to the shelter, their numbers swollen by several of the strays, including Tak, plus Garth and Bunny, who was actually quite relieved to have left the chaos at the pet shop behind. They all sat together in the dogs' home reception area, having enjoyed a meal of cooked diced chicken and shaped biscuits from the restocked store. There was a real sense that this motley gathering was coalescing into a pack and, when everyone had settled down, having noted the looks of enquiry and suspicion being thrown at the rather startling figure of Garth, Tiny had invited him to introduce himself.

"But we can't hear it," called the shaggy black dog, who'd grown quite attached to Garth since his initial fright, and not afraid to speak up.

"You won't," said Garth, "you haven't the advantage of my implant. At least…"

He'd told the story of his imprisonment and torture at the laboratory and several dogs gave cheers of approval to the grey men, who had stopped all that misery. He'd even mentioned Pom, as someone who had had her whole physical and mental being altered by the humans in the lab, and Pom preened and glowed with the attention paid her. "I'm the incomparable Pom," she squealed, standing up with her ears pricked, "your new queen," and everyone looked away embarrassedly, particularly Loki, who groaned.

When the Pomeranian had arrived at the shelter, she was dishevelled and tired, her fine plumage matted with dirt and her claws torn, but on spying Loki she had perked up and made straight for him as he lolled in the door of his pen. To his surprise she lay down on her back with her legs in the air and submitted to his sharply aroused sniffing, then when he was satisfied that she was no threat she curled up on his mat and licked his face subserviently. "I am your queen," she informed him with a sweet whine, "and you are my—"

"I am Loki," he growled, "and not anything of yours."

So it was that Loki now sat on the opposite side of the huddle to Pom, and hoped that very few of the other dogs had noticed that she had decided to camp in his pen.

Tiny sat quietly, his face unmoving and sage. He was impatient for all the historical part of Garth's story to be concluded. He wanted to hear what it was that Garth had been talking about and with whom.

"Hey," called Garth to the shaggy black dog, "what's your name?"

"Shaggy," replied the hound, and there were bursts of laughter.

"Well, Shaggy, would you come and listen, please."

The black dog stood and tiptoed apprehensively across the floor, hoping that this scary mastiff was not intending to put him to public embarrassment for a second time.

Garth knelt and invited Shaggy to press his ear against the implant atop his head. Some of the watching dogs drew breath noisily, fearing a trick, but Shaggy did as he was asked and listened intently.

"Now can you hear it?" asked Garth, standing tall once more.

Shaggy's eyes widened and his tail wagged furiously. "I can hear something," he said. "It's like when you stand at the mouth of the estuary and the sea speaks to you, the waves sounding as if they will go on for ever, building and crashing, over and over. But after a while the waves are like the earth, continuous but still, the sound of time unbroken, and I could hear voices, many voices, all chattering madly, tiny voices."

"Like ants," said Clover quietly to Monty. "That's the same sound I heard from Tiny's disc."

"And did you understand what they were saying?" asked Garth, and Shaggy shook his head disappointedly.

"Never mind," said Garth. "Thank you, Shaggy, you have validated my claim. Do you understand validated?"

Shaggy looked uncertain.

"It means you have shown I am not telling untruths about the noise in my head. And the word I just used that you did not know, that is just another part of what is happening to me. My head is bursting with words that fly into my mouth just when I need them. For the most part, strange words that I don't know until I use them, but when I do they knit together with similar words, and each time that happens my mind feels as if it is expanding. It is something akin to magic, is it not?"

The company of dogs all stirred at that, stretching, emitting low growls and sucking air through their teeth. Was Garth truly endowed with magical powers?

Tiny, of course, knew otherwise.

Garth walked around the little arena that had been made by the assembled canids, who sat but mostly lay side by side in a circle.

He's enjoying this, thought Tiny. *Such a reversal of his fortunes. And why shouldn't he?*

"My friends," said Garth, coming to a stop. "It is not magic." He stood and looked everyone in the eye. "And now I will tell you what the tiny voices were saying, for actually it is the grey men who are speaking, and they are talking directly with me."

Garth walked to the centre of the gathering. All eyes were upon him, even Pom's. "This may surprise you," he began, "but the grey men need our help." No-one stirred, although a number of hackles stiffened. "They tell me that they have unmade most of the eight billion humans on the planet, but there are individuals who have gone into hiding. In particular, these include those humans who were in control of all the others and were masters of their laws and procedures. The grey men have found it easy to work in the cities, for they have colossal versions of their shroud, the device they use to extinguish humans with light. But dealing with humans in the countryside is a more laborious matter, involving single activists with the lanterns you have probably seen used. Now, does everyone understand the words I am using?" Garth stopped and listened, but everyone was too rapt to admit to not understanding all of the language he had acquired.

Only Tiny dared speak: "So what are you saying, Garth, that they need us to go out with their killer lanterns and do the job for them? For that sounds too much like how the humans would employ us, as hunter-killers."

"Not killers, no," replied Garth. "They don't want us to become their foot-soldiers. But they do recognise that we are endowed with great faculties for searching and finding. They are therefore suggesting that we might help them by seeking out these rulers among humans, who they fear are preparing to organise and wage war against them."

"Find them so that the grey men can kill them?" barked Rani. "I'm not sure I want to do that. The humans here in Willow Croft were good to us. Helping the grey men like that would be the same as when some humans, the bad humans, used dogs to catch our cousin the fox, or the deer, boar, otter and a host of other innocent creatures." There came some murmurs of agreement around the room.

Garth walked over to Rani and bent his head down in a non-threatening manner. "Why were you brought here to Willow Croft?" he asked quietly, and Rani recoiled a little without answering.

Garth repeated his question but still she shrank from answering.

"She was taken in a car and dumped at the side of a busy road," explained Loki. "Because she was pregnant. In fact, it was one of the grey men who brought her here."

"Yes, the humans in Willow Croft were likely to have treated you well," said Garth to Rani, "it was their calling. But they held no status amongst the human leaders or rulers, the men that decided who amongst their species should be rewarded."

Garth turned away and walked all around the small arena of spellbound dogs, staring into each puzzled snout, then, "Are there more of you who would take Rani's view," he almost shouted his challenge.

After a very short silence, there came a screech from Pom. "Well, I for one need humans to finish their improvement of me, so if there are surviving humans I want to find them, but not to tell those horrid grey men where they are."

"What is this, this improvement?" asked Garth with the edge of a sneer. "I have watched you being 'improved' for some time now and it is not clear what you mean by finishing it."

"My trainers, they said I had a big future ahead of me," preened Pom.

"Come on, Pom," Tiny insisted from across the room, "what did they actually say?"

She put her nose in the air and did a braggart twirl, "They said I would be huge amongst dogs."

"I think you misunderstood," said Tiny, in a dismal tone.

There was an outbreak of yaps and howls around the reception area then a sudden hush, as the sound of movement outside reached a host of sensitive ears.

Lights crazed momentarily on the glass doors to reception.

"Grey men," somebody whispered.

"Whoever it is, they are speaking the same language as us," remarked Monty. "I'd say it is a couple of humans."

"Oh, wonderful," cooed Pom. "They've come to finish me."

The lights moved on down outside the building and everyone stayed quietly tense until there came a crashing sound from the service entrance at the end, the sound of splintered wood and glass cascading menacingly. There followed quick stealthy footsteps in the corridor from the storeroom and a voice said, "I reckon there's someone up ahead, Jeff. We should 'ave kept quiet." A second voice, presumably Jeff's, grunted, "Bastard grey scum, I told you there'd be some hiding here. I'll do 'em; you go back and around to the front; see they don't escape."

The light of a torch started to grow in the corridor and several dogs began to growl at its approach. But as Jeff's boots became visible in the approaching halo of light the indomitable Pom rushed forward on a wave of hope that here was her saviour, a human who would 'finish' her. In a way, she got what she desired, for when Jeff saw a huge white pom-pom leap out of the shadows towards him his instinctive reaction was to raise his rifle and fire.

Tiny's response was immediate and final. He was on the man in an instant, the intruder slammed onto his back on the shiny linoleum, the great dog's jaws around his throat. But even before any human blood began to flow there came a second explosion of light and sound as the first man kicked in the door to reception, his gun also raised.

"Fuck me, they're using dogs now!" he shouted into the dark, and as his torch lit up the image of Tiny tearing the throat out of Jeff, he took a bead on the great Dane's head, felling him with a single bullet.

When the big black dog crumpled, several of those who watched, horrified, saw the disc at his collar begin to glow, first orange, then red and at last a bright white light, the light throwing out tiny threads, long fine filaments of light that reached across the space until they touched the implant

102

protruding from Garth's skull. The now single line of light steadied and, as it did, the reception area was split by a short but painful burst of sound, higher in pitch than a dog whistle but immensely troubling to all those gathered there. Everyone seemed to be turned to stone, suspended in varying stages of inner turmoil, then abruptly the light went out, it had been mere seconds, and the sound ceased. And with the spell broken a trio of staffies was quick to leap upon the gunman, who screamed and thrashed his limbs as three sets of needle-like teeth tore into his flesh, his cries of anguish cut short by a decisive snap at his carotid.

Their action proved more final than Tiny's had been, for Pom's killer remained largely unharmed, except for a lump on the back of his head and a slight wound to his neck.

"Typical Tiny," said Monty to Clover. "Would never fight acutely even to save his own life. But he's no less a hero."

"But what shall we do with this human?" puzzled Clover, as the man pushed Tiny's corpse aside and struggled to stand up. "He still has a weapon."

"Garth will know, I'm sure," answered Loki, coming up to sniff at Tiny's lifeless body.

"True, it sems that Garth will have all the knowledge we could ever need," admitted Monty, "but Tiny had wisdom, and without Tiny we are disadvantaged."

Garth had watched the whole affair without emotion, even during his mysterious pairing with Tiny's disc, but now he came to the human and placed his powerful paw upon the fallen rifle so that it could not be moved. He called to Tak, who loped over, having been congratulating the staffies upon their kill.

"Please would you take this human away from here to the front gates. Both you and Loki, if you will. You can leave him there," he advised.

"But," argued Loki, "he'll just run away if we do that. He'll bring more of them to shoot the rest of us."

"He won't run," said Garth. "Someone is coming for him. Now can we get rid of the dead human before he begins to stink the place out?"

Loki tugged at Jeff's trouser-leg and, with a wicked growl and bared fangs, Tak prodded him from behind his knee. The man was not going to resist. Having had time to take in the extent of this gathering of canids he was under no illusions as to his uncertain position.

Tak and Loki were given no trouble and, having left Jeff in a state of apprehensive puzzlement at the Willow Croft gates, they were back inside before the dead human had been heaved out into the yard by an enthusiastic group led by Shaggy.

Shaggy was feeling exultant. Garth had treated him with civility, he'd even chosen him for the show-and-tell involving the device on his head, and the black dog was no longer feeling so peripheral, a feeling that had diminished his sense of wellbeing for a very long time. Then, as he glanced away from the main shelter building before heading back, he caught a yellow light building down at the gate, where a grey shadow raised its lantern aloft before all went softly dark once more. Shaggy ran; uncharacteristically, he yearned intensely for that new sense of community safety he had for the first time discovered with the Willow Croft pack.

9. Searchers

Pom was buried at first light. It was more a containment than a burial, since the ground around the Willow Croft complex was too hard to dig. In his search for somewhere to excavate, somewhere far enough from the building that the smell of decomposition would not be offensive, Loki discovered an old stone cattle trough sunk into the ground. It proved a large enough sarcophagus for the Pomeranian, whose body Tak and another lurcher had dragged over the grass.

Pom was covered with a length of plastic sheeting that had become tangled in a fence and the dogs carried mouthfuls of grass and twigs to hold down the plastic.

"It won't keep out the rats," said Monty, "but it's better than being left to rot at a roadside."

Garth and Tak heaved a great log on top of the makeshift vault and, before jumping down, they both raised their legs to give Pom the warmth of their respect.

"We were victims together," said Garth. "I still carry the consequences but she is free of all that. May Black Shuck welcome her as kindly as we all would want."

Tiny's body had been left where he fell, covered by a blanket from one of the pens.

"He was our friend," had insisted Clover, "mine and Monty's. So we should deal with his body."

"You'll need help," said Tak. "He was a big fella."

So it was that, following the disposal of Pom, four lurchers entered the reception hall with Clover, Monty and Garth, their intention being to convey Tiny down the hill to the estuary and launch him on the outgoing tide. It was going to be an arduous way of honouring the grand old dog, but the estuary banks had been his home for many years, and he'd dwelt there in reasonable contentment.

Clover grabbed a corner of the blanket that covered the corpse, noticing as she did that the heap on the floor seemed to have settled during the night, but with the cloth already firmly between her teeth she whisked away the covering.

Everyone froze. There was no corpse, just Tiny's tarnished old collar with the strange disc, which had distorted and warped into a rough nugget of silver metal.

"Gone!" gasped Clover. "Do you suppose…perhaps the grey men…After all, they had left him that disc so he could hear them."

"He hasn't gone anywhere," announced Garth. "He's here, in here." He raised a paw to his head. "Although I think you were correct, Clover, the grey men have most likely taken his body. He seems to have been of particular interest to them."

"How do you mean in here, he's in your head?" It was too fantastic an idea for Monty.

"Monty, my friend, you will no doubt think me crazy, but I once tried to explain to Tiny what it felt like in my head since the grey man touched me with his wand. What I described to him was a place far beyond the limits of my imagination, a room filled with living books that is immense, with the far corners of this room opening out onto a sky full of twinkling stars. When I told him this, I believe he did not doubt what I was saying."

Monty stood with his jaws open, unable to think of a reply.

"And you say he's in there somewhere, Tiny, in that room?" pressed Clover.

"He can be," answered Garth. "When he is not travelling amongst the stars."

To Monty, Clover and the four lurchers, Garth's explanation sounded like the sort of tale to be told around a cosy fire on a dark winter's night. In short, unbelievable. But they chose to accept it because they gained some sense of satisfaction knowing that Tiny might be alive somewhere. And if Tiny had believed it, well…

"Thank Shuck," said Tak. It was all any of them spoke before returning to the rest of the pack, who were eager to know what Garth's next plans might be.

"Just think," said Clover to Monty, "only two days ago I was worried about not having my squeaker to sleep with, and here we are both members of a new pack and having seen off renegade humans."

"It was a comfort to you, that squeaker. I understand," answered Monty, comfortingly. "But that was an indication of your dependency upon your master. We need no such playthings now; we are masters of our own lives. Even I, sceptic that I am, accept how everything has changed." He placed his mouth close to Clover's ear. "But I'm not feeling at all warm about this proposal to go chasing over the countryside in pursuit of the wickedest humans."

Clover leant back and regarded him with surprise.

"Just think about it," said Monty. "This Garth, why is he content to do the bidding of the grey men? We're supposed to be free now, aren't we? That thing in his head, it was put there as a controlling device, wasn't it? Well, who's controlling him now the humans have gone? I'm sorry, I don't like it."

Clover sat quietly and cleaned her claws; she'd been quite excited about the prospect of a long expedition to the northern reaches of the country. She was fleet of foot and sharp of eye; she knew she would be an asset to the search party.

"I'm still of a mind to go," she said. "I need to do something extraordinary to seal my changed existence. Perhaps this will be it."

When the news of Tiny's disappearance first hit the Willow Croft community, there came an initial shock of dismay that spread amongst the whole pack, followed very quickly by fear. Garth had said there was no magic, but watching that strange affair involving Tiny's disc and Garth's implant, and then hearing how Tiny's corpse had shrunk to nothing, to these highly sensitive animals there arose the invisible spectre of hocus-pocus, trickery and hidden forces. Could this be the work of Black Shuck, terrible but ultimately benevolent, or was there something more malign lurking somewhere in the shelter? Everyone trembled for a while until Garth called them to assemble out in the yard, where the bright morning sunshine began to dispel their fears.

"Tiny has not disappeared," he shouted above the noise of screeching crows. "He has gone to join the grey men. You all saw the beginning of his journey, the white fire from his disc that the grey men had given him."

The idea that the grey men had offered Tiny a means of avoiding death was a canny one, and the majority of the gathered canids immediately sat more comfortably in front of Garth, of whom Monty was heard to whisper, "I can see he's properly installed himself as pack leader, hasn't he?"

"Maybe it's Tiny who's speaking," said Clover, "speaking from that room in Garth's head."

Garth heard her but did not correct her. Let them think that way, it was a harmless thought. "To return to my proposal from last night," he continued, "I wish to know who will accompany me on my journey. We shall very likely be going to the far north," he added. This direct challenge brought much muttering, yips and barks, but no volunteers.

"Who are we looking for, exactly?" called Clover. "Every search has to be primed—with a scent or an image. You can't just say 'look for the bad men'."

"The humans we seek are the leaders of humans. They are the most dangerous, since it is they that were responsible for the plans to reach out from this planet. It is these humans who would take war and devastation throughout the stars, which is why I am committed to helping the grey men in this search." Garth stopped for a moment to scratch himself and issue a torrent of sneezes. "Clover, who are we looking for exactly?—I'll tell you. The grey men say this man was the principal leader of the humans who ruled over this land we live in. There are others in other lands; but remember this, our human is tall with white hair, he bears an angry red scar the length of his right forearm, and he walks with a limp, both very identifiable features the consequence of a failed assassination. Now, I will ask as I did last night, did everyone understand all that I just told you, for I am aware we are not all in the same place yet with respect to vocabulary?" He was speaking to the whole pack, with authority and empathy. It brought him swift barks of approval.

"Tomorrow, I leave," he announced. "By twilight barking, I will need to know who is coming with me, who will be the searchers. Whoever you are, you will need to be fast on your legs, keen in nose and ear, and have the courage of Shuck." He paused and then stood tall over them all. "To those who choose to stay, I offer my glad good wishes, for upon you lies the great responsibility of preserving and developing this brave new pack. May the spirit of Tiny remain with you, for he would have been a wise inspiration."

With that petition, Garth ambled over to the entrance gate, lifted his right hind leg and left his mark. No newcomers were to be left in any doubt whose territory this was once he had departed.

10. Dining with Rogues

"How far north?" asked Tak, as they waited for everyone to gather in the yard, some still chewing on the meaty bones that had been dug the previous afternoon from the freezer in the storeroom.

"I know not," answered Garth. "Maybe to the end of the land, it just depends on whether we can overtake them."

"Them?" questioned Tak. "I thought you said it was one particular human that we sought."

"This type of human never travels alone. They need people to guide them away from danger, people to blame when things go wrong, people to massage their ego. He will not be alone, I promise you. But whether we can overtake them, I do not know, for they may have used vehicles to travel. If they have, they will be seen by the grey men, who will tell me."

"But, to the north, even to the end of the land," butted in Clover, "why would they go there."

"It is an empty and wild place where few humans dwelt," explained Garth; "it was chosen by them as the place from where they would launch themselves into space, and as the site of their most terrible weapons. It is also where the grey men suspect the humans may gather to mount a counterattack.

I tell you now, expect to see sights that command great fearfulness, unnatural structures that will look wrong from whatever angle you view them."

"It is also wolf country," added Tak. "We must remember to be respectful."

The expeditionary group accompanying Garth was a dozen strong: Tak and five other lurchers, an Irish wolfhound, three staffies, Clover and Loki. Others had volunteered but were judged likely to be too slow over long distances. Loki, it must be said, was not as fleet of paw as some of the others, but he was an adventurer and the thought of remaining at the shelter was for Loki a notion painted beige. Going into the wild north country promised unknown victuals to be explored and naïve females to be pursued. How could he think of staying behind?

A contingent of dogs had been despatched to assist the bearded collie at the pet store in town and, at Willow Croft, Bunny had been selected to manage the shelter. It restored his sense of honour and he gave a howl of delight. Monty, whose speed over the ground was good only in short bursts, had been persuaded by Clover not to volunteer, and he was glad of her advice, for he had bad premonitions of the direction in which Garth was taking them. Instead, he agreed to act as the shelter's scout, his knowledge of the town below so thorough that he was tasked with rooting out further food sources, for the store at Willow Croft could not last forever and not all those who elected to stay were skilled in hunting for prey.

The search party stayed close to the coast on that first day, it gave them a definite sense of direction, the line of cliffs and then expansive beaches stretching ever away northward. It was only when they reached a great firth that cut across their path that they had to turn inland, a long trek along sandy shores until they reached a man-made crossing, a deserted bridge that rose up high over the water. At the top, Garth called a halt, and they looked down on the city that hugged the shoreline below. A haze of smoke lay over the rooftops and several fires could be seen burning out of control.

"Human work," commented Garth. "Some of their machines and contrivances, too much reliance on heat and unnatural substances. Left without a human hand to command them there will be explosions and devastation. We must avoid cities."

At the far end of the bridge, they were confronted by a group of wild-looking dogs who weaved back and forth across the road. The dominant male was a German shepherd with an ear missing, which lent him an air of roguishness. He crossed to the side of the road as they drew near and peed against a metal stanchion to emphasise his claim to the territory.

Garth stepped out in front and both dogs went through an extended examination of each other.

"Kilmorack Strays," growled the big GSD. "This is our patch, as you can gather. You're not local, are you?"

"Just passing through," said Garth.

"Come far?"

"Far enough."

"Long journey, eh? Long enough to forget your manners." The GSD seemed to be teasing Garth rather than threatening.

"I mean not to offend," said Garth, "but I sincerely do not understand."

"There are thirteen of you," said the GSD. "We can handle thirteen." He looked round at his pack, about ten rough characters of fairly ragged appearance, long-legged and lean.

"What do you say?" he called, and several stretched their necks and howled in response.

Garth stiffened and curled his lip a little to reveal his brutal canine teeth.

"You have come far," said the GSD, "to be so ignorant of our convention here in the north east."

Garth said nothing, while Tak and the others, sensing a challenge, readied themselves to fly into battle.

"All who cross the bridge into our domain must bring good cheer and entertainment. It all begins with a nose-to-nose and ends with a compelling story. In return, we will offer replenishment. That is our custom. As I said, you are fortunate we have enough food set by to satisfy thirteen travellers."

Garth relaxed. "Indeed that would be welcome, I'm sure."

"There is no option to refuse," added the GSD. With his nose, he indicated the side of the bridge. "It's a long way down."

As Garth drew himself up in indignation the GSD roared with laughter, as did several of his compatriots. "Just my bit of fun," he chortled. "We don't see many strangers around here. I couldn't resist it."

Garth relaxed and advanced to touch noses with the GSD; and when the others saw that they followed his lead and fell in behind the Kilmorack Strays, who led them off into the cover of broom and heather that terminated the bridge.

The meal that was provided consisted principally of fish, and the GSD, who gave his name as Ham, explained that nearby was a salmon farm, which offered easy pickings. "If you don't mind getting your paws wet," he laughed.

"So, I must honour your tradition," said Garth, "and conclude this gracious meal with a narrative that shall entertain you."

"We don't know narrative, although I guessed gracious," said Ham. "A saucy tale would do us fine."

"I have nothing like that to tell, but the story of our journey should amaze you if wonder and surprise will suffice."

"As you will have noticed, we do not follow all your words," said Ham, "but if you can keep the tale simple for us simple lads and lasses I am sure that wonder and surprise will do just fine."

And so Garth commenced by introducing his fellow travellers and explained how they came to know each other. He then gave snapshots from his own history and, when mentioning some unpleasant detail from his time at the laboratory, several of the Kilmorack Strays put their paws over their eyes and whimpered.

"So that explains the odd swelling on the top of your head," proclaimed Ham, triumphantly. "When first I set eyes upon you I wondered, has this fellow been dealt a mighty blow with a chunk of wood or, noticing his confident swagger, perhaps his brain has grown so huge he wears it on the outside of his skull."

"I'm glad I'm already forewarned that you are given to jest," said Garth with a sharp look, "or I might take offence at your observation."

"No offence," responded Ham. "But we do not go much on false dignity here."

"That swelling, which you remarked upon," continued Garth, "is at the nub of my story. It is a device inserted by the humans as an experiment to find out if they could command me at will, even contrary to my will or neglectful of my natural ability to execute their wishes."

"How foolish of them," exclaimed Ham. "They had only to ask you. Surely they would know we are an intelligent species."

"It is the way with humans. If they want to find something out, however pointless is their curiosity, they will go to the ends of the earth to find it, at whatever the cost to others. They have technology—you know technology?"

Ham and several others nodded sagely.

"So they have technology, and having it they are compelled to use it. It seems the technology makes them do things they'd never thought of before. So this device in my head is a piece of their technology. Although of course, it is no longer theirs. Which brings me to the more current part of my tale, which involves the grey men, who are here exactly because of the humans' advances in technology."

Mention of the grey men brought a few growls and moments of rapid ear scratching from both the Kilmorack Strays and Garth's own team of searchers.

"What have the grey men told you of their purpose for the Canidae?" Garth spoke directly to the strays, causing them all to stir and shuffle, and eventually look to Ham.

"They say we are the future," said Ham. "They say there is no need for strife amongst us, that there is plenty in the world for all, and without greed we shall prosper."

"That is our understanding too," agreed Garth. "It is our turn to take charge of the world and arrange it as we believe it should be run. That is the message I am receiving from them."

"You talk to them!" Ham sat up, astonished.

"That is the rest of my story. I said it would surprise you."

So Garth told of the moment when the grey man touched his implant with its wand, the changes that subsequently took place in his head, the commotion of knowledge, and the reaches into deep space that he carried within him. Everyone who listened leant forward on their claws, their eyes wide, several of them panting with a chill unease.

"It is because of the grey men that we are making this journey. We are seeking out the most dangerous of the humans for them and our reward will be to have finally mastered the world on behalf of us all."

"Is that it?" Clover whispered to Loki. "I detect some human thoughts in that speech, which Garth has not previously shared with us. I hope I am not over-reacting, but the word megalomania just popped into my head when I was grasping for an apt description. Do you know it?"

"It is the lust for power," Loki hissed. "Take care."

"And you talk to them all the time?" asked Ham, fascinated by Garth's disclosure.

"From time to time," answered Garth. "They send me information to assist our search."

"And you go onward north, I assume." The GSD licked his lips, thoughtfully.

"To the farthest places if necessary."

"We have passed by that way on occasion," said Ham. "It has been made an uncanny place, a green landscape high above the sea, poisoned by strange buildings that have a wrong scent about them, and with large objects that soar on flames into the sky uttering a sound like the sky itself is tearing apart."

117

"If that is where they hide, it will be their last refuge," asserted Garth. "Now, the day is marching on and we must go further before the humans gather strength to attack. We thank you mightily for the sustenance."

A chorus of friendly barking was given in response to his thanks and the Kilmorack Strays rose as one to escort the searchers back to the road.

"You will have much to tell at twilight barking," suggested Garth.

"But who will believe us?" asked Ham.

Garth crossed the road and issued a hot stream of pee on the stanchion marked earlier by Ham, before stepping out at a pace with his tail held erect, his team of twelve hastening to keep up.

"Cheeky old fantasist," laughed Ham, watching the party disappear up the road. "Well, lads and lasses, how was that for an entertaining lunch?"

11. Scavengers

Monty was feeling out of sorts. When the search party had disappeared from view over the hill, he took himself off to his pen and curled up with his nose under his paws. First, Tiny had gone from his life, then his friend Clover had taken off on a mission he feared would end badly. That Garth, he was too confident, too powerful with the magical device in his skull, it was clear he meant to become some kind of top dog over them all. It didn't bode well.

He lay on his rug and dozed uncomfortably until Shaggy's unkempt muzzle poked around the door.

"What's up, mate?" asked the black dog, sniffing at Monty's tail. "Miss your bitch, do you? I know I would if—"

"Clover is not my bitch, you piece of..." growled Monty. "And you'd have no chance with her, you tatty mongrel, I promise you."

"Sorry, mate, I was only…"

Monty uttered a sharp bark of rebuke. "Leave it, Shaggy, I have things to do."

The shelter was already feeling claustrophobic for the dog who had quickly acclimatised to an outdoor life. Monty had always spent much of his time out of doors when the blacksmith was at work, sitting out front watching life on the

119

street, or just rooting around the neighbourhood to see what was what. More recently, he had valued his excursions with Clover, going ratting in the back yards of abandoned buildings or simply exploring the sea shore aromas of the estuary beach. The shelter was too static now that the commotion that had followed Garth's arrival was over. He got up and pushed past Shaggy. "Things to do," he repeated. "No time like the present."

This is uncanny, he thought to himself as he crossed the front yard to the gate. *These slick little phrases. Was my master in the habit of saying no time like the present? I don't recall. So where did it come from? Perhaps I have a library in my head, just like Garth's.* It was an intractable question and, being a pragmatic soul he decided not to pursue it, for he had a very real purpose in front of him.

Taking the road down the hill to the town, Monty began to cheer up. It was a bright sunny morning and the sky was atremble with the optimistic cry of laverocks. There was no traffic to watch out for and he was free to consider the task that had been set him. It was not urgent just yet, there were plentiful stores at the shelter, but he thought it prudent to scout out potential food supplies in advance, so that anything promising might be identified, even concealed, for collection at a future date. Anything that was going to last, at least.

He remembered the last time he had come down here, the evening he had met Tak, and he felt glad that Clover was in the company of half a dozen lurchers. They seemed a decent lot to Monty, and he knew he was usually slow to warm to strangers. He was enjoying being out in the sun; he strutted along, feeling at last that perhaps he hadn't a care in the world and that all would come good after all.

Finding himself among the commercial centre of the town, Monty began to assess the likelihood of making a good find in each of the premises he passed. He hadn't had enough opportunity to learn to read, and the names on shopfronts meant nothing to him, but his nose was sufficient when it came to reading the scents of what lay behind those open doors.

Some of the doors, and some of the windows too, had been smashed, and Monty guessed that there had been other scavengers in these parts—human scavengers with tools to break their way in. But the grey men had been all through this town, he was sure of that, and he didn't anticipate meeting any humans.

At the end of one street, a couple of blocks from where the blacksmiths' had stood, he picked up an interesting aroma, drifting on the still air. What was that? It was familiar and it spoke of food. Toast and jam, that's what it was, hot buttered toast and strawberry jam. The blacksmith used to toast bread on a long fork over his furnace, and he would share delicious pieces with Monty. Oh, happy days, he remembered, salivating.

Without thinking, his mind full of happy memories of the time with his master, Monty followed his nose. If there was toast, someone was making it, and that was more likely to be a human than a grey man. But perhaps it wasn't toast he could smell, just something like it that smelled equally delicious, and there might be other tasty things to be had. Caught by the fragrance, Monty was like a fish on a line and mounted the kerb. A door was ajar at the front of the dwelling from whence came the alluring odour and he peeked inside. It was dark in the hallway but he could see a light coming from a room at the end. There were plastic bags stuffed full of things wrapped in coloured paper, stacked all along the hallway, and Monty sniffed delightedly as the intoxicating tang of bacon from one of them excited his nostrils. Crumbs, what else might there be in this place? He tiptoed along the hall, listening for any movement. But so what if there were humans here, it didn't necessarily mean danger.

Before Monty reached the door to the lighted room, two voices, distinctively human voices, began arguing.

"Is this all the shit they left behind? A half mouldy loaf and a pot of home-made jam."

"They always had a well-stocked fridge, Joe, I thought there'd be something decent in there."

"An' that's what you told me, you fucker, you said there'd be some nice steaks waiting for us, defo."

"Obviously someone's beat us to it, Joe. Not my fault. They always had meat in the house, promise."

"Course it's your fault. An' there was me all ready to barbecue a nice piece of sirloin. It's months since I 'ad a juicy steak."

"But we got plenty of stuff out in the hall, Joe, we found some really decent stuff."

"It ain't grub though, is it, 'cept for a bit of maggoty bacon. An' all that dosh and jewellery we found, that's no use now really, come to think of it."

Monty stopped before reaching the open door. Best get out of here. There was nothing to find here except for a couple of tetchy humans. He backed down the hallway, keeping his eyes on the open door. Halfway down, his tail caught the side of a carrier bag with something heavy inside, and it toppled over.

"Whassat?" cried one of the men and rushed outside into the hall. "It's a bloomin' dog," he shouted to his companion. "Good boy." He bent and clicked his fingers at Monty who stood resolutely still.

The second man, Joe from his tone, burst out from the lighted room. "Grab it Billy," he roared. "Bring it 'ere."

"Nah, Joe, we don't want to be bothered with a pet right now, it'd be awkward."

"That's fresh meat, that is," insisted Joe. "I can see at least a couple of steaks on that little bugger."

Joe pushed past Billy and started to wave a wooden club at Monty, but the dog simply ducked and backed away with a snarl.

The man crouched down and put out his hand, placatingly, an invitation that Monty couldn't refuse, so he darted forward and sank his upper canines into the man's palm, his lower set of teeth making a corresponding penetration when his jaws closed fully around the hand.

Joe screamed and dropped his club, the air in the corridor on fire with his anguish. It was the moment when Monty thought to run, but Billy gave a flying tackle and grabbed his tail, winding him and hauling him back over Joe's supine body.

His rump now the seat of a great ache, Monty found himself thrown down on a bare kitchen table, beneath a bright lightbulb, held down by two thick hands around his neck and a knee in his groin.

"Right," said Joe, wiping his hand free of blood on Monty's thigh, "keep 'im still an' I'll smash his head in with this." He raised the club high over Monty.

"Stop," yelled Monty. "The grey men are coming. They brought me to find out who was hiding here."

The club hovered in the air.

"A talking dog," exclaimed Billy. "I'd heard about these. They're the aliens' doing. Like he says, we'd better make ourselves scarce or it'll be curtains for us."

"Fuck the aliens, I'm starving," roared Joe, and he raised the club once more.

There came the sound of the front door crashing open against the wall in the hall and, climbing on a chair, Billy threw himself through the broken kitchen window into the garden.

"Come on, you bastards!" yelled Joe, advancing to the hallway, the club held out in front of him. "I'm ready for ya."

But he wasn't ready for the black streak that launched itself from the hall floor, sending him backwards into the room, where he collided with the table.

"Shall we kill him?" Shaggy asked Monty. He stood on the man's chest, his fangs teasing at the man's agonised scalp.

"Let's go," replied Monty, letting go Joe's wrist, with which he had stopped the man fending off the black dog. "There's nothing here for us."

Regaled by a torrent of curses, the two dogs trotted out to the street.

"That was so stupid of me," hissed Monty, when they were well away from the dwelling. "If Tiny had been with me, he'd never have let me go inside, it was so foolish of me." He stopped and rubbed his head against the black dog's shaggy mane. "Thank you," he said. "What were you doing there anyway?"

"Don't thank me," said Shaggy, "thank Tiny. Do you remember, when he arrived at the shelter, he said that as a member of the pack we'd always have someone looking out for us? Well, I could see you were in no frame of mind to be thinking straight, so I followed you."

"Thank Shuck for Tiny," said Monty, "and for you, of course."

"We should go back," said Shaggy, "back to the shelter. We can come back tomorrow, the two of us."

12. Complaisants

When the rain started, Loki wondered whether it would be best to go back to the shelter at Willow Croft. Not that the prospect of being there was terribly attractive, but it would have been a sight more comfortable than here in this sepulchral forest of pines, where the branches were spitefully loading themselves with huge drops of rainwater before releasing them on the party far below.

He huddled in a drift of pine needles with Clover as they all stopped for a rest.

"Where's Garth?" he asked. I haven't been at the front with you, I haven't set eyes on him since we were with those curious strays.

"He's probably off marking again," she complained. "He's been like that all the way since the bridge. Did you see him? It's ridiculous, he can't be expecting to claim all this as his territory."

"Perhaps it's so he can find our way back more easily, or just let others know we've come through peaceably and moved on."

Clover shook her head but said no more. It was probably wise of her for, at that moment, Tak ran up, having been off scouting the way ahead. He'd assumed the role of Garth's lieutenant and shown himself as highly adept at slipping away in front to establish the most advantageous tracks, as well as noting those to avoid.

"There's a camp a little way in front of us. A human camp, in a clearing. Some of their weird houses on wheels are still there, and some low buildings under the trees. Oh, and a fire is burning, in the middle of the clearing. I saw someone moving, dogs I think, but I didn't engage before telling Garth. Is he back yet?"

"Back from where?" asked Loki.

"He didn't say, exactly, just that the grey men had been talking to him."

"Talking? Talking about what?" demanded Clover. "He hasn't said anything to the rest of us."

"He didn't tell me either," admitted Tak. He paused and looked to see if anyone was listening. "Only, he did say he needed to meet the wolves. Something about getting back to his roots. I remember him mentioning the need to negotiate— do you know that word?"

"Now that is interesting," said Loki. "What on earth would he have to negotiate with the wolves? We are on the edge of wolf territory, of course, but as fellow Canidae we certainly shouldn't expect to be negotiating a way through it."

"Best wait for him to tell us," suggested Tak. "He's been a bit sharp with me the last few miles when I've quizzed him about what lies ahead."

"Here he is now," said Clover. "I recognise his step on the underbrush."

Garth came up to them at a rush. "The light's fading," he gasped to Tak, "so what's your recommendation?"

"I think I've found somewhere where we can be dry for the night."

"Lead on," commanded Garth. "I'll gather the rest of my doughty pack."

"I hope you heard that," whispered Loki to Clover. "His pack of all things. You chose the right word back at the bridge with the strays."

"I'm still a loyal member of Tiny's pack. I'm just waiting for him to appear from inside Garth's head." In a fit of pique, Clover shook her head so that her ears clapped noisily against the side of her head.

"I don't think it works like that," said Loki. "I got the feeling that Tiny is somewhere a long, long way away. Perhaps the place the grey men came from."

They followed Tak along a soft path of pine needles and merged with the other dogs, who had already been assembling in a tiny clearing, and they all fell in behind the tall lurcher. He sprang through the straggly bracken with the others close behind, slowing only when flaming spasms from the fire became visible between the narrow trunks of the trees.

"Don't tell me that canids have learnt how to make fire," said the Irish wolfhound. "That would be something."

"It wouldn't be permitted," snapped Garth, running up. "That would be too much of a risk. Now move on."

They all pushed through the tall grass that bordered the clearing. The rain was easing off now and they stopped to shake the accumulated raindrops and burrs from their coats, at last drifting forward on apprehensive legs in ones and twos, cautiously towards the glow of burning logs. At the centre of the fire was an entire tree whose trunk glowed with an intense heat, and it was clearly this that had kept the fire going.

Someone was reclining on an old mattress just beyond the singe-point of the fire's intensity, an ancient golden retriever with a grey muzzle, large black dugs and a significant paunch. Oblivious of the haphazard raindrops that hissed onto the fire's scattered embers, she seemed to be snoozing; but she sat up with a groan on her arthritic limbs when Tak and the wolfhound, having picked their way forward through the hot wood ash, announced themselves with a gentle prod of their noses.

"Oh," she yawned. "Visitors."

She stared through rheumy eyes at Tak. "Are you the leader of this new contingent of revellers?" she demanded. "Only everyone's away at the moment. They're so fed up with Mr Dog."

"I'm the leader here," growled Garth from behind the lurcher.

"And where's Mr Dog?" asked Tak. "Your leader, I take it."

At that, the old retriever flashed him a myopic look of scorn. "Where have you lived your life, sonny," she sneered, "in a cave, on a remote island? Mr Dog is human-made food for dogs, disgusting stuff full of sawdust. The humans who came to stay here brought a supply meant to last months; they'd come to start a new life together. Didn't your human have those little silver trays with the picture of a rabbit on the front, meant to give you an appetite for the muck? I told Toby to go and fetch us some real rabbit, something with fresh blood and chewy bones, not the rubbish made from stuff the humans usually threw away."

"I didn't have a human of my own," confessed Tak.

"Strays!" yelped the retriever. "You're a bunch of wandering strays. Look—we've nothing here of value, we're just a harmless gathering of likeminded souls minding our own business. We don't want any trouble."

"These are not vagabond strays," interceded Garth. "This is my pack and we are on a noble mission. But if you have a warm and dry place for us to spend the night, and perhaps some decent food, we would be very grateful."

The old retriever settled back and gave Garth as good an examination as her eyes would allow, her nose working overtime. "You smell strange," she ventured, her lip curling to expose dirty yellow teeth. "Something uncommon about you, and it's not just the pig's ears you're wearing. You've not been brought here by those creepy grey men, have you? I watched them slinking about the vans over there, going in places which weren't theirs to enter, and when they came out our humans had vanished. First we knew was their huge frisbee coming down out of the sky, right there in the middle of the clearing. Three or four of them, there were, climbing out of that thing, each with those weird lamps on poles that shine bright even in the daytime. They sat with us all evening and when we awoke the next morning we found ourselves like this, changed, talking in the way of humans. I was wondering what they'd do next when, without a word, they went off again in the frisbee. It rose straight up, like a laverock, but before it was high in the sky they shone a light on to the tree and that's how we have the fire, you see. The others who came later have kept it going with sticks and pieces of human rubbish. It gets very cold here at night, you see."

"Who are these others?" asked Garth quickly. "More grey men?"

"Word got round that we had a settlement here. It's become a bit of a draw in the retriever world. The humans had held a show for golden retrievers just a few walks south of here, at a place where our breed began, years ago. Hundreds of us beautiful creatures brought from all over to be brushed and cosseted and paraded in a ring. And when their humans were removed they were all a bit lost, just left there with their rosettes and nowhere to go. Many had come a long way, some from other lands, and didn't know how to get home, so they came here. It's been quite a party ever since. Of course, most of them are sorely missing their humans, so they've turned to each other for comfort—non-stop frolicking and zoomies ever since. Those of us who were already here have rather enjoyed their company, it felt like we'd been left in a dark place ourselves after our own humans vanished."

"Well," said Garth, a look of alarm on his face, "we've not been brought here by the grey men, as you feared, nor are we seeking to canoodle in party mood. It sounds to me as if the grey men did not explain much to you, but I am talking to them all the while and I shall relay their wise words to you in due course. So, where is everybody?"

"I told you, Toby's gone to the warren to catch us fresh meat. A lot of them went with him, too many to keep the hunt quiet I reckon, and the rest have gone for a snooze in the washing houses or the vans. Like I said, they're tired from all the fun they've been having."

"What are these washing houses?" asked Tak.

"Those low buildings under the trees," said the retriever, "where the humans would wash themselves. We go there for drinking water, but there are piles of cloth the humans used to dry themselves, and they make cosy places to sleep."

"Some of our group would like to visit those houses," said Tak to Garth. "There have been very few streams to drink from since we left the bridge and I've noticed some long tongues since a while back."

"Good idea. You organise that, Tak, while I go and find this Toby."

Toby lay stretched full length in the deep grass of a second clearing just a tennis ball's throw from where the old retriever bitch was resting. He was a large red-coated dog with an immaculately groomed coat. Garth made exaggerated panting noises as he approached so as not to startle him.

"Hello," said Garth, lying down alongside the retriever. "Toby?"

Toby glanced up and with a frown focused on Garth's implant and floppy pink ears. "Oh, is it fancy dress this afternoon?" he asked in all innocence. "I think I'll go as an Ethiopian red wolf."

"Have you ever met an Ethiopian red wolf?" asked Garth, nonplussed.

"My humans kept a small zoo," explained Toby. "I used to sit near her and do tricks to keep up her spirits until we could help her escape. Just somersaults and stuff like that—would you like to see?" When Garth didn't answer he continued with, "By the way, did Nell send you?"

"The old bitch by the fire?"

"Yes, that's Nell. Good with the pups is Nell. She's had plenty of practice, you may have noticed."

"And did the red wolf escape."

"Oh, that's a splendid story I will share with you. But later. Yes, she did, she's come north too, but has had a bit of bother being accepted in wolf country. I expect that will improve now we can all converse as one community."

"What are you doing here?" asked Garth.

"My humans joined their own new community to escape something called the rat race, though I can't say I'd ever seen rats racing. But I do remember them going on and on about it—the rat race I mean. Anyway, they and others decided to live hereabouts and live off the land."

"No, I mean, what are you doing here, on this slope, hidden in the grass. And where are all the others, all your companions?"

"No patience, you see. I told them we must lie low until the rabbits thought it safe to come out. The warren's just over there, look." He nodded towards a sandy bank riddled with burrow entrances. "But they quickly grew bored and went off to the river for a swim and Shuck knows what else. I'm stuck here on my own, left to catch supper for all of us."

"No luck yet then?" Garth looked around for rabbit corpses and found none.

"Well," sighed Toby, "I'm not really much of a hunter. Retrievers retrieve things, you know, things other folk have hunted. Other than that I'm a lovely boy, that's what my human said, and I do enjoy being lovely."

Garth cringed and, to change the subject said, "There's a rabbit now. It's sitting up sniffing the air and not picking up our scent. Could you catch it, do you think."

"Oh, look at him," chuckled Toby. "what a sweet little chap."

Garth gave a loud groan and the rabbit hopped back underground.

"You frightened him, the poor little mite," complained Toby. "I don't know if he'll come back now."

"I think you need help," said Garth. "I'll be back in a while with some friends."

Two lurchers and the three staffies put on a display of hunting that dazzled the watching Toby, who shuddered every time there came a sharp squeak, meaning a rabbit's soul had been despatched to rabbit heaven. Nonetheless he ventured to help carry their catch back to the clearing with the fire, the successful hunt accompanied by a throng of returning wet retrievers who shook themselves furiously dry in front of the glowing embers.

Strips of rabbit flesh were joyfully mixed in a large enamel basin with kibble from a sack of Chappie, and there was just enough for everyone to at least have a taste of the fresh meat.

Garth perched on the old mattress between Nell and Toby, while the rest of the travellers and the golden retrievers spread themselves agreeably around the fire, which brightened the gathering dusk with its continued intensity.

"It's story time," said Toby, licking the last taste of rabbit from his greasy lips. "Our tradition, only I'm not sure it's something old enough to be a tradition. I'm still grappling with the meaning of words."

"It's the same for us all," remarked Garth. "It's just that I have an advantage, being able to talk directly with the grey men, who make things very clear to me. Perhaps that should be my story."

So, with a nod from Nell, who was clearly accepted as the dominant elder amongst the retrievers, Garth for the second time that day told how he came to have the implant in his head and how the grey man had changed its function to enable constant contact with the aliens. To finish, he gave the example of the grey men requesting help in finding the human pack leaders, and how this had led them north to this forest. Toby listened avidly, his eyes bright with wonder; Nell too paid close attention, but with eyes half closed and her lip turned back in a sardonic curl.

"So," she began, as soon as Garth stopped speaking, "it was the grey men who sent you on your noble mission, was it? So why don't they seek these wicked humans themselves? They can travel in the sky and see everything below."

It was a question to which Garth could not find a satisfactory rebuff. It had been the same when Tiny and Rani had both challenged him, and all he could do was extol the canids' virtues in seek and find. It was a response he repeated now. "We are best suited to executing this endeavour," he bragged, "it makes the best sense."

"It seems to me that you have simply changed your master," said the old bitch. "That device in your head, it is still being used to command you; they have not set you free."

"We are all free now," insisted Garth. "Have not the grey men explained it to you? The world is ours now and we must take hold of it and make it work harmoniously. We are all responsible for ourselves now."

"I don't think anyone here is thinking like that," interjected Toby. "Most of us are unhappy that our masters have disappeared. No more regular meals of fresh meat, no more sleeping on a firm mattress between two warm bodies, no belly rubs and a kind word and biscuit at waking. What you are suggesting doesn't sound at all appealing."

"So what will you do," asked Garth, sounding horrified.

"What we are doing now," snapped Nell, with applause coming from the other retrievers. in the shape of a round of enthusiastic barking. "Enjoying each other's company, living life as it was, in a place our humans intended us to be, for as long as we can. And then, when the time comes, we'll have to think about what next."

"But that's not, that's not—" gasped an exasperated Garth.

"Right?" Nell gave a high-pitched laugh. "Look, stranger, there is no right or wrong way, only a this way and a that way. You'll discover that in time, I'm sure. Now, I'm of a mind to sleep. I suggest you and your friends find somewhere to bed down, there are still plenty of spaces in the vans and the washing houses where you can enjoy a warm, dry night. Please thank your friends for the rabbit; my lad Toby will hopefully have learnt from you the trick of catching them." She glared at the hapless retriever, then, "Oh, just one thing more before I shut my sorry eyes: I've been watching you, Garth; please stop making your mark all around our encampment. It is not your territory."

13. Wolf Country

Loki had an upset stomach. He'd grabbed a couple of mouthfuls of Mr Dog before they left the encampment. With a griping belly, he fell back behind the others almost as soon as they set out through the forest. Clover walked with him, she felt more confident talking to Loki than to the lurchers and wolfhound, even the staffies; they'd all sprung to attention when Garth barked out the instruction to get moving and it left a nasty taste in her mouth. Clover had admired Loki's reluctance to submit to orders, even if the manner of his delay had led to him feeling unwell.

Anyway, it gave her an opportunity to voice her disquiet with respect to Garth. "He's still marking like he has a bladder problem," she complained. "We'll need to find water soon or he'll have run dry."

"I'm feeling rather dry myself," said Loki. "I slept out all night next to that fire, with a nice young retriever cross, very nice she was, but I've felt parched from the moment I woke up."

"I have no sympathy," smirked Clover, with her nose in the air.

"But," added Loki, "speaking of the fire; when we first approached that camp, did you hear what Garth told the wolfhound? I've been wanting to talk about it ever since."

"No, I had stayed at the back instead of running up to the leaders like nosy you." Clover was feeling miffed about his admission of a night-time dalliance.

"Nosy gets to know," he quipped. "Anyway, what I heard Garth say was that we wouldn't be permitted to learn how to make fire. The two of them were looking down on the fire at the centre of the encampment, and he said we'd be forbidden because it would be too much of a risk. Now, who do you imagine would be so determined to stop us as to forbid it?"

"The grey men?"

"Of course, the grey men. And you know why, don't you?"

Clover thought for several paces. "You tell me," she said, "you're the canny one."

"I've been exploring the words in my head," said Loki. "Life isn't all willing young bitches. And what do you find when you see how words connect with each other to make new words? You get a story. The humans called it derivation. So I've been doing some of this derivation while on this march, and in answer to your particular question, we won't be permitted to learn how to make fire because fire leads to explosions, and explosions need explosives, and explosives lead to fighting equipment and fighting equipment become weapons."

"You are so clever, Loki."

"But you understand don't you? Fire can be a good thing, like at the camp, but it can lead to the creation of terrible machines, which in the wrong hands will be used destructively."

"Oh!" Clover was looking worried and whimpered a little.

"Which," continued Loki, "brings us to the grey men. They are here to stop the humans taking all that destruction out into the stars. We all know that. And they certainly don't want us to learn how to make fire, like the humans, and become a risk to them all over again."

Clover walked on carefully, suddenly aware that they'd almost caught up with the rest of the pack. "He's doing it again," she said, spying Garth lifting a hind leg against a tree stump before stalking off into the forest.

"Marking the trail?" suggested Loki.

"I'm not sure," replied Clover. "Just how much is he hearing from the grey men, I wonder. That he knew they'd stop us learning how to make fire, it's as if he's being passed a set of rules."

"With which to rule us?" suggested Loki. "He clearly has ambition. I would also agree with that old retriever bitch, that Garth has simply been passed from one master to another. We need to continue this expedition with caution."

"With an open mind, Tiny would have said." Clover was still hopeful that Tiny would reappear magically from out of Garth's head.

The travellers had come to a halt and Loki and Clover suddenly found themselves in the thick of the throng. There was no sign of Garth and Clover asked Tak why they had stopped.

"We're well inside wolf territory," he answered. "Garth's gone ahead to check that we're not going to stumble into any special places. You know the wolves are very jealous of certain areas where particular family things are done? Well, he wants to make sure we avoid them."

It sounded plausible to Clover, although she'd never heard of this before, and Loki just shrugged when she glanced him a questioning eye.

Garth was at that very moment standing on the edge of a stony cliff, unexpectedly high above the land below, which gave him the perspective of a broad valley, thick with rowan and silver birch, and richly watered by two foaming rivers that stretched and leapt to the horizon. His eyes gleamed in the midday sun and he arched his back in a movement of delight.

"If I pee here, all this will be mine," he said to no-one in particular, licking his lips and nodding to himself.

"It's not yours to have," said a dark voice, the words wrapped up in a wet growl. "First, this is traditional wolf territory, and second, the wolf nation has accepted the word of the grey man, that there is enough for all to share without conflict."

Garth did not turn to face the speaker, but raised his hackles and stood as tall as he could. He had come through enough terrible things in recent years to eschew fear now.

The massive red wolf slid out from the trees on huge paws and positioned herself next to Garth, so close he felt her chin whiskers against the side of his face.

"It fills me with awe to see this country," she remarked, "for I too am a stranger in this land. When first I arrived here, I was denied a place, for I come from very far away. But with the coming of the grey man everything is changed, and I am at last a wolf among wolves who will share to all who come in peace."

Garth turned his head to assess the nature of this beast, easily half as tall again as a grey wolf, it seemed to him, with a tail more like that of a fox's brush than a wolf's, thick and tipped with jet. This wolf was lean and muscular, with a close-fitting coat of shiny russet, white stockings and a white rump. He could appreciate she was a splendid animal, if a daunting adversary.

"I am Garth," he said, with no fear in his voice. "I am passing through this land on a quest. I lead a pack of travellers on a mission that serves the grey men."

"I am aware of that," said the wolf. "My name is Bala. I have been tracking you all morning. If you intend to continue north, you have challenging terrain ahead of you and I shall guide you. There are places you must not tread upon or defile with your own marks. Ignore my warnings and you will suffer certain death."

To Garth, relinquishing his charge over the mission was not to his liking, but he saw how it might be turned to his advantage. Rejecting Bala's help would, however, be foolish, for he had heard tell of the mysterious ways of the wolves and to incur risk simply out of a desire to preserve his pride did not make sense.

He led the red wolf back through the trees to where the others waited, the sudden appearance of this spectacular creature setting them down on their hindquarters in awe with a bump, the dogs all jumping with fright at first, seeing this huge beast with sparkly eyes and an open mouth filled with razor-sharp teeth, and they sat awkwardly and defenceless, bewildered by Garth's apparent unconcern. Loki let out a long beagle howl of incomprehension.

"This is Bala," said Garth in his most confident tone. "I have asked her to guide us through the next stretch of our journey, which the grey men have warned me is wolf territory, where passage requires sensitivity toward their customs."

Bala said nothing to contradict Garth's hubris but silently eyed each of the travellers in turn, then turned to the northern sky, raised her snout high and gave a long stentorian howl that shook scuttering wildfowl from the underbrush.

She looked back at Garth and the pack, quietly explaining that it had been a signal, a warning that strangers were about and intending to cross the land. "Courtesy," she said, "it is a word I have only now come to know and understand, although it is something we are familiar with in my homeland. If you meet any denizens of the way ahead, remember, courtesy will smooth your passing, for its essence is the showing of respect, which works both ways."

"A wise wolf," whispered Clover to Loki. "You'll get on well."

"That's enough of your cheek," said Loki. "But she is without doubt an impressive-looking canid." He knew that observation would inflame Clover with jealousy, then he thought better of it and nuzzled her ear.

No-one had demurred and Bala took them on a path that none but she seemed able to detect, there were no indications that it had been used before yet they found themselves free of obstacles; no snagging fronds or courses of loose stones slowed their passage, even though they were walking through an increasingly rocky terrain that sloped steeply down the side of the valley which had so impressed Garth.

At the bottom of the hill, the trees thinned out and they left the pines behind them. Ahead were shiny wet banks of vivid green grass and bracken that bunched along the line of silvery boulders bounding a river. Having climbed down for some time they were still high over the water, which rushed white and untamed over rocks, sleek black spines that jutted menacingly through the foaming cascade. Beyond the river the country marched uphill again, but less dramatically so, the gentle gradient populated with deciduous trees which looked less forbidding than the forest of firs. There had been no sighting of grey wolves, but it was the question of how to cross this crazy river that worried the weary dogs.

To their left as they surveyed the hungry waters the land rose in a great stony outcrop, the river racing over its edge in a tumultuous waterfall.

"That is our crossing," said Bala. "I am too large for it but all of you…" She quickly looked at everyone to gauge their proportions. "Yes, all of you should just fit, although you" (she peered meaningfully at the wolfhound) "you may come out on the far bank a little damp."

The crossing was a slippery ledge beneath the curve of the falling waters. The staffies were to go first, not because they were the bravest but due to their size. But because they were indisputably brave they fought to be the first to run through, although Bala made them wait, with intervals between, so that the safe arrival of each of them could be confirmed before the next took off. The first to go, a feisty brindle, disappeared after a few yards, her colouring merging with the spray, but then came a gruff bark from Bala, who had seen the plucky dog hop across rocks onto the opposite bank.

Loki was selected as the next after the staffies to try the run. He feigned nonchalance and clambered up on to the ledge, exaggerating a slip as his pads failed to grip the stone.

Clover squealed but Loki turned and threw her a cheeky bark that encouraged her to follow him. She shrugged off the nerves that had been troubling her and raced after him, catching him as he jumped down to the grass on the other side. They both shook themselves vigorously to expel the spray that had doused them, finding Tak beside them when they'd finished. Tak seemed pleased with himself, he was as dry as a bone and was keen to show off his prowess at running the waterfall. He stood tall and stretched his neck in search of admiration.

"Tak," said Loki quietly, "we're not watching you. But someone is." He flicked his eyes in the direction of the trees behind them. Three pairs of yellow eyes glittered unmoving from the shadows, three wolves hidden unmoving in the tall grass.

"Don't stare at them," said Clover quickly. "Remember courtesy."

The wolfhound had now arrived and he was dripping wet, his wiry fur sparkling with droplets. He shook himself next to Tak and the lurcher was immediately drenched.

"What is that human saying about pride?" said Loki to Tak with a gleam in his eye.

"At least, I didn't fall," snapped Tak, peering through the descending screen of water, where they could all make out a murky image of Garth struggling to stay on four legs, the shelf having been seriously wetted by the wolfhound's clumsy run through.

"He'll be peeved," said Loki. "Perhaps we can look forward to a more humble Garth from now on."

"But what about Bala?" asked Clover, suddenly remembering the red wolf's comment.

When the last lurcher had made it through the water tunnel, everyone's eyes were on the red wolf. She turned and began to walk downstream, and Garth suddenly felt wretched—had he been hoodwinked? Loki had pointed out the watching grey wolves amongst the trees; had Bala simply brought them to this place to be prey for her cousins? Were they to be sacrificed for some pact she had made to earn her acceptance in wolf territory, and what she had said about respect, was there a hidden meaning to her lesson?

"Here she goes," Loki was saying, "just look at those legs. She could have been a deer."

Bala had slunk away from the river a little way, her carriage low, then turning she ran towards the racing current and took off in a high, graceful leap, a red flare against the clear blue sky.

She'll never make it, thought Garth. *It's too wide even for the most agile of deer.*

But as she descended in a graceful arc, little more than halfway across the torrent, and thinking she would be swept away before his eyes, Garth jumped back astounded, the red wolf springing lightly on her thickly furred paws from the rocks that broke the waters' surface, and sailing on to the safety of the river bank.

"That was an amazing show," congratulated Garth, who ran to her, his tail wagging with relief.

"At my home, our common food is the giant mole rat," said Bala. "But the humans have taken so much of our land for their goats and cattle we have to seek further afield for other food, which increasingly is antelope. To catch an antelope one has to leap like an antelope and I have had much

145

practice." She sat and steadfastly licked her paws clean of blood where the lethal rocks had wounded her.

"Grey wolves are watching us," said Garth quietly.

"I have seen them," she replied. "But remember, as Canidae they will have heard the same words of the grey men as yourself. They are no threat unless we trespass on their sacred places. Come, we must press on; call the others from their rest."

The journey was easier now, principally because of the soft light that came through the leaves of the deciduous plantation, where during the morning the pine forest had seemed gloomy and monochrome. Garth and Bala led the way through rocky gullies and over treacherous mossy mounds where the contours of the ground were concealed beneath virulent green encrustments. Bala made no conversation but kept her eyes on the way ahead as well as all around; Garth too was unusually taciturn. He was thinking about Bala's comment, that they and the wolves had heard the same message from the grey men. But for the wolves, the message had been simple and finite, whereas Garth was having difficulty keeping up with the flow of voices in his head.

They seemed to be testing him. That instance of self-aggrandisement, his expression of ambition atop the cliff, when Bala had rebuked him, he was sure they'd put that notion in his head. And other examples; he traced the journey they'd made, all the way back to Willow Croft. *That's not me,* he decided. *I've never been thirsty for leadership, or power and the acquisition of territory. They are watching me—from the inside! Planting thoughts in my head and looking to see what I might be capable of doing.* He growled to himself and Bala stopped, contemplating him quizzically.

"Am I tiring you, is the pace too fast?" She sat on her haunches.

"No. No, it's these damn voices in my head."

Bala tipped her own head on one side in a questioning motion.

Having seen the two leaders pause their stride the other dogs had also come to a halt, assuming this was a rest stop, and Garth threw himself down on a cushion of sorrel.

"You've never asked me about this thing in my skull," he said, "nor my ridiculous piggy ears. Well forget the ears, they are just a failed experiment and work almost as well as any dog's, but the implant in my head was put there by humans who wanted to see if they could control my every thought and action."

Bala drew back her teeth and snarled. "And all through history humans have called us the wicked wolf, the horror in the woods. Pah!"

"What troubles me now—these constant voices of the grey men—is the fear that far from having set me free, the grey men are using me somehow, in their own experiment. They touched me with their strange wand and my mind was instantly free of the human's hand. I was grateful, energised, renewed, but increasingly I have felt the presence of an old remembered feeling. A sense of manipulation."

"Then tell them to stop," said the red wolf.

"That's easier said than done," replied Garth, with a shiver. "This will make no sense to you, but there is a friend of mine, a wise great Dane, who through me has been taken to dwell in their domain, their home in the stars. I hear his voice from time to time. He tells me not to thwart the grey men for, to his cost, he has learnt that their power is immense.

He also urges me to make my way here in this world, to enjoy the natural delights of our homeland, for where he is located life is bland and featureless. And that is my current problem, for the grey men have made clear that when my mission is completed, they wish to take me with them. Am I destined always to be a laboratory specimen?"

Bala hunched and closed her eyes, eventually opening them with the platitude, "There will always be a way out of this for you, I am sure. I was imprisoned for years in a zoo, a world away from my home, suffering the indignity of being stared at by gormless humans every day. But I had friends amongst the local canids, who effected my escape."

"I wish I had your optimism," groaned Garth. "Yet, for the moment I am free, where for a long time I too was held in a cage. So let us press on. Soon we shall need to stop to eat."

14. Shaman

Garth had read the situation right for, after only another mile or two, Clover ran to the head of the column and solicited a halt.

"Apart from Loki, no-one had any breakfast before we set out this morning," she opined. "And he's brought most of it up anyway. We need to break our journey and find something edible."

They were in the midst of a grove, having stumbled down a stony sheep track for the past half hour. The trees here were mature rowan, oak and chestnut, providing a canopy of shelter from the north wind, which was turning increasingly cool as the afternoon grew old.

Garth looked around speculatively. "What do you suggest, Clover?" he asked. He'd seen pheasants wandering among the saplings that bordered the deeper forest a short run away. She'd spied them too.

"There might be a mouthful or two, but they come with feathers," she said. "A bit of a trial, those feathers."

She said nothing more on the subject just then because Loki had broken away from the pack, tearing up a short rise from the track and hurtling into the grove, barking exasperatedly at a small dark shape that seemed to cut its way like a knife through the bark and acorn cups that littered the ground. A feathery tail undulated as it ran.

"Squirrel." Announced Bala. "We can eat squirrel."

"But can we catch them?" asked Clover, who'd spied Loki returning rather disconsolately, and empty-mouthed.

"We may not be given the opportunity," observed Garth, as two athletically built grey wolves trotted from out the shadows of the grove. They made straight for Loki, their movements supple and determined, and, as he offered nervous submission, his tail under his belly, the male wolf took hold of him by the scruff of his neck and hoisted him into the air. Loki was not a small dog, not as big as the collie Clover, but he was a solid character, yet he looked to be as light as a feather hanging from the wolf's jowls.

The two wolves then proceeded to the head of the group, the she-wolf acknowledging Bala with a quiet, "Hello Sister, you have acquired an oddly assorted pack." Loki was then dumped on the ground by the male, who spoke gruffly in a loud voice, "He insulted us. He made to hunt in a live creche with no regard for our young." He looked Bala directly in the eye. "As pack leader you must choose his punishment. You know the ways of our forest kind."

Garth, who, standing in Bala's lee had been obscured from view, now strode forward and, nose to nose with the she-wolf, who had drawn herself up to her imperious mostness, also presented his most powerful bearing. "Honourable Mother," he began, "proud Canis lupus, I am the self-respecting leader of this pack of travellers. If we have offended you we beg your forgiveness, but no insult was intended." He lowered his head in deference before continuing.

"The humans had a saying that to err is human. Since we have been gifted human speech I am aware that we have also acquired certain human attributes, and I might venture that to err may also be canine. We beg your good nature will allow you to overlook our inadvertent error on this occasion."

"You speak strangely," said the she-wolf. "A mouthful of unusual words. We have the same language as you but your tongue is more…"

"Instructed?" suggested Bala. "It is because he has the voice from the stars in his head."

The pair of grey wolves seemed fascinated by Garth, and their eyes remained fixed upon him in silent contemplation, until the she-wolf broke the tension between them.

"Two-heads," she said, "you speak honourable words that we cannot disdain. I recognise that you have an impetuous pup amongst your pack, and we should not seek to punish his lack of restraint, although I am sure he had been forewarned. But such is the way with juveniles."

Loki was fit to burst, his hackles stiff. He was no pup and he was not wont to feel shame. But Clover held on to his ear with her sharp incisors and urged him to stay put.

Like a change in the light, the two wolves, who'd had their heads pressed together, suddenly relaxed, and the she-wolf faced Garth at his own level. "Two-heads, I see from the dust on your coat that you have travelled far and will be hungry. We offer you and your pack our hospitality; we have rabbit and venison in plenty, and a stream with the clearest water to drink. Do follow us; we would welcome your company should you decide to stay, for we have been troubled these last two nights by strangers who come with unwelcome intentions."

The she-wolf led them through the grove and out the other side, where grass and cloudberry bushes provided cover for their paths into another section of the interminable forest. Back amongst silent firs once more, they walked quietly toward a hollow where several more wolves lay together on fallen fir and old cones. Three wolf cubs were playing with some of the cones on a hollow log, too engrossed to look up when Bala and the dogs emerged from the wide swathe of grass, but the adult wolves tensed, prepared more for fight than flight.

"Everyone calm," called the she-wolf, "we bring Two-heads to our community and he will ensure our luck will change, as the old stories foretell."

"They mistake you," said Bala quietly to Garth, "but don't correct them if you want there to be no conflict."

"As we walked I have been looking in the store of knowledge in my head," said Garth, "since first they used the name Two-heads. This knowledge I can reach is mainly human and, unless I have found something in error, it appears the humans told stories of a mythical two-headed dog who had mysterious powers. Perhaps the wolves know of this or a similar story and are deceived by the appearance of the device in the top of my head."

"They are indeed an inscrutable race, these grey wolves," said Bala, "and I can imagine they have many inexplicable beliefs. Just be careful not to let them feel they have been deceived."

"Please join us, gracious Two-heads, and ask your pack to recline with us. As the grey man has declared, the Canidae is one nation now." The she-wolf stood to the fore of the group and called in yet more wolves who were out patrolling in the forest. It was time to eat and the she-wolf opened the proceedings by launching an enthusiastic assault on the corpse of a stag that had been left in the grass.

Garth and Bala sat close to the she-wolf, who never volunteered her name, and they ate quietly on the fresh carcass, looking up infrequently, with a care not to offend by being over-familiar with their glances at the family of wolves.

It was the she-wolf who spoke first. "This voice from the stars that you hear. The grey men came from the stars, is it their voice in your skull, venerable Two-heads?"

"Indeed that is so," Garth replied; "another voice too, a good friend who has died within the passing of a few suns only."

The she-wolf visibly recoiled. "You speak with the dead? Then you are truly the one spoken of who has come to save us." She stood immediately and gave a shrill howl to her pack, all the wolves in the glade sitting up with ears pricked.

"I give you Two-heads," called the she-wolf, "the shaman our elders foretold, he comes to save us from the predations of the men from the sky. Give thanks to the forest that shields us and the earth that nurtures us." There came a rally of barks and other guttural noises from the pack and she turned three times in the grass and lay down.

"The men from the sky," said Garth, "the grey men? But surely they mean us no harm, they have given us a new consciousness, and a voice."

The she-wolf studied him silently for a while and then replied, "If it is they you speak with, they are concealing their thoughts from you. Their words have two sides, like a smooth stone in the shallows of the river, one side to the light and the other hidden from view."

She lay back for a moment and regarded the sky. The afternoon was almost done and the last few bright beams of sunlight were struggling to penetrate the trees.

She sat up again and leant toward Garth. "He comes at dusk. His lantern is dimmed. And he stands and watches them, the cubs."

"Just watches?" Garth wanted more.

"He wants one of them. He has asked and, of course, been refused, but he comes again and I fear he will take what he desires. We shall, of course, resist, but he has the lantern—and many more of his kind besides."

"But why? The grey men have opened the world to us, given us freedom and a sense of empathy throughout the Canidae."

"When first he came, he had two large bubbles with him, they floated in the air beside him, and in one was a badger, the other held a squirrel. The bubbles had clear walls and we could see both creatures were alive. When he noticed the cubs, he put his hand in the light of the lantern and pulled out a third bubble; it was empty. Then he asked for a cub. He said he was collecting specimens that did not exist on his world and he wanted to take them away in order to understand them."

Garth stood clumsily and gave a roar. "Never!" he shouted. "I know too well what is meant by wanting to understand. No cub of yours will be taken to a laboratory."

"Or a zoo," added Bala. "What can we do?"

"He has the lantern," said Garth, "but he cannot be invincible. Every living thing has a weakness—I just have to think. We have a little time before the fall of dusk, and he may not come tonight anyway. I must go somewhere quiet and think."

The grey man was clothed in a long ash-coloured cloak that dragged on the leaf-litter at the edge of the glade. It made the only sound that came from him as he approached, walking like a shadow torn from the gloom under the trees. Considerably taller than a human, he wore a loose cowl over his head and shoulders, which hid his face, the only visible parts of his flesh being the grey hand that grasped the pole of the lantern, and the other hand that held a rod.

The she-wolf went to meet him and he touched the back of her neck with the rod so that they might talk. "Man from the stars," she addressed him, "we are fortunate that you have set free our tongues, and rid the world of our persecutors. But we cannot enjoy this bounty if you take our future from us, our young, who are our joy and our succour in later life."

"You can have other young," the grey man's voice in her head was dry and unfeeling. "You are not old. There are many other females too." He took a step toward the three cubs, who curled up asleep. "I will have one," he insisted, reaching into his lamp for a fresh bubble shape. "I have waited for too long."

"No," said Garth, firmly, pouncing in front of him. Even without the rod pressed into his back the grey man heard him clearly, for Garth's implant served as their connection. "No," he repeated, "you will not. If you try to take a cub, you will find that your soul will be forfeit to this pack of wolves."

None of this conversation could be heard by the wolves or the dogs of Garth's pack. But they all saw him reach forward and grasp the grey man's rod, dead in the centre, his powerful mastiff's jaw clamped tight. His baleful eyes fixed on the grey man's face, just a shadow in the blackness of his cowl, and he spoke determinedly, mind to mind with the Derin. "I have a firm hold of this wand," he said. "At this moment, I could release it and you could walk away with it undamaged. But I need you to know that if you persist in attempting to steal a wolf cub, I shall bite down on it and break it in two." At that, the grey man's lantern flared and the device on Garth's head glowed with a brief fire.

"Put down your lantern," Garth demanded, "down here amongst the grass. And relinquish your wand to me. If you do those things, we will accompany you to wherever you entered this forest, for you can't find your way without the lantern in the dark. I also promise to give back your wand if you agree never to return. If that promise is broken, your soul will be forfeit."

There came a deluge of words into Garth's head, harsh alien words that he could not understand, although he well knew their intention; his head throbbed and he felt the rod grow warm in his mouth, and for a moment he thought he was back at the House of Hell, having wires threaded into his brain. Then the rod cooled and his head cleared, the Derin let go the rod, and kneeling, lay down the lantern.

The journey to the grey man's craft took half the night. He'd entered the forest far to the west, where the treeline stopped and a long sandy plain stretched inland from the sea in the north. Standing under the cold light of the moon, Garth and Tak, who had carried the Derin's rod between them, shivered in the sea breezes from the north. It felt exposed and they imagined a great hand could sweep them from the plain in one swift movement. But it was only the wind they could feel, along with their imagination building upon the mystery of the grey men. Yet they ducked instinctively when a light brighter than the moon appeared above them, descending rapidly and stopping just as decisively a short distance from the ground.

"I'll take the wand," said Garth, and ran with it in his jaws a hailing distance away. Then he gave a great bark that flooded the night with sound, and Tak and the two wolves who had shown the way through the forest all raced back towards the trees. The grey man watched them, unmoving, while also watching Garth, who jammed the rod into the sandy soil, his head on one side and the rod gripped in his teeth, before running in a dash to catch up with the others.

They didn't stop until they were concealed once more in the forest. Neither did they look back to see if they were being chased, although they all caught a glimpse of the bright frisbee shape lifting at an unfeasible velocity into the night sky.

Garth's return to the glade was met with howls of welcome and approval from the wolves but he went straight to his company of dogs, turned three times in the grass and made clear he wanted to sleep. Tak fully expected they would have sat and told the tale of their expedition to the other dogs but, well, Garth must have had his reasons and, being a rather laid back stray accustomed to all eventualities, Tak also stretched out his fine limbs and drifted off to an untroubled sleep.

Tired as he was, Garth's mind would not shut down and, after jiffling about restlessly with his eyes closed, he propped himself up on his forelegs to find Clover sitting in front of him with a question in her eyes. It was not the question that Garth had anticipated; that would come later. "What are you going to do with the lantern?" was what Clover wished to know. "Only I find it rather scary to see it there in the grass right next to us, knowing what it could do—maybe even unmake us dogs if we're not careful with it."

Garth hadn't given the lantern any thought other than that he needed to disarm the Derin. "I'll have to give that serious thought," he replied, lamely as it felt. "In fact, there's a lot I need to understand about the grey men," he admitted. "I've been turning over every manner of thoughts all along our path since Willow Croft. Lately, as I considered how we might dissuade the Derin from taking a wolf cub, I have benefitted from the many wise words of Tiny."

Clover sat up, suddenly very interested in what Garth had to tell. "He is alive then?" she exclaimed.

"It is something else," said Garth. "I cannot explain it. Maybe he has joined Black Shuck, I cannot tell. But Tiny has come to know the ways of the Derin quite well, and he informs my thoughts."

Clover lay down, her chin on her paws; it seemed Garth was ready to talk more. Some of the others had been woken by their conversation and shuffled closer, better to hear. Seeing this, Garth raised his voice so that all of his pack might listen to his tale.

"Do you remember, back at Willow Croft when I first spoke of this mission to the north? There was some scepticism about the motives of the grey men, or the Derin as they call themselves, some doubt that they really needed our help in finding the runaway humans. I argued that our proficiency in searching, using our extraordinary natural senses of hearing and smell, surpassed the Derin's skill. It made sense to me that we were better suited to find those men in the countryside than were the aliens."

He stopped and there was a frisson of nervous anticipation amongst the dogs.

"Yet," he began again, "I had my own doubts nonetheless, and communicating with Tiny…"

There came some yips and snuffles of surprise at this.

"…speaking with Tiny I am now convinced that the task set us was a sham."

A flurry of angry barks arose from his companions, and several of the wolves sleeping nearby looked up with ears alert.

"We've come on a fool's errand, is that what you're saying?" demanded Tak. "I'm minded to chew off those piggy ears of yours, Garth. It is not my nature but I am most angered by your deceit."

"It is Garth who has been deceived," interceded Bala. "I think I can understand what the grey men have been doing."

"But do let me tell you my thoughts," said Garth, "and you can then let me know if they are the same as yours. I call them my thoughts but, as I have said, they are informed by Tiny, who sees how the Derin conduct their empire in the stars. For me, it is a terrible discovery, to find that I have gone from being a prisoner, to enjoying glorious liberty, and back again; from a puppet of wicked humans who sought total control over me, and then to freedom, but a false freedom in which other beings seek to use me for their own ends."

"All of us have asked, from time to time, what is it the grey men really mean to do here? We know their aim is to rid the stars of the threat posed by the humans, but what will follow?" He paused, not really expecting any suggestions. "Well, according to Tiny, who admits to knowing only a part of the story, in each land in our world they are creating what I can only call a stooge, a term you may not know but which is a servant, someone they have given authority and access to greater knowledge than the average canid, their servant who will rule for them over a particular area. Their claim to have chosen canids as the higher species is true, but it involves a risk and they need somehow to ensure that we never present a challenge to them, in the way that the humans did. Because of this device implanted in my brain they can communicate with me, and it was because of that they have selected me as their stooge in this land. So long as I carry this device in my head, I cannot be free, for they tuned it that day when Tiny rescued me, and I am perpetually sealed into their awareness."

"Naturally, I am feeling sorry about this revelation, if it be a true one, for I had begun to enjoy my freedom after escaping Wickhurst, the place you know as the House of Hell. This revelation also means that I no longer intend to continue the quest for the fugitive human, which was clearly devised as a test to see how I would perform as a leader."

Groans came from all around the party of dogs.

"So, what should we do, go back?" whined one of the lurchers. "And will we still be the West End Strays if we go back? I'm feeling rather confused."

"Bugger that," said Loki, who relished and enjoyed flourishing the human expletives in his new-found vocabulary. "I came on this mission for the adventure. I'm not going back to sit with a bunch of nursing bitches in a boring pen. I say we keep going."

"I agree," said Bala. "I want to see the northern ocean, it may present me with a means to return to my homeland, although that is very far from here. Humans used to travel on the water to distant lands, so why not a homesick red wolf from Ethiopia?"

"But what about you, Garth?" She turned and licked his snout. "If you are a prisoner of the device that rules your brain, what can you do still to enjoy our new freedoms?" His reply did not come as a great surprise.

"I intend to stay here, with the grey wolves. They seem to regard me as something special, a shaman they said, someone with supernatural powers, someone in their tradition who is connected with the spirits of the earth, the trees and the sky; just as they are creatures of nature themselves, beings who identify closely with the natural world. I am not tricking them by assuming that role, I believe that through my implant I may bring some advantage to them from my connection with the Derin—and with Tiny, of course. We also have the grey man's lantern, and I intend to discover how it works; it may prove useful in defending the pack."

"But your paws," said Tak, "you will need the opposing finger and thumb to hold up the lantern pole."

"The grey wolf is remarkably resourceful," answered Garth, undeterred. "I'm sure they will find some way. I know I can't expect to hold it in my teeth."

"That reminds me," said Clover, "aren't you going to explain how you defeated the grey man last evening?" It was the question Garth had earlier anticipated from her.

He scratched a piggy ear to tease them with his delay, then took to an elaborate washing of his rear end.

"Garth!" shouted an impatient Clover, "everyone's waiting for you."

Garth ceased his toilet and sat on his haunches. "Well, it was really Tiny who saw off that particular grey man," he replied, his tone tantalising and secretive. "So, am I allowed to tell you what advice he gave me?"

"For Shuck's sake," bellowed the wolfhound, "get on with it."

Garth snarled briefly at the wolfhound and then relented. "I was communicating with Tiny, as I said."

"Ye-es," chorused the impatient canids together.

"He explained something extraordinary to me."

There came a further expression of exasperation from the dogs, the three staffies doing crazy zoomies across the glade and waking the wolf pack by stumbling over them as they slumbered.

Garth stopped fooling and spoke without hesitation. "According to Tiny, who watches them all the time, each grey man is unable to function without his wand. It contains all the record of his past and a map of every one of his possible futures. It is his store of private information, for the brain in a Derin's head is limited in size, used mainly to manage his body and limbs, or to search in the knowledge in his wand. Without his wand, each one which is his and his alone, a grey man cannot make his way in life and would be cast out from normal community."

"So," interrupted Bala, "there was a conversation going on between you and the Derin who wanted the cub, and my guess is you said either he would give up his quest or you would snap the rod in two."

Garth nodded vigorously. "It was no choice for him. I just hoped that Tiny had made a correct study of his hosts, wherever he is. It seemed to work."

"I just hope you have made a correct study of these wolves," said Clover, "and that they will truly welcome a dog, impressive beast that you are, the Noble Holmegarth of Aquitaine, to dwell among them."

15. The Persistent Labradors

With Garth now faced with having to explain his intentions to the she-wolf, the twelve dogs had to decide whether to continue north with Bala or find their way home. Loki had already made his intention clear, and Clover announced she also would continue their journey, if only to keep an eye on Loki, of whom she had grown rather fond. Tak was all for going back, although he worried about finding an easier way across that foaming river. He missed the easy-going life of the West End Strays and those of its members he'd left behind. The three staffies said going back was too long a journey, while with hints of the sea already suggested in the south-flowing air, going forward couldn't be worse. The wolfhound, like Loki, craved adventure and new sights.

With a single bark to Garth and the she-wolf, the six lurchers set off with Tak leading. He was to take the route they'd led the grey man the previous night, hoping that the broad sandy plain beyond the forest might lead to shallower crossings of the river.

Bala stepped out in front of the remaining six, although they now moved in the manner of wolves, spread out through the undergrowth and sweeping forward broadly together. They continued like that for a day and a half, taking a diversion now and then to chase prey for sustenance, for they no longer felt any urgency in their quest. They slept in the open, for there was no beast they feared, and the night air was mild.

"He wasn't a bad sort, Garth," said Loki, unexpectedly, waking to the sound of crows in the trees. "I'm not the sentimental sort but I feel sad for him. But, you know, that is in itself a strange feeling, not something I could put into words before. I'm sure I did have those kinds of feelings but I would never have realised it."

"It's because of the awakening," decided Clover. "It's the same for me. So many new words and ideas flooding into my head, I'm sure that before long it will be full." She wrinkled her nose. "Hey, do you suppose we'll need a rod, like the grey men, somewhere to keep all the things our heads can't hold once they're full?"

In answer, Loki put his paws over his ears, and Clover laughed.

"I have a feeling right now," she confided. "Not one of your new kinds of feelings. Call it a canine's second sense if you like, but I'm sure we'll meet Garth again."

Around midday on the second day, with the salty tang of the sea now strong on a forceful northern wind, they climbed over a flinty ridge, drawn by sounds they couldn't at first believe, the barking of dogs at play and the occasional human shout.

What met their eyes was even more difficult to accept as real. Beyond the ridge lay an expanse of flat land bordered by thin stands of mountain ash and silver birch. It had been largely colonised by grass and cat's ear, and ran for the length of a football pitch, uninterrupted by rocks or streams. In the

165

corner nearest to Bala and the dogs were some of those bales of straw that have been harvested by humans in the shape of a giant wheel. They seemed to have been long abandoned, for the straw was grey in places and weeds grew from their tops. One or two had been tumbled onto their sides by the winter gales that frequented this part of the country. None of that was exceptional, but the gathering there of a cohort of ebullient dogs was not what Bala and her companions expected to find. Some of them lay indolently stretched out in the sunshine beside the bales, animatedly talking amongst themselves, while others were running back and forth with noisy excitement. Such was the travellers' first view of a large group of Labradors, their clumsy gait unmistakeable, their attitude boisterous and the air full of their energetic barking.

A short distance in front of the Labradors, a little further into the field, stood two humans, flanked at the sides and rear in a kind of close, by what looked like a guard of more Labradors. They faced out into the field and, at a barked signal from one of the Labrador guards, one man flung a ball away in the air. Seeing this, the dog at the head of the guard detail chased after it in obvious delight, catching the ball and swiftly returning it. Meantime, the second man was urged to throw a ball for another dog from the group.

This routine was being repeated over and over until, seeing the men were flagging, the red Labrador currently at the head of the guard detail called a halt and the two humans were escorted back to fling themselves down on straw from a bale.

"You go ahead," said Bala to the dogs, "Labradors can be a bit jumpy and they may take exception to a red wolf joining their games. I'll come down when you let me know it's safe."

Just the wolfhound and Loki scrambled over the crest of the ridge and trotted in their most unthreatening step towards the mostly black and chocolate throng, tails wagging to signal their affability.

"Ho ho," called one of the Labradors as the pair were spied, "strangers. Not come to steal our balls have you?" he threw loudly at Loki. "Only you look a bit beagleish to me, and beagles have a reputation for thieving balls."

"I'll have your balls, mate," replied Loki. "Disrespecting the beagle family. Only I see the vet has beaten me to it."

"Ha ha," chortled the Labrador. "I like a quick mind, Mr Beagle."

"Loki," explained Loki. "Pleased to meet you…"

"Bobbo," said the Labrador. "Silly name, but then I had a silly master. Tried to negotiate with the grey men until they put him in a bubble and floated him up to their flying machine. Still, maybe that means they did something other than unmake him. Hey," he said, seeing Loki was paying him close attention, "have you seen those things fly? They look just like frisbees. I wouldn't mind having one of those to chase."

Typical Labrador, thought Loki. *Nice fellow but clearly his awakening hasn't improved his intellect.*

"So what did you do to keep the grey men from taking these two humans?" Loki took a good look at the men, who lay gasping and perspiring in the straw. They were naked from the waist up and wore trousers that seemed more befitting a city environment.

"You tell him, Rafi," called Bobbo to a muscular chocolate-hued dog. "Rafi was there when it happened," Bobbo said in an aside to Loki. "I was busy digging out a rabbit burrow. Well, a fellow's got to eat."

"There were three humans," explained Rafi. "She had foam on her jaw after having spent a hectic time chasing tennis balls, but she was voluble and eager to tell her story. They came in a...a..."

"Truck," prompted Bobbo.

"Yes a truck, one of those things with the back left open, and they had a German shepherd tied up in the back. He looked really unhappy to be there. They came from that place near the cliffs, the place where they set giant silver sticks on fire and throw them up into the sky. It's too noisy to watch. Anyway, we didn't know why they'd come here, they had never bothered us before, but when they saw us the truck rushed towards us really fast and we had to scatter to save ourselves. Then they stopped and got out. They had guns, and they were pulling the GSD on a rope, and they went into the trees over there. I called to the GSD but it turned out he wasn't awakened, so he couldn't tell me what was going on. Then they disappeared into the trees, and after a little while we heard a shot and the GSD cried out, and then there was another shot and the men came back without him."

The wolfhound turned a couple of agitated circles upon hearing that and declared he would tear the men apart, but Bobbo shook his head and said everything was under control.

"Yes," continued Rafi, "That's exactly what Ben wanted to do when he followed them into the trees to investigate. He found the GSD with his front legs tied together and a big hole blown through his head. That's Ben," she said, indicating a very large square-jawed Labrador. "Well, Ben ran back and told me and very quickly word spread amongst the rest of us who weren't off looking for food. Without needing any explanation we charged as one at the men as they neared their

168

truck, looking our meanest with teeth and gums fully exposed, and roaring as we ran. One of them, we call him the scar man, had got into the truck and slammed the door. The other two had taken fright, dropped their guns and run round the back to the other side of the truck." Rafi stopped to lick her nose; she was becoming distressed by her own tale. "That's when Ben showed what a brilliant retriever he is; he left the others and ran round the front instead to confront the men. We heard them shouting in fear. The scar man heard them too and opened the door for them, but Ben hurled himself at the door, closing it with a bang and we all managed to herd the two humans away from the truck, growling and menacing as best we could."

"Ben sounds like an impressive character," remarked the wolfhound.

"If we ever have any need for a pack leader, he's the obvious one," said Bobbo. "But we get along just fine, don't we Rafi, we're all friendly fellows here."

"We're not all fellows, Bobbo," corrected Rafi. "However much you'd like it that way."

"Why do you call the one who got away the scar man?" asked Loki, quickly steering the conversation away from Rafi's disgruntlement.

"Ah," replied Rafi, "all three humans had bare arms, it was a warm afternoon like today, and he—scar man—had a long red scar on his arm, I thought he must have had a difficult meeting with a wolf. This is wolf country, you know."

"We know," said the wolfhound, and looking at Loki he nodded back to the ridge.

"Talking of wolves," said Loki casually. "We have other travelling companions waiting back there, one of whom is a red wolf. I'd like to call her down here, is that acceptable to you, seeing as you're all friendly fellows?" He winked at Rafi.

"She won't eat our ball throwers, will she?" asked Bobbo nervously.

"I doubt it," answered Loki, "she's still full from the two bears she ate last night."

Bobbo looked horrified then saw the laughter on Rafi's face. "You are playing with me, Loki," he said. "Of course, there are no bears here. Oh fine fellow that you are. But call them down, your companions, and the wolf. I'll quickly tell everyone there's no need for concern."

"This is a very satisfying arrangement you have here," remarked Bala to Bobbo, when introductions had been made, ears sniffed and rear ends examined. "Oh, don't worry," said Bala, seeing Bobbo's pensive expression, "we don't plan to stay. But you have all that you want: shelter, plentiful prey to catch, and captive humans to provide you with your favourite recreation."

"Recreation?" asked Bobbo. "Well, yes, we do feel we've been made anew, I suppose."

"Exercise, sport, play," corrected Loki, who was building up quite a library of words of his own.

"Yes," agreed Bobbo, "many of us were feeling a bit lost without our humans to throw a ball. It made what was a good way of life here feel a bit tasteless after a while. Capturing those two humans has really been the cream on the biscuit. And for a change, they're ours to command. No more having to sit for a treat; not that we have any treats, of course." He feigned sadness then brightened. "They're not very happy having to eat raw flesh, I've noticed. Not country men, of course. Most of us dogs lived in the countryside before coming here, so the outdoor life has suited us well. Everyone here got word, one way and another, that we'd set up this camp, and they've come here knowing what sort of life it would be. But most of all, we all like being here as company for each other, for generally we didn't have bad humans and they were being missed."

"So," inquired Loki, you mention bad humans. "Well, did you find out from your two captive humans why they killed the GSD?"

"They're humans," said Bobbo. "Why would they need a reason?"

"And since you've been here there have been no visits from the grey men?"

"I saw the frisbee once," said Rafi, "over the forest, but it didn't stop. It went toward the place with the silver sticks and just stopped moving for a while before going up into the sky."

"And the humans had never bothered you until they came with the GSD?"

"No, they were too busy making big noises and flying their machines, the ones that buzz with moving wings like a horse fly."

"Is the scar man the only human left at the place you described?"

"I don't know," said Rafi.

"We just don't go there," explained Bobbo. "It's scary down there."

Bala was aware that the Labradors found her scary too. They'd been pleasant and welcoming, greeting her with a wild thrashing of tails, but as many as there were of them, they still reacted with a flinch and an instinctive show of teeth whenever she moved unexpectedly. She was beginning to feel uncomfortable, trying not to set them off and, hungry as she was, she decided to forego the offer of rabbit meat and be on her way.

"Shall we go and see for ourselves?" she suggested to Loki, who was preoccupied in getting to know a jet black bitch who was presently licking his snout. He didn't hear Bala but the three staffies responded immediately. They in their turn were feeling awkward amongst all these Labrador retrievers, it was something to do with rivalry in the best family dog stakes. "We won't find it scary," chirped one, "we're staffies."

It was the wolfhound who prised Loki away from his new female interest. "Come on," he said. "You're the brains now Garth's no longer with us."

But it wasn't Loki whose brain excelled that afternoon, although he was not displeased to be overshadowed.

16. Possibly the Last Human

Bobbo's scary place was a half hour's walk beyond the Labradors' encampment, an easy trot down the grassy track the men must have taken with their truck. It was set some way below the top of the rise from where they first saw it, a plateau mainly of bare rock that reached to a sharp edge—at least they assumed it was an edge, for beyond it glittered the sea, the sharply delineated edge suggesting that it was in fact the top of a cliff.

The centre of the plateau was pockmarked with tufts of grass and nettle, but for the most part had been concreted over. Two runways for aircraft formed a cross over toward the assumed cliff edge, and at the plateau's eastern end there had been constructed several concrete single-storey blockhouses, one massively tall building painted grey, and three circular platforms, also of concrete. The three platforms bore garish scorch marks and were heavily blackened. In the middle of one had been erected a high lone gantry of dull metal, from which swung several loose pipes. Another lay on its side across a second platform. Various odd-looking vehicles were scattered around the plateau, some with pipes attached to tanks, and a helicopter stood, its rotors unmoving, close to the gantry.

"It does look scary," said Clover. "I don't know why, but I feel it in my gut. It just feels wrong."

No-one contradicted her.

Their view to the west brought Clover a little relief from her unease. From the end of the concrete bleakness, a slope of unbroken green rose up to a horizon of trees, and on the slope a large flock of sheep busied itself undisturbed, enjoying the fresh grass underfoot.

The only other sign of life was to be found at the end of one of the runways, where a solitary man was unloading things from a truck and carrying them to a light aircraft. He had a white head of hair and he was wearing shorts and a T-shirt, and even from a distance the dogs could make out the dark imprint of a long scar on his arm.

"That's him, we've found the scar man," squeaked one of the staffies, in his excitement letting out a series of excited barks.

"So, he does exist. The grey men were not telling lies after all. But what do we do now?" asked Loki, to nobody in particular. "It seems we have found our quarry, but without Garth we can't alert the grey men."

"What we should do now," said Bala, "is do our best to hide. Look!"

Alerted by the staffy's bark the man had reached into the back of the truck and pulled out an automatic weapon. He crossed the apron of the airfield and set foot with a limp onto the grassy slope, where Bala and the dogs had pressed themselves flat against the ground. Still at a distance he raised the gun and loosed a volley of shots that raked the wet-nosed grass. Loki heard a dull thump and a groan, and knew that one of the bullets had found its mark, but he daren't move until the man turned and walked back to the truck.

It was Bala; one shot had caught her in the shoulder and her red coat was already fast changing shade as blood seeped through the fur. She pushed Loki away when he went to examine the wound. "We must stop him," she said. "It looks as though he is preparing to leave."

The man had stowed his gun in the light plane and, climbing into the truck, drove at speed to the blockhouses. He emerged from one a few minutes later, now dressed in some kind of brown costume that covered his body. From one hand swung a briefcase, while in the other he carried a long tube, which the watching dogs correctly assumed to be some kind of weapon.

This time he walked, leaving the truck standing immobile, setting out in a direct line for the plane.

"He's going to escape," said the wolfhound. "Loki, think of something."

"I'm thinking, I'm thinking," snapped Loki, "but all I can think of is a pack charge. Come on." He stood and raised a great beagle howl that echoed around the plateau. "Let's go," he shouted, starting to run down the grassy slope, the wolfhound close behind him, uttering his own most terrible roar.

But the man, upon hearing the din, stopped and hoisted the tube onto his shoulder. There came a puff of smoke followed by a sharp crack and a whooshing sound, and the ground in front of Loki flew up into the air, knocking both him and the wolfhound head over heels backwards. They lay unmoving as the man took careful steps towards them across the concrete apron, a long knife in the hand that had carried the briefcase.

Clover wailed. Was this how she was going to lose her friend? It was not, and she took off at a dash, her sudden appearance slowing the man's approach to the grassy bank. She streaked across the hill like a streamer of black smoke, she was beyond the length of the airfield in no time at all and ascending the western slope. In his daze, Loki heard the sound the sheep made when they realised that they were about to be disturbed from their grazing.

Clover ran without changing her pace, all around the back of the flock, causing it to shift en masse away from the trees, then racing forward she snapped at the sheep furthest down the slope, so that one or two broke from the flock and began to run downhill. Being sheep, others quickly began to follow, until Clover had organised all of them into a fast-moving column.

Down they came in a clamorous white stream, the sound of their hooves like a distant rumble of thunder, as Clover directed them onto the airfield, their cloven rush becoming an ominous rattle on the concrete. Bala and the staffies had sat up, watching in amazement, as the sheep were teased out by Clover into a curve that swept past the astonished man, then were turned back around behind him by the fluidly sprinting dog, so that in what seemed no time at all, he was encircled by a maddened, bleating mass of ruminants, his progress towards Loki and his path to the aircraft both now impossible.

"Brilliant, Clover," exclaimed Loki to no-one in particular, his head aching. "But...?"

The sheep were jostling and stamping, mightily displeased at having been disturbed from their peaceful grazing; some part of the woolly barrier was going to give sooner or later and Clover's quick-thinking act of skill would have been wasted. The man had dropped the long tube and was now waving a handgun above the heads of the sheep, looking for Clover, without whose presence the sheep would soon disperse. In frustration, he fired the gun in the air and several sheep bucked and reared in fright, the secure ring of imprisonment quickly breaking.

Clover ran speedily to turn them back, her whereabouts for a moment exposed, and the man took careful aim on her glossy black form.

"Oh no," muttered Bala, watching.

"Oh yes," croaked Loki, sitting up carefully, his whiskers twitching. He'd seen the giant frisbee rise up over the edge of the plateau from the sea. It climbed quickly in an unwaveringly perpendicular trajectory then slid forward over the airfield. The man did not see it, he was trying to hold his focus on Clover, which was blurred by the movement of chaotic sheep. So it was that he failed to see the stroke of intense white light that pierced the afternoon sky, a silently extruding stream that flowed from the alien craft and returned with him spectacularly dispersed within it, like dust in a beam of sunlight.

Without pause and without a sound the giant frisbee sliced through the clouds like a hot knife through butter and vanished before the dogs even realised it was moving.

"They knew all the time where to look," said Loki. "Garth was absolutely correct in his thinking. But you were magnificent, Clover." Loki rested his chin on the back of her neck and she felt his hot breath through her fur.

"I've always wanted to do that," she sighed, "but being only half-collie I never got the chance."

"I saw a thoroughbred collie running on that slope," said Bala, and Loki wished he'd said it first.

"Do you think that's the last human, then? The last we'll see of them?" asked the wolfhound.

"Possibly the last," said Loki thoughtfully, "but there are many lands in this world, so I can't say for certain if they've all been swept clean."

"I'm beginning to think I'm perhaps the last red wolf," groaned Bala, whose coat was now soaked with her own blood. She was having difficulty standing. "I need to go, to return home. There is only one ocean to travel, although it has many different names in its different locations around the world. It will carry me; it is my way back."

She struggled to her feet.

"You can't—" breathed Clover.

"I can't stay here," murmured the red wolf, "I don't belong even with the grey wolves," and she began to drag herself across the grass.

"Wait," called Clover and the staffies together, the collie rising to her feet.

"Let her go," said Loki quietly. "What else can we do for her? We are on our own now, no humans, no aliens to help us. She is in control of her own destiny." He paused then gave an uncharacteristic sigh of regret. "Unlike our friend Garth, who is equally on his own, even amongst the wolves. There's nothing we could do for Garth. With that device in his head, surely he will be easily found by the grey men, and when they do find him, how will they use him? I have worried about that ever since we said goodbye. With that thing in his head, he can communicate with the aliens, and they with him—as they have planned all along. That gives him immense power amongst the Canidae, although it is not truly his power; and if he uses it in any way contrary to the wishes of the Derin they will know, and there will be consequences." Loki licked his lips regretfully. He'd rarely spoken at such length before, and he hadn't finished yet.

"Garth has the lantern, of course; that gives him a unique strength, more than they ever intended him to have. He may yet use it against the Canidae to reinforce his dominion over them, or he may even be a threat to the grey men. No-one can predict. I just hope that whatever happens to Garth is his own choice, guided by fate and his good canine nature." Loki paused a second time, taking a deep breath and staring down the slope to the airfield for a long minute before continuing.

"Look here," he needed to stop his companions from being hopelessly emotional, he could sense it already, "there's nothing we can do for Bala except allow her to take the path she has chosen. Fortunately she has only the natural world to deal with. The wolves we met in the forest would approve of that."

The six dogs sat and watched the red wolf slowly make her painful way across the barren airfield, her fox's brush of a tail low in the dirt, her white stockings streaked red. On the far side of the plateau, she stood for a long moment at the cliff's edge, staring out at the scurrying of the oceanic highway, then, in the blink of an eye she was gone.

Part 2
Intervention

17. Hooked

"Clover and I would rarely go for a race like that," puffed Monty. "She knew she was faster than me and she didn't want to bruise my dignity."

"You miss your bitch, don't you," growled Shaggy. "I know I would if she were mine."

"She's not my bitch. How many times…oh, never mind." Monty broke off, his attention taken by a seal pup that was sleeping by the side of a rock. "Don't go near that one," he said to his friend. "They've fearsome teeth. I once saw a dog have its entire chest taken out with one bite. Taught me to be careful where I went swimming."

"Let's turn back," suggested Shaggy, "the tide's coming in and then we might find ourselves swimming with the seals."

They scampered along the flat, empty beach and up the short causeway onto the links, Shaggy moving ahead of Monty, who found himself suddenly to be limping painfully. The black dog looked around before tearing back down the track that led to Tiny's old shack. Monty was sitting with one leg raised into the air, and he was biting at his upper thigh, clearly experiencing some kind of torment.

"What is it old friend?" asked Shaggy, running back. "Those flexible joint tablets we found proving to be no good?"

"It's this thing, by Shuck it's tied my back legs together."

A length of plastic fishing line had wound around both limbs and hobbled him. One end of the line was attached to a fishing hook that had become embedded in his thigh, and every time he had struggled to run its barbed point had dug deeper.

"What's happened?" Shaggy sniffed at the hook. "Who did this?"

"It's a human device," explained Monty. "A hook. The humans tied them to thread like this, with the other end attached to a pole. It's for killing fish."

"Well, hold still," instructed Shaggy. "I can't get a grip on the hook but I can bite through the thread so you can walk again."

It was a fiddly task but not beyond Shaggy's capability and, in no time, Monty could move both legs freely. The hook dragged on his flesh, however, and every step was painful.

"We'll get help back at Willow Croft," Shaggy reassured him. "Get it out somehow."

The two dogs crossed the railway tracks, automatically hesitating and listening for a train that no longer ran. From there, their route lay through the centre of town where once Monty had led an easy life with the blacksmith.

"It had become a habit," observed Shaggy. "Us still watching for trains."

"I'd call it conditioning," countered Monty.

The two dogs had developed a friendly rivalry as new words entered their heads in response to the need to describe

184

something. It had become a compulsive game, although neither yet knew the word compulsive.

"That's going to be our greatest challenge, in my opinion," remarked Monty, "now the humans have gone."

"What is?" asked Shaggy. "The railway or fishing hooks?"

"All the stuff the humans left behind, dangerous things, things we have no way of understanding. Fishing hooks, yes, but worse things. Machinery, things that move, things that explode, substances that burn or poison. Since we can't yet read we won't know what's inside all those things in packages and bottles when we go looking for supplies. Everything is potentially dangerous—that's how we are going to have to think."

"Like that," said Shaggy, "that machine at the next corner."

A car was parked at the kerb, its engine running. It was the first car they'd heard in weeks.

"I thought the grey men had taken all the humans from town," exclaimed Monty, for the moment forgetting the pain in his leg.

"Perhaps this one has just returned from the country and they missed him—or her. Remember what Garth said about finding humans in the countryside."

The two dogs slunk low to the ground, trying to be invisible, remembering their last encounter with humans. But they reached the car without incident and stood, ready to run, but not knowing what to do next. Shaggy gave the vehicle a good sniffing, mounting the kerb and examining it from all angles. He reported that it was undoubtedly empty, which didn't make them any more certain about their next move.

"Let's just make a run for it," suggested Shaggy. "The human must have gone indoors."

Monty looked up at the nearest building and froze, a growl deep in his throat. "You know where we are, don't you?" he croaked, and Shaggy looked up at the building in front of which the car had been parked. He shook his head.

"It's not somewhere that I recognise," he admitted.

"I've been here several times over the years," explained Monty. "It's the vet's. And look," he said anxiously, "there's a light on. That's where the human went."

"Well," Shaggy shook his ears with intent. "Now isn't that a coincidence, considering your current problem."

"Huh, I'd call it providence, actually," replied Monty, "although finding a vet in these circumstances is not necessarily to be thought providential."

"Oh, stop showing off, will you." Shaggy showed his irritation at Monty's new erudition by taking a pee against a wheel of the car. "Look, you need help, and vets can be helpful, you know. They had a good reputation at Willow Croft."

Just then the light in the window was extinguished and a short while after the front door to the building was opened. The young man who emerged had long hair tied in a pony tail and carried a small black case. He wore strong leather boots and a padded coat, and he ran down the steps to the road as if in a hurry.

"It can't be a vet," hissed Monty, "it's just a boy human. No whiskers, see. Let's just go."

"He's rather tall to be a boy human," argued Shaggy. "He might just have had a good scrub. I used to look smooth and glossy whenever I had just been groomed." He snorted wistfully.

They were standing at the rear of the car, hoping not to be noticed, but the human went around to the back to open the boot and found the two dogs huddled there.

"Well, hello there," he said, cheerily, and realising he wasn't a threat Shaggy wagged his tail. Monty did not; instead, he shrank back. A vet was a vet as far as Monty was concerned, even if he looked like a boy human, and Monty had quickly smelled this human, confidently confirming his profession from the aroma of disinfectant and vaguely familiar chemicals.

"Here boy," said the young man, crouching and holding out his hand for Monty to sniff. Then, seeing how the dog recoiled, "What's the matter fella; are you hurt?"

Monty stood as tall as he could. "Just a little bother with an unwelcome piece of metal," he replied, his voice sounding thick and wet to the vet, who jumped back a little, it was his first meeting with a talking dog, and a talking dog with an extraordinary turn of phrase too.

Still crouching there, he almost fell over backwards when Shaggy nudged him in the knee, stuck his nose in his face and demanded, "Are you a vet? Because my friend is hurt; it's a fishing hook."

Recovering his wits, the young man straightened up. "Yes," he said, "I'm a vet. Well, only just, I qualified a couple of months ago." He laughed, feeling ridiculous to know he was explaining himself to two dogs. He'd always talked to the animals that came into his care, but replies usually came as nuzzles or purrs.

"Shall I take a look?" he asked Monty, gesturing at the bloody patch on the dog's leg. Without waiting for an answer he opened the car door and switched off the engine, then briskly crossed the pavement, the black case still in his hand. "Come on, pal," he called to Monty. "Need a carry?"

Shaggy ran in front of them, being the first to reach the top step, while Monty refused to be carried and dragged himself, putting his weight on just three legs.

In the surgery that old feeling of dread was fairly immediate, and was quickly dramatised by a bout of flatulence, Monty's emission of a foul odour being greeted with exaggerated coughs by his friend. The vet discreetly opened a window.

Lifted onto a shiny steel table, Monty watched the young vet search in his black case for some instruments, which he lay on the table. *Things designed to prick, cut and tear,* thought Monty, but the vet left them untouched, saying, "Let's have a look at you." He parted the fur on Monty's thigh and peered closely. "A clean wound," he said, "But you know these things have a barb, don't you?" Barb was a new term for both dogs, and Monty simply gave an indeterminate yap in response.

The vet went to a glass cabinet to remove a small bottle and a hypodermic needle, turning back to find Shaggy on his hind legs, his front paws on the table edge and his lips drawn back to show his teeth. "You're not sending him to meet Black Shuck!" he yelled. "Put that back!"

The vet, already quite used to difficult dogs, could only guess the meaning of the reference to Black Shuck, but he recognised canine fear. "This is so it won't hurt your friend," he explained, "when I manipulate the hook. It's what we call a local anaesthetic."

"All right," said Shaggy, "but if he is sent over what you humans call the rainbow bridge I'll kill you."

Monty's leg was growing more painful. "Just do it, please," he said in a tiny voice. "Black Shuck would be better than more pain from this hook. I have developed a great deal of empathy towards fish." He spoke with a laugh and the vet was astonished at his wit. This was all too weird, even after the arrival of the aliens.

It took only a couple of minutes to retrieve the hook, the anaesthetic doing what it was supposed to do and the vet working dexterously with nimble fingers. A couple of stitches later, Monty felt brave enough to jump to the floor.

"Hey," called the vet, "no more of that for a while, please. By the way, what is your name?"

"I'm Monty, and he's Shaggy—because, of course, he is," replied Monty. "And who are you? I can't call you Vet."

"Oh," answered the vet, "I'm Francis, or—" He rapped his knuckle against his temple. "Perhaps I should say Frances."

"You just did," said Shaggy, who'd already been wondering if there was something wrong with this human, he had dark lines around his eyes that looked as though they had been painted on, and his lips were a bright shade of pink. What is more, he now seemed to be confused in his thoughts.

"I'm sorry," said Frances, "but I have to rush. I only came back for my equipment and the suppressor."

The two dogs stared with vacant eyes.

"I've been up at Hopetoun Farm," explained the vet. "With the cows—nobody's there to milk them and they'll become ill and die if left unmilked."

"Are there no calves to milk them?" asked Monty. "That'd be the simplest solution."

"I don't think you understand," replied Frances, hurriedly. "Their calves are taken away and, if male, will be killed for meat, in order that none of them get to drink the milk that we want to bring to market for ourselves. Accordingly, there are no calves you see."

The two dogs said nothing but stared, feeling rather disconcerted.

"I've been up there all day, milking," explained the vet. "Now I'm going to try reducing the generation of milk with this suppressor." He held up a plastic bottle of coloured liquid. "It's my own theory, so wish me luck. If it works, so long as the cows don't produce another calf they won't start making more milk; but if they do, the calf can have it, as nature intended."

"Hopetoun Farm, that's quite near Willow Croft, isn't it?" asked Monty, and the vet nodded, clutching her case and heading for the door.

The dogs didn't ask but followed Frances down the steps and hopped into the car as soon as the door was opened.

"I want to see if the cows can talk," whispered Shaggy to Monty.

"They won't," he whispered back. "Only the Canidae have been awakened. You knew that didn't you? The cows are too dumb. But tell you what, this vet could be useful to Willow Croft."

"Yes," gasped Shaggy, his eyes wide with thought, "with all the dangerous things the humans left behind, like you said, we might need him from time to time."

Frances started the engine and hoped she could keep her head clear enough to drive. Seeing the two dogs sitting on the back seat talking to each other it had suddenly hit her how weird life had become. *And I was talking to them,* she said to herself, *without question. Has all this aliens stuff caused me to lose my mind?* She turned round to speak then thought better of it. *No, I'm not going to apologise to a pair of dogs for not having had canine seatbelts installed.*

18. Milkmaid

"Well, this is all new to me," gasped Monty. "It seems rather impertinent to my way of thinking." Impertinent was currently one of his favourite new words, a word he flung at the puppies at Willow Croft if, uninvited, they colonised his bed, or at any dog who couldn't wait their turn at meal time.

Frances had hooked up some cows for their afternoon session of milking, and the dogs were bemused by the unflappable manner in which the cows entered the stalls, permitted the vet to wash their udders and submitted to suction caps being attached to their teats. It was this entire process that raised Monty's cry of impertinent.

Frances saw the concentration in the dogs' eyes and laughed. "I'm a regular milkmaid, aren't I," she quipped.

Monty looked at Shaggy and they both made a canine equivalent of a shrug.

Frances saw the awkward gesture. "Are you cold?" she asked. "Perhaps you should go and wait in the barn; there's straw there."

"There's something very wrong with that vet," said Monty when they were outside. "His signature smell doesn't work for me. Out here in the open all the vetlike niffs aren't so strong and I'm able to test his body odour. But it's very weak, unacceptably faint for a healthy young man. I'm beginning to ask myself whether we really want him at the home, he could prove a liability."

"I'm glad you said that," replied Shaggy. "When I confronted him over that needle, I got close to his face. The skin was a strange texture and had odd-smelling colours on it. What sort of sickness is that, do you think?"

Entering the barn they climbed into the loft and settled down on some bales of hay. Monty went quickly to sleep, no doubt tired by his recent ordeal, but Shaggy remained alert. There was movement amongst some further bales, which had been broken open. *Rats!* thought Shaggy. *Haven't enjoyed a rat hunt for ages.*

He crept across the loft floor, his belly almost touching the wooden boards, his legs outstretched so that he was balancing on his claws, and his nose whiskers twitching feverishly. He passed under a slender piece of wood and immediately his head shook with a cacophony of voices, the sort of shrill, quick voices one might expect rats to have. He moved quickly beyond the wood and the sound stopped. *Can't be rats,* he decided. *Monty just reminded me that only canids can talk.* Shaggy stood up and shook loose straw from his back. The long piece of wood beneath which he'd crawled protruded from a heap of tossed hay that was piled against the wall of the loft, and Shaggy gave it the customary sniff of examination always afforded new objects. Close up he could see it was smooth and shiny, decorated with intricate patterns that occasionally flickered as if they were alive. Then he recoiled, his teeth bared, there was a sinuous grey hand curled around the further end of the rod, the three fingernails yellow and pointed.

The figure that lay covered by an avalanche of hay didn't move and, just to make sure, Shaggy carefully parted it with his nose. A grey man, his back against the wall and his feet stuck out in front of him, slept soundly in a warm cocoon of hay. His shrivelled grey nose protruded from the darkness of his cowl, there was spittle on his thin lips and an empty bottle of Scotch lay beside him.

Shaggy withdrew as silently as he had come and crept back to his slumbering pal.

"We must warn the vet," he said urgently, his paw on Monty's chest to rouse him. "We can't let him be unmade when he's been so good to you."

Monty opened one eye and sniffed the air. "You're sure it was a grey man? It's not a dead human, is it?"

"Come on," urged Shaggy. "He may wake up soon." He prodded his friend with a nose to the ear and jumped down onto the stack of bales below. Monty rolled rather than jumped, he was feeling dopey, but the fall woke him at last and they scampered back to the milking shed.

With a large syringe in her hands, Frances was administering the last of her coloured transfusion. "Nearly done," she grinned, seeing the dogs arrive.

"Good," said Shaggy. "We must go. Hurry. There's a…there's a…"

"He made it into the barn, did he?" laughed Frances. "I'm sorry, I should have told you about that."

"Grey man," finished Shaggy. "Asleep in the loft."

"Asleep? Then we're quite safe," said Frances. "I guessed he'd drink all of it. At forty per cent, that whisky will have knocked him out well and truly. I dare say it will have been his first ever taste of the stuff. A good single malt too."

The dogs stood with mouths wide open.

"You gave it to him, and he didn't use his lantern on you?" Monty was astonished.

"He came in here earlier when I was finishing the morning session. Startled me—the first of them I'd seen up close. He seemed fascinated by the milking process and watched for ages. Then he pointed to the tanks and beckoned me to let him have a sample of milk. Well, I couldn't do that but there is always some spillage, which is collected in a pail, so I took some up in a jug and passed it to him. He had just one swig and turned green, I think he believed I'd poisoned him and he made to threaten me with that rod thing he was carrying. That's when I took the whisky out of my coat. I'd found it in the farmhouse and couldn't let it go to waste. I offered it to him and made a smiley face to show it was good." Frances gave the dogs an exaggerated smile as she finished wiping a cow's flank with disinfectant. "And that's how you found a drunken alien in the barn."

"So he never attempted to use his lantern on you?" The dogs had never come across a human exception before; both had witnessed the unmaking of several humans.

"He came with the intention of harming me, I'm in no doubt," answered Frances, "but something about me puzzled him; maybe my difference confused him and he wasn't sure if I was a legitimate target."

"Your difference?" exclaimed both dogs together.

Frances laughed. "Yes of course. I'm transgender. I started life as a male and I'm on my way to being female."

"You mean," said Shaggy disbelievingly, "you've been to another vet to have your—"

"Not yet," answered Frances. "And not likely now there are no or few surgeons left hereabouts." She frowned. "Still, there is one good thing to come out of all this, there's no-one around to make fun of me or call me bad names because of what I am."

"But," Monty interjected, "when dogs are taken to the vet to have their wherewithal removed, they don't become bitches."

"It's more complicated than mere surgery," said Frances. "I'm just glad I managed to confuse the alien. Here, help me turn the cows out, we should get going before our friend wakes up. He may have changed his mind about me. I'll come back tomorrow to see if I have been at all successful with my suppressor."

"Are there more animals to see to?" asked Shaggy.

"There were some pigs, I let them out of the yard. Pigs can survive. They'll forage. And the chickens, they're happy to have been freed from their cage. So long as the fox keeps away."

"Do you think we should have a word with the local foxes?" Shaggy asked Monty.

"What!" exclaimed Frances, overhearing. "You've got foxes talking too? What on earth is going on? First talking dogs speaking the King's English, and if that isn't enough we now have the tod chattering away in the woods. Whatever next?"

So, back in the car, Monty explained to the vet what the grey men had done, their purpose for visiting Earth and their promoting of all the Canidae to be the new dominant group of species, including foxes. "And no," he said to Shaggy, "we shouldn't go asking the foxes to leave the chickens alone. Foxes got to eat. They don't kill for sport."

"Actually, I wouldn't mind some fresh chicken myself," muttered Shaggy. "But the feathers—ugh!"

Frances was quietly turning Monty's tale over in her mind. She'd seen the grey men arrive in the town and was aware that the population was dropping rapidly, but the extent of what was underway had not occurred to her.

"So," she said at last, "this thing is total, then. Everyone gone. Just me left alive on this planet." Her hands gripped the steering wheel. "Actually, I can't believe it," she declared. "They've left me, they'll leave others. Nothing is ever absolute; the universe is too chaotic for that to be the case."

'Will I ever understand what she just said?' wondered Shaggy, while Monty made his mind up to investigate the nature of the universe.

The vet drove back into town and stopped outside the veterinary surgery. "Is this okay for you?" she asked the dogs.

"We can walk from here, it's not that far," replied Monty.

"Where is it you live, only I don't want you to strain that wound for the next twenty-four hours." Frances stayed in the driving seat. "Come on," she said, when Monty didn't answer. "I can pick up my meds later. Tell me where you want to go."

Their arrival at Willow Croft caused a flurry of excitement. Monty had arranged a schedule of lookouts and the two spaniels on duty ran around in a frenzy, barking their heads off to give warning to everyone inside the shelter.

Oh no, thought Monty. *That's not what I wanted.* He jumped from the car as soon as the door was opened and ran to remonstrate, while Shaggy watched, amused, then turned back to the vet.

"Where are you going to live? Now there's just you, I mean." Shaggy was remembering the earlier conversation he'd had with Monty concerning the value of vets.

Frances hadn't given it a thought. She lived alone in the centre of town. Why would that change?

"I was just thinking," said Shaggy. "It might be risky to stay in town, if your home's there. The grey men could be back. From what we know, they do seek out those humans they've missed. In fact, one of our friends has gone on a mission to help them find such people. Besides, it will be lonely living somewhere where there's no human comings and goings, won't it?"

"I won't be lonely," asserted Frances. "I've never liked other human beings very much; it's one reason I became a vet, to try to undo some of their wrongdoing with the animal world. There being fewer people about won't cause me any distress."

"Oh," sighed a disappointed Shaggy. "Well, if you do feel the need for company, always remember this place. There's somewhere here that used be home to the Willow Croft vets. You could have that."

Frances did not take up Shaggy's offer but drove back into town, leaving the two dogs to relate the story of their day's adventures to the rest of the Willow Croft pack. Shaggy's idea that the vet might be persuaded to join them occurred to several of the dogs, some of whom were feeling nervous to think that they were now entirely responsible for their own wellbeing.

So when her car drove into the forecourt in the middle of the next day, spirits were raised and several of the dogs ran out to meet her, with wagging tails and a spring in their step.

The corgi on guard duty was taken by surprise when the car appeared at the shelter entrance, and forgot her new power of speech, instead dashing about hither and thither, barking hysterically.

Frances ruffled Shaggy's ears and stroked Monty's stiff coat when they approached and she stood, her hands on their backs, taking a long critical look around the shelter.

"Do the aliens ever come up here?" she asked, and both dogs replied that they had never seen them up here above the town.

"The streets seemed full of them last night," she confided. "I hid in a cupboard, hoping they wouldn't detect me, and I could hear them slinking about the outside of the building. It made me think of your suggestion, Shaggy."

"Then, as I drove out to the farm to check on the cows, one of the aliens stood in the middle of the road and pointed that rod thing they all carry, pointed it directly at me. I was expecting to be hit with a death ray or something but all I heard was a sort of musical whining in my ear, and nothing stopped me."

"So, you've decided to join us?" asked Monty.

"I might be safer here. You might find me useful too," she grinned. "I'd also like to know more about what it is like to be given the gift of speech, whether it is good thing or if you find it a burden. Either way, I am mightily impressed by your vocabulary and articulation."

Frances went late in the afternoon for another survey of the cows, and reported back that their milk production had begun to reduce. Fatigued, she sat with Monty, Shaggy and a couple of poodles on the front porch of the shelter, where the sun was still warm.

"What will happen to them?" asked Monty.

"If I can stop their need to be milked, they can be turned out into the fields. I don't know how well they can survive as wild cows, they've been wholly domesticated, but I can't nurse them forever."

"We were domesticated," observed Monty. "But we've survived—so far."

"So what actually happened—your transition from non-speaking to fully voiced, in fact to being fully conscious, if you don't mind me asking?" Frances bit upon a pasty she'd had in the freezer at the surgery and, fascinated by the meaty aroma, Monty took a moment to answer.

"This sounds very feeble, but I don't know what they did. Nobody does, except our friend Garth, and his awakening was rather special. There was a light, we all agree on that, and some kind of machines were present, but other than that it was like magic, as some still believe."

"And this light, the use of what you describe as a lantern, that is central to what you call unmaking?"

"That's what we've seen. It looks very simple."

"It would have to be," laughed Frances, "given there are—or were—billions of humans to be unmade."

"There are a lot of grey men. Tiny, our friend, told us that. Thousands, maybe millions. They've come in huge frisbees. Shaggy and I saw one when we were foraging."

"And tell me, how does it feel to be awakened?"

"Like going from being blind to being able to see for miles," butted in Shaggy. "It's not just seeing, either, it's knowing too. Now, I call that magical, even if Garth says it's not."

"And how about you?" asked Monty. "What made you transition from a man to a woman?"

"That too is very hard to explain," said Frances. "I was born with this sense I was in the wrong body. As I grew older and was able to think about it logically, I've gravitated towards the view that it was a consequence of all that plastic in the food chain. My mother must have ingested so much that it affected me in the womb. No-one ever came out to confirm that as a cause of gender dysphoria, but scientists researching plastic pollution have evidence that working closely with plastic can affect the human genome."

"That must make you angry," said Shaggy.

"Just part of the chaos in our corner of the universe," smiled Frances. "Anyway, I'm comfortable with myself."

Yes, thought Monty. *I'm pretty comfortable with the way I am now.*

In fact, life at Willow Croft was, for everyone there, generally agreed to be comfortable. Nevertheless, there hung in the air a sense that something remained unfulfilled, a feeling that they had suffered a loss, in spite of having gained the ability to talk and to reason. It was the latter, being able to reflect upon events, that drew each of them to the conclusion that they were troubled not by pining for a life with a human master but by thoughts about the search party. Even though the Willow Croft pack had been a newly constituted entity, its rapid deficit of Garth and his team of twelve had been keenly felt. They had left for a journey imagined to be fraught with hazard, and they had been gone now for what seemed a very long time.

19. Fox

The year had passed almost into autumn, when Jake the bearded collie brought the strays who had been tasked with managing the cockapoos up the hill to Willow Croft. Order had been established at the pet store, and despite their scorn for the breed, the strays had found the cockapoos generally to be good company.

"Our food supply has seriously depleted," Jake told Monty. "There has been a problem with rats, and this bunch"—he nodded at the handful of cockapoos who'd accompanied him—"don't seem to have a taste for ratting. In addition," he groaned, "a skulk of foxes has been coming around regularly and demanding their share. *We're all one family now,* they said, the cheeky blighters, *share and share alike.* Only they've got nothing to share. In times past, we'd have chased the lot of them out of the county, but with these grey man craft buzzing about over our heads I was reluctant to let that happen."

"Yes, there's been a lot of frisbee activity of late," said Monty, thoughtfully.

"Well," Jake began, "I was wondering if Frances might bring what supplies we have left up here for us, if her travelling machine is still working."

"I've told you—often—it's called a car. But yes, I'm sure she would do that. She keeps going down into town to find her meds, something she needs to 'keep stable', as she calls it."

"Really? Have you seen her horse?" asked Jake. "I'd like there to be a horse up here at the croft. Oh, that's what I meant to say: we would like to move up here for the winter, if there's room, make it our base until the others return and we can go back to life as the West End Strays. I suppose there's been no word?"

"Not a whiff," said Monty; "and yes, there's room I expect." He ignored Jake's misunderstanding about the stable, just as he ignored those made by his pal, Shaggy, and all the other residents of the shelter. By human terms, Monty had become quite erudite; he'd learnt how to deeply mine the store of knowledge that the awakening had gifted him.

Every evening at dusk since the search party had left, Monty had sat out on the hill above the croft, up from Pom's tomb, and listened out for twilight barking. Up here the air was clear in every direction and he could listen in on conversations passing from town to town and farm to farm. Where the lines of communication crossed there was sometimes a confusion of messages, with more than one voice becoming entangled, but Monty kept his ears tuned to the more distant sounds, canine utterances that he hoped would provide news of Clover and the others.

On the very day that Garth had headed off, Bunny had expressed a desire to spend time with Monty, hoping to grab some of the gloss of authority that Monty so easily enjoyed. His humiliation in the encounter with the strays was a source of lingering shame and he felt that no-one would respect him as the appointed manager of the shelter. Being seen as an associate of Monty would, he hoped, give him reflected credibility.

But Bunny was destined never to sit with Monty on those busy evenings on the hill. Out trying his skills at hunting rabbit, late that same morning, in the hope he might impress the other members of the pack, he had spied three beagles floundering in the crazy water of Butcher's weir. From their pawprints, it seemed they had been stranded for a while on a small muddy island and were attempting to regain the shore. He immediately jumped in to rescue them, but for all his bravery all three were swept away, despite Bunny having seized one in his teeth for a precious moment. He returned to Willow Croft with a sore head, which in a week had developed into oral blisters and an intense fever. Monty, assuming charge of the centre, isolated the poor creature in the home's greenhouse, where he shivered his lonely way to Black Shuck after no more than ten days.

That was, of course, before Frances had come into Monty's orbit, although all she might have done would be to ease the hapless doodle's pain.

Sitting there in the long dry grass, Monty reflected on the considerable changes that had been wrought upon his life. First, there was the coming of speech and higher consciousness, that's where it had begun, but there were also the unpredicted consequences, changes both mundane and extraordinary: membership of a new pack, for example, for which he had assumed leadership, the discovery that humans could cross from one gender to another, and recognition of his feelings for his long term pal Clover. *I didn't have those feelings before*, he insisted. It was an issue that kept coming up when he had time alone to think. *Or if I did, I didn't know I had them.* How was she doing anyway, was what he really wanted to know.

"Lost in your thoughts, pal?" said a reedy voice, and for a moment Monty expected to see a grey man standing there. But there was no rod touching his back to facilitate speech, only the sharp visage of a vagrant fox, its eyes twinkling and roguish, its ears tall and erect; they were turning this way and that as it examined all possible avenues of attack should there be trouble coming. But the fox's eyes were implacable; Monty felt as if he'd been pierced with a spear.

"Hello Tod, how go you this fine evening?" Monty chose familiarity, to be in the new spirit of companionship.

The fox relaxed and swished his thick tail in a conspicuous show of self-possession.

"I have run far with a tale to tell," he said in a sing-song voice, which made Monty think of the stream that ran babbling over pebbles into the estuary. "I have friends to speak of and deeds to sing about. I seek sustenance and a quiet bed for the night before I go to find my own kin. It has been a long day." The fox sat in the grass and wound his tail around him, looking questioningly at Monty. "Any news in the air tonight?" he asked. It was the first thing he'd said that made any sense to the Airedale.

"It has barely begun," answered Monty. "Just local news of associations made and new sources of food discovered. I was hoping for something rather different."

"News of six proud lurchers, perhaps," said the fox, shrewdly. "Six canids brave enough to confront a human huntsman with a weapon, six large dogs with the compassion to rescue a brother fox. Six proud lurchers heading home on twenty-three legs, maybe that's what you're wanting to hear about."

Monty was a long way now from ruminating about his own life. He stood on all four legs and growled a deep, dark growl. The fox stared back at him, its eyes flat and unreadable.

"Just six dogs, you say, six lurchers. You didn't mention a collie—did you forget?"

"Six lurchers is what I say and six lurchers is what I mean. Fox knows his mind; I tell you straight." He sat and licked his paws, his thoughts elsewhere. "Come to think of it, there was a collie," he said slowly, focusing again, and Monty jumped. "She was a fine creature, saved another dog's life by all accounts, a black and white dog she was travelling with. Mmm, yes, they decided to stay for a while. I can tell you where, if you're interested."

"Do you have any names?" Monty was half-disappointed but also hopeful. At least, Clover could still be alive—and Loki too it seemed.

"The three-legger, as is, goes by the name Tak, does that mean to you what I thought it might?"

"I have been waiting for a lurcher named Tak," said Monty, "together with a band of a dozen other canids, but the Tak I know has four legs. Are the lurchers of which you speak close to home?"

"Closer than yesterday," said the fox cryptically, "and no farther than a fox can run without a meal. Tomorrow, well before twilight barking, you should see them. One of them is wounded—he has an arse full of buckshot. They told me to run ahead while he rests, and I could smell this place from miles back." The fox suddenly crouched down and started to scratch itself with a ferocity that must have been painful, and only then did Monty notice the coil of thin wire wound tightly around its neck.

"You are hurt," he said, and the fox showed its teeth in a spasm of pain that it had been hiding. "We have a human who can help you," Monty suggested. "Come."

"Do you think I am out of my head?" snarled the fox, on its feet now. "Humans kill, not help."

"The world has been turned upside down," said Monty. "Our human lives to help the animal population. Trust me, if I speak lies you can have whatever revenge you think is fitting."

As he led the fox down the hill, Monty tried to remember all six lurchers that had accompanied Garth. There hadn't been time to get to know them well, even to learn all their names. Names weren't something that had been important before the awakening, one relied on scent and demeanour to recognise another dog in those times, but knowing language had introduced more sophisticated social behaviours. Monty wasn't sure whether that represented progress.

Fortunately, Frances was on site and, although unused to handling foxes, she succeeded in retrieving the wire from around the animal's neck. It had bitten deep and the flesh of his neck was severely broken. "This will sting," she said to the fox.

"Perhaps you have something to help take the pain away," said the wily fox. "A piece of chicken breast, perhaps, or a freshly killed rat."

"There are plenty of rats down in the town," said Monty. "My friend Jake can show you if you like."

"There you are," said Frances, showing him the wire. "It's a common snare. You were lucky to get out of that."

"I didn't get out of it did I? You have it in your hand."
The fox looked at Frances scathingly. "It was the lurchers that
saved me. The big one called Tak, he pulled out the stake to
which it was attached, buried deep it was, then we had to run
for it, because the hunter came after us with his gun. It was a
tense moment, with buckshot flying over our heads, but we
made it away. I then had the problem of living with a wooden
stake dragging behind me. Would have rather cramped my
style." He coughed and winced. "Any sign of that chicken
breast?" he entreated.

Frances grimaced. "I'm so glad I could help you," she said
testily, and to Monty, "Jesus, you could think he is human."

"Come," Monty urged the importunate fox. "I'm sure you
need a drink and, while we have no chicken breast, I can offer
you rabbit. It's mealtime anyway, and you can sit with us all
and tell the rest of your story."

20. Laboratory

After quitting the wolves' retreat, Tak and the lurchers had run far to the west, so far that they skirted the source of the river that had been a potential barrier to their journey home. There, they found themselves in mountainous country of bare rock and towering slopes, and for the first week they slept their nights in caves and gullies, with swooping bats irritating the air above them. Food had to be caught, and they dined on squirrel and wild goat, the experience of catching and killing their prey unfamiliar to half of their party, who had relied for sustenance on scavenging and the benevolence of animal-loving humans.

On the seventh night of working through the mountains, Rex, a slim brindle dog with a greyhound's face, sat up with a start. He'd been tasked with staying awake in order to call the alert if danger approached. The lurchers had bedded down high up in a cave, overlooking a valley with a long lake at its centre, the cliffs on either side of them and on the other side of the lake peppered with the dark mouths of other caves; so many and so regularly arranged that they must surely have been made, Tak had remarked. Rex realised while shaking himself out of a doze that he had been aware all along that there were lights in those cave mouths, aware but not prescient. Now he saw them clearly; they were fires, or flaming beacons. He stood and walked out to the cave entrance, his nose busy in the air.

Aromas of charred meat and human sweat wafted across the valley, carried on drifts of wood smoke and steam. Rex stood for a while, salivating a little at the rich smell of freshly cooked venison and hot fat. Then he remembered his duty and crept back inside.

"Tak, Tak," he whispered sharply into the big dog's sleeping ear. "Humans, quite a number of them I gather, close by."

Tak roused himself carefully; on an earlier night he'd got up in a rush and tumbled down the ravine where they were lodging. He too walked to the cave mouth and stared into the distance.

"They're on this side too," said Rex. "Humans."

"I smell them," confirmed Tak. "But so many. Does this mean that the grey men have gone away, or that they have simply missed this lot?"

"Out of a total of billions I suppose this isn't many." Rex ducked. "Hey, look out!"

The two lurchers stepped back into the shadows of the cave and flattened themselves to the rocky floor, their eyes focused on the brightly lit frisbee-like craft that sped in a smooth line down the middle of the valley.

"Here you are," said Rex. "They've come to take this lot. It must have been a runaway community."

The frisbee stopped abruptly then moved sideways towards the opposite cliff wall, a loud chorus of voices reaching the dogs from the humans who were hiding there, as though someone had turned up the volume of the background chatter that had already been evident to the dogs' keen ears. A light came on and swept the wall, each cave highlighted in turn, the human figures stark like matchstick men in its cool glow. They stood frozen while the light was on them, then it moved on without noticeable incident and the figures were animated once more.

"Did you see," asked Rex, "were any unmade?"

"I couldn't tell," said Tak. "Probably. But I still smell human on the air."

"There are some either side of us," said Rex. "Maybe…"

At that point, the light was shut off and the frisbee shot across the valley towards the dogs.

"Quick!" snapped Tak, "back inside and don't let any of the others move."

Again, flat to the floor, Tak and Rex whispered an explanation of what was going on to the other lurchers, who all lay like stone carvings and probably appeared to be a heap of boulders to anyone peering in. Then the light came on again and the dogs in their turn felt its soft touch through the cave opening. Once more there rose a buzz of human voices before the light went away from the cliff and the valley was dark once more.

The Derin craft withdrew silently in the direction from which it had come and the dogs looked out to find the fires in the caves were still burning, distant figures moving around in their flickering light.

"I don't want to know what's going on," said Tak to the others. "This is grey man business and grey men are not a threat to us. But there are humans, out of their normal environment, and they will be unpredictable. I can hardly believe we came in here unnoticed. But be ready, we'll slip away before it's fully light and follow the river we saw from the ridge, the river that feeds the lake."

The sky was a wan grey, lit only by a waning moon when Tak led his party down through the loose boulders below their cave. The fires in the other caves had been extinguished and the dogs saw no signs of life in those they passed. At last, a trail emerged that ran parallel to the lake, and they stepped out quickly, in haste to quit the valley, once a place where they had felt safe to rest but now redolent of mystery and hidden threat.

The lurchers were almost silent as they trotted in a close group, until one dog, a black and tan, skipped off to the side with a clipped yip to Tak. He glanced back and saw her squatting in wispy grass. "Hurry," he called, thinking, *At least there's no-one to complain about what's being left in the grass.*

But there was someone, someone standing stiff behind a dead tree trunk, a human, a smallish human, in fact a human child about as tall as Tak was long. It carried something, a spear, held awkwardly in its hand.

The black and tan dog had finished its defecation and was scratching earth and stones over its deposit with its back legs. As it turned to rejoin the other dogs the child, who seemed not to have noticed Tak and the others against the dark waters of the lake, rushed forward with its spear raised high.

"No!" barked Tak, running forward, and the human stumbled to a stop. The spear, Tak saw, was roughly made, a thin shaft cut from one of the few trees in the valley, whittled to a point that would have been unlikely to wound severely. The child gripped it tightly in its three fingers.

"You are dogs!" cried the child, a boy in his mid-teens, "and you speak. Is this another test?"

"I don't know what you mean," answered Tak. "We are simply passing through this valley, on our way home." Then to explain, "All dogs can speak now. We do have a little trouble with our *s* words, on account of our long tongues, which tend to make us sound as if we're sneezing, but yes, we are growing better at speech by the day."

"So, they didn't bring you here," said the boy, his tone disbelieving.

"They?" Tak didn't elaborate but he knew who the boy was referring to. "I am Tak," he said, "and I brought my pack here. It has been a long journey."

"I am Marcel," replied the boy. "The aliens brought me, brought all of us." He looked back at the cliffs. "Two hundred of us, all under twenty years of age. And they did this." He held out the hand that did not grip the spear. It was no longer a normal human hand, for it had only three long fingers and was missing a thumb. There was no sign of a wound, no scarring or regrown tissue; it was as if it had always been thus. "We are all like this now," said Marcel, disconsolately. "We have been told to test ourselves, to find our peak. When we have reached our peak, we shall be put to propagate ourselves." He looked Tak in the eye to see if the dog understood. "They check on us every day; to measure evolutionary potential, they say. We are imprisoned here; we cannot go anywhere freely outside this valley, it is like being—"

"I know," threw in Rex in his sourest tone, "like being a dog chained up in a yard."

The lurchers were all beginning to feel uneasy, and there began some rapid twitching of tails that Tak could not ignore.

"We must go," he said to the boy. "We cannot help you."

"But you can't go," the boy insisted. "There is a…a…plug in the end of the valley. Go back the way you came."

The dogs all groaned. They had come over the mountain tops and to return that way was a dismal prospect.

"Let's investigate this plug," said Tak and the others all gave small barks of agreement.

Without a further word to Marcel, they left the boy, who watched them until the shadows swallowed them and they became indistinguishable from the motion of the wind on the waters of the lake, where a slight breeze had arisen.

The further they walked the less was there evidence of caves in the cliffs above them, and the dogs felt more relaxed as they progressed. The valley was narrowing all the time, the grey cliffs ahead seeming to come together to provide an impenetrable wall.

"It can't be wholly closed off." Tak sought to reassure the others, who were muttering unhappily. "The river runs in at that end, I'm sure, and anyway, what that boy said about a plug; a plug needs a gap to fill, doesn't it, as do we."

The lake too was narrowing to a sharp point, squeezed by the convergence of the rock walls until it melded into the river that fed it, and as the day was growing lighter the dogs could see at a distance the foam made by fast running water. The sound it made grew louder with every step they took.

Contrary to how it had first appeared, the two cliff faces did not quite meet. On one side, the dogs discovered the noise made by the water was the result of a cascade that frothed down over a wall of loose rocks, the roar of the falling torrent

214

given note by the chinking of the stones, making a kind of wild music together. But this tumultuous spectacle occupied less than half of the gap between the leaning cliff ends, which sought to pinch the air between them. What blocked the rest of the passage out of the valley now engaged everyone's thoughts, for it was so incongruous a phenomenon, a translucent bubble over a metre in width. It hung suspended by no visible means and slowly spun on a vertical axis, the growing light in the sky above causing it to radiate all the colours of the rainbow, wandering streaks that flared and faded, only to repeat further around the sphere. This fine filigree of colours suggested something organic, an organism with a network of nerves or fluid dispersion, and several of the dogs shivered, feeling its presence quietly sinister.

"Well," said Tak, contemplating in turn the cascade and the bubble, "I'm not going to chance clambering up that waterfall. The rocks look loose and besides, they are covered with green slime. Break my leg and I'm never getting home." The others nodded their assent, and proceeded in turns to pee on the bank of the stream that ran from the torrent into the lake, just to show their contempt for that artful avenue of escape.

"Anyway," Tak blew air threw his nostrils, turning to the sphere that blocked their way, "it's only a bubble. A very large bubble, I admit, and a bubble I don't like the look or scent of, but still a bubble. And what do we do to bubbles? We poke them and they burst." He was sounding more confident than he felt, but still he cautiously approached the uncanny sphere, put out a foreleg, and pierced its lustrous skin.

All of the dogs cowed down at the great blast of air that came from the space in front of them, everyone hunched and falling in agony from the high-pitched whistle that, for no more than a second, seemed to split their skulls in two. When the air had calmed once more they crawled to their feet, shivering with fright and then filled with elation to find the way ahead lay clear and unblocked, their tails wagging furiously with relief.

Tak was the last to stand, and he stood unsteadily, his right foreleg gone, severed at the elbow. As with Marcel's hand, there was no evidence of wounding, no blood, no broken skin. Even the fur that covered the end of the shortened limb looked firm and dense.

The others quickly became aware of their leader's attempts to hobble around at the head of the group. "Tak," said one after another, "are you in pain?" "can you walk?" and, in an attempt to be level-headed, "use your tail to help you balance." They were so busy running around him, keen to examine his changed anatomy, sniffing and giving encouraging licks to his face, that no-one but Tak noticed the grey man who stood unmoving in the spot where the giant bubble had hung. He moved forward, his rod held out in front of him, and with it he touched Tak's back between the shoulder blades so that the big lurcher could hear him speak.

"You will not come here again," came the voice. "This place is not for the Canidae. You have almost the entire world, but not this place." He twisted the rod and Tak felt the voice grow in his head like a warm cloud. "Know that the energy from the sphere is in you, just as the knowledge we give you is yours to use, as well as your strength. For you are made strong," said the grey man; "you will be known as mightily strong, and on three legs you can run with the wind. But do not dare to lose another, for if you do your strength will be forfeit and you will never see beyond the stars in your sky." With his other arm, the grey man pointed out through the gap where the bubble had been. "Go, quickly, the way will be clear for only a very short time."

"Run!" shouted Tak, "run through." And the dogs raced for the space beyond the opening between the cliffs. Just one or two looked back when they had gained a distance from the exit, seeing a large translucent bubble hanging in the air between a tall fissure in the rocky landscape behind them.

Leaving the river, which cut away from a high plateau of grey rocks, they ran across an undulating plain and did not stop until the land dipped down and they could see a green expanse of trees and grassy slopes stretching before them. They stopped, out of concern for Tak, all of them with tongues hanging long and pink, wanting to see how their leader was managing the journey on three legs; but he was full of good humour and quipped, "Did anyone see me falling behind?" Then, with a yelp to register that he had something pithy to say, he asked, "Remember as puppies, when we burst bubbles on the floor of the fish market after it had been washed?" There were looks both of recognition and anticipation from the other dogs. "Well, what did we usually use to burst them? he demanded."

"Our noses," came the chorused reply.

"So, don't anybody pity me," said Tak, licking the stump of his foreleg. "It could have been much worse."

21. Woodsman

They ran through misty glens and along verdant hillsides, all of the lurchers highly athletic runners, with Tak showing no handicap from the loss of a leg. Indeed he outstripped his companions, continually stopping and waiting for them to catch up. "I am on fire," he muttered to himself. "I am made mightily strong."

For two days, they ran in weather that turned its face away from the sun, rain falling in shrouds of droplets no larger than the particles of fog, the dogs' backs glistening with a silvery covering.

"It's called mizzle," crowed a black lurcher with ghostly blue eyes, "I looked for the word in my head and it just, well, popped out." The dogs were still coming to terms with their new facility for understanding, although it had been many weeks since their own awakening.

"We must be getting closer to home," said Rex. "I recognise this weather."

Heading into a pine forest to find somewhere secure and dry for the night, they almost ran into the walls of a cabin hidden in the shadows. It was in fact not a cabin, but a shelter all the same, a structure composed of horizontal logs built in the almost square space between four evergreens, the corners of the building fixed by groove and gravity to the trunks, with more logs for the roof, all camouflaged with deep moss.

"Wait!" urged Tak, and they ceased in their hasty search for shelter from the ceaseless dripping of rain from the trees.

A stealthy examination both outside and in found the structure empty, although an extensive search for scents, six snuffling noses poring over every inch of earth floor and wall, confirmed recent human occupation.

"When I was very young," said the blue-eyed dog, "I lived with a human family—until I was thrown out for developing a prolonged stomach upset, that is, may Black Shuck curse them all—and they had their own young who used to build camps like this in the wood behind their house. Perhaps this is such a human child's den. Somewhere now used to hide from the grey men."

"It is human made, certainly," acknowledged Tak, "but look, what do you see there?" He indicated a shotgun and metal traps hanging from nails in the roof. "Not a child's den, after all, and I think we need to find somewhere else to shelter."

With increased caution, they crept on beyond the wooden den, following faint trails made by deer across the forest floor. The rain was at last signalling a pause when they emerged into a clearing, just a stone's throw from a parked vehicle that sat in the middle of a muddy track. There was no-one behind the wheel and no sound of human footsteps could be detected.

Nevertheless, "We must keep going, quickly," insisted Tak, and one by one the dogs sped across the open space, glimpsing as they ran the seemingly endless avenue between the trees that had been made by loggers.

"Do you suppose there are humans still working here?" asked one of the lurchers, as they sheltered from the track for a moment behind a tall stack of cut timber.

"I can't imagine it," said another. "They surely will be too busy just surviving to worry about working. But it is likely woodsmen who knew how to build that den."

They moved quietly on, forced by the anonymous topography of the forest to stray in a direction well away from their intended route south, the light in the sky insufficient to act as compass. Without thinking, they each periodically marked their route, stopping to raise a leg against a tree before scampering to catch up with the others, and they checked that they had not doubled back by sniffing at the base of trees for traces of their own scent.

With barely a word or a growl between them as they padded on, they passed two more of the log dens, neither of which seemed to be occupied, and had just spied a third when they were halted by a series of sharp barks and a brittle keening that wounded the calm forest air.

"By Shuck," declared Rex, "that startled me. There's evil afoot, without a doubt."

"I didn't hear evil," said Tak, "I heard extreme pain and despair in those barks."

With ears pricked and noses trawling the air for clues, they shuffled forward through a carpet of pine needles. It was the black and tan who first made contact; she ran forward, caught on a scent, her nose bobbing as if she was attached to the flow of an airborne aroma in motion. It led in a path dictated by the drift of forest air to a slight bank of earth and pine cones, a place pockmarked with rabbit holes, where a fox crouched immobile, its face at an angle, one sharp ear pricked and the other flattened against the ground.

The fox's jaw was held in a rictus of agony, but as the dogs approached it relaxed and spoke through heavy gulps of air.

"I heard you. For a long while, I could hear you, but I feared you would pass me by."

The fox's voice sounded strange to the lurchers, the timbre of its vowels to their ears peculiarly slurred and musical, when they had since awakening been used to their own more guttural speech, and they put their heads on one side as they concentrated on what it was saying. But what they did not have trouble figuring out was the nature of its plight, for the earth had been scratched and deeply furrowed where the fox had attempted to free itself from a wire snare, a cruel device that led from its neck to a stake that had been hammered into the ground.

"Rex," exclaimed Tak, "you were right about there being something evil here, for evil has been done to our brother fox."

And without hesitation, Tak grasped the end of the stake in his teeth and leant back, his hind legs at an angle, and he tugged and tugged, arching his tail to focus his strength, each jerk on the post breaking the earth around it; but it had been buried deep and was not inclined to be pulled free.

"I hear footsteps," said the black and tan dog. "Heavy footsteps, coming this way in a hurry." Her whiskers twitched as she tried for a scent.

Tak didn't cease his toil, yet it seemed the stake would never budge. "Oh Shuck," he grunted, "grant me strength," and as he called for help from the canids' mythical spirit he recalled the words of the grey man at the end of the valley. So, with renewed energy and foam on his lips, Tak pulled once more until the stake flew skywards from the earth, taking the fox with it for several feet. There came a roar of anger from behind them and the sound of booted feet running heavily. Rex grabbed hold of the stake and ran, pulling a choking fox behind him on a windmill of little legs, and the lurchers fled as one in a cloud of pine needles, ears flapping against their heads and tails outstretched.

A loud explosion overtook them before they'd reached the shadows and shot peppered the trees on either side. But no human, and in this case a large, heavy-set human male, could outpace a fleet lurcher determined to escape. The dogs ran in a wide circle, every one of them intuitively anxious not to travel too far from their entrance to the forest, there having already been too many diversions to their route home. That circular flight brought them back to the track where the Land Rover still stood. There was no sound of anyone chasing them.

They stopped before venturing an exposed crossing, the injured fox out of breath from being dragged behind Rex.

"My friend," the fox panted, "it is not my way to be ungrateful, I am not the churlish kind, but I cannot keep up this pace. If I were freed of this piece of wood, I could do my best to match your speed."

Rex looked at the snare mechanism and saw it was fixed to the stake by a metal plate held by screws. The metal plate, which was corroded brown with rust, had a half ring to which a swivel was attached, and that was connected to the wire. There was no way any of the dogs could bite through either the swivel or the steel wire.

"We must remove it from around his neck," said Tak, but when he looked closer he found the wire had cut deeply into flesh and was too embedded for his teeth to grasp without seriously injuring the animal. He examined the metal plate and the swivel.

"What would a human do?" he asked himself aloud.

"A human would seek tools," said the fox.

"A human has fingers and a thumb to grip those tools," countered Rex, wryly.

If we had Garth with us, thought Tak, *he could ask the grey men for advice.* He recalled once more the grey man's words, the resolution that he must use the knowledge he'd been awarded through his awakening. *But I know myself what has to be done.* He bit his lips in frustration and squealed at the hurt, darting off in a cloud of vexation to pace upon the track. As he walked he kept his eyes and ears open for the appearance of the car's owner.

But I'm still only a dog, he thought, *a dog who thinks he has become something better. What a fool, such conceit.* He hung his head and his ears flattened against his cheeks, his tail hanging low. Then his steps quickened and he ran back to the others, dramatically inspired. "It's not just knowledge," he said to them, their faces puzzled by his sudden animation, "it's thinking. We've always done thinking, but without the foundation of knowledge. Tools are what's needed, you said so," he was almost snarling. "Well, we can use tools, if we work out how best to use them. All of you, stand guard while I look in that vehicle. We may have only a little time."

To the other lurchers Tak's disjointed statements sounded as if he had gone mad, but they did as he commanded, for he

223

was clearly in earnest and, anyway, they had learnt always to trust his judgement.

The Land Rover was one of those with an open rear section covered by tarpaulin, and it took Tak no time at all to wriggle his way underneath it, into the back end of the car. It was full of a forester's workwear and equipment, including a rope, chainsaw, some heavy chains, and a bowsaw. None of these caught his eye, but a metal spike that lay loose in a drain in the floor was quickly seized in his mouth, and he jumped down with it to the track, where he dropped the spike to examine it closely. It was one of those implements wrought to split wood and had evidently been used thoughtlessly, for where the hammer would drive it into a log the metal had split and torn. If he had understood the concept of luck, and perhaps he did, Tak felt that Shuck had smiled upon him at that moment.

Taking up the spike again, he jammed it into one of the holes in the vehicle's front wheel, where a circular pattern of openings had been engineered for some function unknown to the dog. Then he called to the fox to come close.

The wounded creature looked exhausted, but assisted by Rex it dragged itself out from the trees and onto the track, Rex holding up the stake to take the stress off the fox's neck. When asked, he passed it to Tak, and the big lurcher nudged the fox as far back from the vehicle as the steel wire would allow. Then, carefully and gradually, Tak manoeuvred the half ring of the rusted plate over the end of the spike. It took him several attempts, for his mouth was clumsy, and by the time he had succeeded he was panting heavily and his mouth was bloody.

There was still no sign of the driver of the Land Rover, but Tak took a moment to walk up and down the track for a moment before returning to the car. "If this goes wrong and I'm caught," he said to Rex, "go south without me. Take the fox to Monty; I think Monty has the brains to find a way to help him."

Then, without waiting for Rex to reply and first telling the fox that he must remain still, Tak grasped the end of the stake in his teeth, wedged one end inside the wheel rim, and began to lever the metal plate, which was hooked onto the spike. In his mind, he believed that by doing this he could pull out the screws holding the plate, but the harder he pulled, all he achieved was to break off the end of the wooden stake. The fox, its eyes popping in his head, was in agony, the tight wire pressed further and further into his flesh as a consequence of what Tak was doing to save him.

"Leave it," he croaked. "Sadly, it is beyond your strength."

"But didn't you know?" laughed Tak, letting go of the stake to spit wood fragments off his tongue, "I am mightily strong." He certainly did look mad in that moment.

He took hold of the stake once more, adjusted the angle he was pulling, and gave a mighty wrench. The screws still failed to budge, but there was movement, the rusty metal plate giving up the half ring, which flew off and dinged the poor fox in the crown of his head.

Dazed, the fox sat back on its tail, barely conscious of the lurchers gathering around the car.

"Someone is approaching, there are heavy footsteps," said one.

"Then run!" barked Tak.

"Take the woodcutters' track, it is the fastest route out of the forest," counselled the fox in a strangled voice. To Tak, it was unwise advice, for they would be exposed, but the lurchers were already running, their paws throwing up dust.

Tak and the fox crawled underneath the Land Rover, seeing a pair of legs run up in tall leather boots. The boots stopped and they heard heavy breathing, then the sound of a mechanism being closed together. Then boom, the roar of both barrels of a shotgun shocked their ears.

Tak peered out and down the track. The lurchers were well away now, but the dog in the rear was limping. It was Rex.

The ratcheting, closing sound came again and Tak looked out once again as the man raised his gun a second time. *Remember, you are strong,* Tak said the words in his head just before he leapt from beneath the vehicle, his one outstretched forepaw like a ramrod in the man's throat. He went down like one of the trees he was used to felling, the back of his bare head making fateful rendezvous with the spike that Tak had left in the wheel, his gun uselessly shooting down pine cones that anointed his fresh corpse.

With contempt, Tak ignored the man and coaxed the fox out into the open. "You must come with us," he said. "Somehow we will find a way to remove that wire. It can't be far to home now; we have travelled for many days more than when we first came north."

They sauntered along the track to catch up with the other dogs, who had stopped in a quiet place for Rex to examine his rump, which bore a swathe of black spots across his close fur. "Oh, look," he said to Tak as he approached, "I'm turning dalmatian."

22. Up the Garden Path

She managed to hook her left canine under the edge of the panel. The treated wood tasted of tar and smoke and she felt nauseous, but she persisted, managing to tear off a long strip, which she placed on top of the small pile she had already broken from the shed wall. That was four panels she had weakened, wide enough for a collie to squeeze through once it was open.

If he wakes up soon, I'll see if his overfed girth would also make it. She got up and went to sniff at Loki's mouth. There was still that ugly reek of venom. Or was it herself she could smell? For an age she had licked and sucked where the adder had struck, wiping her long tongue clean on a sack, feeling disgusted to have had that filth upon her. But at least the man had left them a dish of water, with which she had rinsed her mouth repeatedly. And, thank Shuck, Loki seemed to have survived.

Not for the first time, Clover wondered whether they had made a mistake, thinking they could travel alone, just her and the beagle cross. But having watched Bala drop away over the cliff she had felt she must do something positive, there was no reason to stay in the forbidding environment of the airfield, and neither she nor Loki were attracted by the plans made by the staffies and the wolfhound.

Was this sentimental desire to go back to their roots anything to do with having been awakened? She certainly didn't share that feeling, but then those dogs were all breed entire, whereas she had two places of origin.

The wolfhound had been the first to declare his intention. He'd always been drawn to travel and adventure, and now he'd set his mind on travelling to Ireland, wherever that may be. Similarly, the staffies hungered for the source of their identity, and they declared they would accompany the wolfhound, hoping to discover the location of Stafford, which was bound to welcome three well-travelled sons.

"But there won't be any humans to make a fuss of you, if that's what you're thinking," sneered Loki. "Just another load of pushy little oiks like you, all fighting for food and the most fecund bitch."

The staffies didn't care, they said they were going anyway, to act as a protective militia for the wolfhound.

So Loki and Clover, having no desire to travel further on, were left with the prospect of travelling home together, back to Willow Croft and—What? Safety? A new life?

"I'm not fussed," said Loki languorously. "Perhaps we can retrace our steps and meet up with Garth. I like Garth. We could have some fun with him."

But although Loki's tremendous power of smell fetched them, without deviation from their original trail, all the way back to the pack of wolves, Garth was no longer with them.

"It was like the story of the goddess Bavu," confided the she-wolf, "when the moon came down to seek a bride. Only on that memorable occasion, the suitor was rejected, and the great she-wolf stayed to lead her pack to several victories in battle. Unlike Garth."

"What, Garth has a mate now," cried Loki, astonished. "I never would have guessed."

"No," chuckled the she-wolf, "it was the grey men's ship from the stars that descended, brighter than the moon. It came almost to the earth, over there by the birch trees, then a shaft of light delivered two of them onto the grass."

"Oh Shuck," groaned Clover. "Did he try to escape? Only I know he was unhappy with the way they always knew his thoughts."

"He was unhappy with this place. He yearned to do great things and we are a quiet people, content to live our lives in the natural unfolding of time. More than once he set out on his own, searching, searching…So when the giant frisbee came he was curious, and after they had talked to him he came and said goodbye, then left without a moment's hesitation. He said he had been told there was a test that he had passed, and that it had never been intended as a trick. I was sad to see him go, for he had gentle magic, and when he said the grey men have great plans for him, through which he will win his freedom, I knew he won't return. They took the lantern with them, and for that I was pleased. It didn't belong here."

"And neither did Garth," said Loki, "which he must have realised."

The pair stayed for a short while before moving on, both feeling too disconsolate to entertain thoughts of remaining without Garth. Before they left, the she-wolf alerted others of her kin in the forest that they would be passing through, and when they reached the ferocious river there was a young wolf waiting on the river bank to see them safely though the waterfall.

"See," chided Loki, as they mounted the opposite bank, "it wasn't necessary for you to worry about us taking this journey. It's been fine. Apart from us not seeing Garth."

"They must have another task for him, poor fellow," snivelled Clover.

"I'm afraid that seems to be his lot," agreed Loki. "It's become a way of life for Garth, made to undertake tasks and challenges. At least, he'll be prepared for anything with his history."

But the two dogs were not prepared for what next befell them. Choosing not to climb up to the heights above the river, they headed across the easy ground of a deciduous plantation, the very landscape that Garth had looked out upon with such proprietorial thoughts the day he first met Bala.

Trotting at a relaxed pace the two dogs found it easy going, the ground smooth, with thin patches of grass their only obstacle. But late in the afternoon the trees fell away and they felt suddenly uncomfortable, finding the land had been recently tilled, and the presence of humans palpable.

"Listen," said Loki. "I'm sure I hear chickens. And I've just realised I'm very hungry."

"Leave it," insisted Clover. "It would be unwise. Stealing chickens is risky at any time, but out here in the wild, with humans being unmade everywhere, who knows how they would react?"

"But I have their lovely peppery aroma in my nose, and it's talking to my belly." He would not relent but began to creep on his stomach between two rows of freshly weeded turnips, Clover reluctantly only a tail's distance behind him.

There was a cottage. They saw it before they spied the chickens, which strutted and clucked in a wire coop across a stony yard. The cottage was small and painted white, although the white had turned green with moss and lichen, which lent it a natural camouflage under some bending willow. From an open window came a man's voice, singing something vaguely operatic.

The two dogs crept under the window and headed for the chicken coop. Before they reached it, the cottage door opened and the man stepped out to empty a teapot into a bucket. He cleared his throat with a loud rasp and spat, which made the pair of would-be chicken thieves flinch, then he retreated back indoors.

Loki and Clover had in the meantime sought shelter, hiding behind the woodpile that was stacked under the window.

"Come on, Loki," said Clover, "when the man was gone, it's too hot in here, the sun's been on this heap all afternoon." She backed out into the sunshine only to hear a shriek from Loki, and saw a red and black snake slide from under the furthest log. Her friend was already feeling sick when he emerged.

"What do I do now?" was the last thing he said for a good while, for a wooden club swished down from above and knocked him unconscious. Looking up, primed to dodge, Clover saw a wide black shape drop down from the sky, she was grabbed by the tail, and in a trice she was trussed up inside a sack.

"Let me out of here," she shrieked, thrashing and snapping at the sack. "Let me go!"

"Wow," came a man's voice. "If it ain't a talking dog. Now, that must be worth something. After my chickens too—I'll show them."

He hadn't been back after securing the latch on the shed door, and Clover had listened to him stomp away into the distance, singing a song about going fishing, while assiduously she attempted to draw the snake venom out from the two punctures in Loki's shoulder.

The dawn chorus was in full-throated delivery before Loki stirred, opening first one eye and then another, blinking in the single shaft of light that angled through the shed's narrow cobwebbed window. His head throbbed in unison with the pulsing ache in his swollen shoulder. His first words were typically profane when he saw the bald patch where Clover had torn the fur to get at the wound. But she didn't care, it meant he was on the mend.

"Can you stand?" she asked, and Loki, impetuous as ever, scrambled quickly onto all four paws, immediately giving a cry of pain and sitting back down again.

"The man who hit you," Clover explained, "came back in the night, I heard a nightjar churring loudly just outside the window. Morning is still only just starting, so I expect we have a little time, but only a little."

Loki groaned to hear this. "And then what?"

"I don't expect there to be a then what, because I mean us to be gone. Drink plenty of water, it is clean, and imagine you have a bellyful of those chickens that got us into this difficulty. There will be no food for us before we leave." Clover gave Loki a look that meant, *Do not argue.*

"A way out of here has been prepared, but I need your help." Clover showed Loki the small pile of wood before turning to resume ripping at the wall panels, which she had reduced almost to the thickness of cardboard during the night. Loki sat on the sack and shivered, and the collie worried that he had developed a fever, until he complained of the coldness inside the shed, and how a draught was making his whiskers tremble. For herself, Clover hadn't noticed how cold it was, she had worked up a temperature from her endeavours, and she scolded him for being too precious.

Roughly an hour later Clover began to feel anxious. They had to escape now, before the man woke and came to—she imagined all manner of wicked things. She prodded Loki, who had dozed off.

"Come," she said, "it's time," and she bent to the spot she had been preparing and broke away a large piece of one panel. With her snout to the space, she peered out and sniffed. It was going to be a sunny day. The air was sweet with the aroma of wild roses and—what was that more pungent smell? She saw the man's boots first, then looking up she spied the whole of him, sitting on a bench with a pipe smoking in his hand. He didn't seem to be aware of her, for he hadn't moved, but she felt his eyes upon her all the same.

"Well," said Loki. He had risen to his feet and was standing close behind her. "I'm ready. Are we going, then?"

"Hush!" she hissed. "Look. We can't."

Loki took a quick look through the hole she had made and gave a growl of disappointment. "After all your work," he said, prodding the pile of wooden shards with a paw. "Such a shame."

"It's more than a shame, you idiot, it means we're likely done for." Clover gave a great shake of her tail.

"Well," said Loki, "I think I'm up to it, we'll just have to go out the other way," at which he jumped up onto an old table bearing a trug and flower pots, and with a shudder used his paw to sweep aside the insect-encrusted cobweb that covered the window, where a spider had its eight eyes set upon a struggling crane fly. "Come on, then," he called down to Clover, before squeezing through the window's slender space and jumping to the ground.

They crouched in the grass to catch their breath and to decide their escape route.

"It was that draught that first alerted me," said Loki. "Then, when I saw that crane fly hit the web, it struck me that there was no glass in the window. And you, you said the nightjar was churring loudly; well, I didn't think a shy, reclusive bird like that would come so close to a human dwelling, so it was likely the window was open for you to hear it out in the woods."

Clover was speechless, she didn't know whether she was angry or grateful. This Loki, he was…he was…

"You're not the only dog with a brain," Loki said with exaggerated immodesty. "Anyway, I think I deserve one of those chickens, I can hear them over there."

"If you've a brain," snapped Clover, "you'll think again. Now, assuming you are up to it, get running." She spun in the grass and took off at speed, Loki waiting for only one more moment to give a beagle howl of triumph, just to tease the man with the pipe.

23. Reunion

With the day's new sun clearing the trees to the east, they were able to strike a course that was near enough due south and, despite Loki's constant complaints about being hungry, about how well a fresh chicken thigh would go down just now, and how he could see hundreds of rabbits under the trees just begging to be caught, they ran unceasing until Clover stopped in a sudden lurch to the side, her nose buried in a clump of tough grass.

Loki was glad of the halt, his wound was aching, but he now was scared that something was wrong with his companion.

"Trouble?" he enquired, and Clover looked up, her eyes bright with excitement, her tail swishing to and fro.

"It's him," she replied, "Garth."

"How long?" Loki asked, feeling a frisson of delight himself.

"Stale," said Clover, "and there's no respondent, so I know what this means."

That was disappointing for both of them.

"Remember how he was always marking?" Clover put her head on one side as she recalled complaining about it on their way north.

"Well, I think we've found our original trail."

Although it was not the fresh scent, they had hoped it would be, since that would have meant Garth was near, it did prove to be a welcome find, for they had unwittingly stumbled upon a map of the route home. By following Garth's excessive practice of posting urine, they would be led back to the bridge, and beyond.

Suddenly they felt more relaxed. The man at the cottage seemed not to have noticed their escape, there had been no sounds of a chase, and with the sun now warm in the mid-morning sky the day felt comfortable, even for two dogs with empty bellies.

"Let's press on," suggested Clover. "Perhaps those ruffians at the bridge will share some food with us."

The thought of there being food ahead enabled Loki to forget the ache in his shoulder and he bounded ahead with his ears flapping like tiny wings.

Coming down out of the forest at last, the ground crumbling and sandy, Clover's attention was diverted from thoughts of retaining a foothold when it was seized by laughter, laughter that was quickly offset by a loud yowl. With no-one yet in sight the sounds had an eerie quality, cutting through the forest, and when a ginger cat came pelting up the track towards them its appearance made both dogs' hackles rise. They stopped to see where it was headed.

"Get you next time, you thief!" came a rough voice, and the cat put in a spurt before disappearing into the trees.

There was a group of largeish dogs gathered on the empty road to which the pair emerged. Only one them, a scruffy GSD, resembled anything close to what Clover would call a ruffian. She recognised Ham, the leader of the Kilmorack

Strays, who was telling some tale to the other half dozen who milled about on the road.

"That's Tak and the lurchers, if I'm seeing clearly," exclaimed Loki. "What fortune, so long as they haven't eaten everything."

Then Tak saw the two dogs approaching and ran to meet them on his three legs.

"Come, hurry," he said, giving them both a sniff of welcome. "Ham has freshly caught fish. We've only recently arrived too." He pranced with excitement. "What a find, seeing you two."

"You're in luck," said Ham, when they joined the group. "We saved the biggest fish from that damn cat's grasp, and we were arguing over who shall have first bite. But, I understand from Tak, you were in the party that continued the quest to find the most dangerous human, the one that Garth spoke of. Tell me, did you succeed? For if you did, the salmon is yours."

"We completed the task," replied Clover, her head held low with modest pride, "but please may we eat before I tell you the tale?"

"We want to hear your story too," said Loki to Tak. "I'm glad to see you all here, but to find you have lost a leg, that is a sorry sight indeed."

"It was a good exchange," laughed Tak, "for now I have great strength as well as being fleet of paw. But yes, I will explain all. For now, everyone has a stomach to fill and a rest to take. I see from the foam on your lips that you have run hard. And as you will notice, Rex has been wounded. We also have a new companion, and one who needs help that we

237

cannot give." He indicated the fox, who sat on the edge of the group, a little disconcerted to be out on the road with no cover.

They sat with the rest of Ham's strays on a slope overlooking the firth, sharing their stories and filling their aching bellies. Their stories of brushes with humans caused some consternation amongst the strays, who hadn't encountered any locally for quite some time.

"I thought the grey men were here to eradicate them," commented Ham. "Are these just a few they've missed, perhaps?"

"What I find interesting," said Loki, drawing out his words to sound knowledgeable, "is that these men were alone. I mean, there were no female humans to be seen, yet human men generally keep a female."

There came murmurs of speculation from the other dogs.

"I think there were females in that valley, in the caves I've described," said Tak. "The boy we encountered used a word that means reproduce, and to reproduce they will need both male and female humans."

"But only there, you say," insisted Loki. "Neither you nor Clover and I saw females in the forest." He decided to think further on this mystery. If only he could speak to Tiny, he would be able to explain. Meanwhile, he had polished off a whole side of salmon and found his appetite still demanding. The meal had lacked something and he knew what it was.

"Oh," he yawned, "that was splendid. And don't you find it strange how we've all sat here together in easy conversation? Something that not so long ago we would only do in a dream. We shall have to take care not to become humans." At that, the fox looked distinctly uneasy, then realised it was Loki's humour. If he knew Loki better, he'd be aware that his next statement was far from being a jest.

"But how much better a meal it would have been with some fresh kelp to line my belly." Loki rolled on to his side and licked his hairless stomach.

"Kelp you say," Ham saw an opportunity to tease. "There's plenty kelp down on the shore below here. We use it to hide our waste in a pit in the sand."

Loki recognised that he was being joshed and said nothing. But after a minute of two, he edged closer to Clover and said, "My wound is beginning to make my leg go stiff, I think I'll go for a walk," and he stood and with an extravagant limp wandered off down the steep hill.

Seconds later, Clover darted after him.

It wasn't far at all to reach the sandy beach, and they arrived together.

"Ah, Clover," said Loki. "I can take care of myself, you know."

"I don't know," she replied sharply, "and nor do you."

"We're being watched," whispered Loki, oblivious to her criticism, as he bent to grasp a juicy fresh kelp stem in his teeth.

"I see it," said Clover, the seal's head bobbing in the calm waters, its liquid eyes glistening and its whiskers long.

"No," corrected Loki, "along the beach."

A stone's throw from the two dogs a flint cottage sat half submerged by the scrub and hogweed that grew down to the shore. A thin whisper of smoke rose from the chimney and the door was open. A man in dungarees stood in the doorway and leant on a stick. Seeing that he had been spotted, he stepped down from the door and began to walk slowly toward them.

239

"It's another one of those lone men," said Loki. "But he doesn't appear to be dangerous."

"How would we know?" Clover prepared to run.

"Hello there strangers," called the man, cautiously nearing them, his hand held open in a gesture of friendliness. "Hungry?"

He stopped when he saw Clover lift her lips to show her teeth, her ears flattened to her head.

"It's all right. Look." He took a biscuit from a pocket and held it out in the palm of his hand.

Clover turned her head as a signal of rejection, but Loki made a grab for it and chomped it as if he was starved.

"Hey, pal, what's the matter—are you hurt?" The man had spied the matted fur on Loki's shoulder, where there was still considerable swelling.

"Come on boy," he coaxed, "let me see what I can do for you."

Loki sniffed the man's hand, all the way up his wrist. There was something about him that said that he was no threat. In fact, he gave off a sense of empathy that Loki recognised from other dog-friendly humans.

Still suspicious of the man's intentions, Clover stayed back, her tail between her legs, but when Loki began to follow the man, she determined that she was going to keep him safe.

It was a small cottage with just two rooms on the ground floor. A fire glowed in the grate and a plump tabby cat snoozed on an old sideboard. She awoke and stared at the dogs for a minute then discounted them and resumed her sleep. The man went to a cupboard and selected cloths and some small bottles before calling Loki to him. He touched Loki's wound, gently parting the fur.

"Mr serpent got you, did he?" muttered the man to himself.

"I believe it was an adder," replied Loki, and the man just nodded, not in the least amazed to have a talking dog in his kitchen.

"I've had a number of dogs in my lifetime," said the man. "I've always wanted to be able to converse with them. And now, well, mmm."

When he had cleaned Loki's wound and expelled the pus that had collected there, the man filled two bowls with the remains of a grouse stew. Clover had, all this while, sat alert by the fire, with one eye on the cat and the other following the man's every move. Satisfied that there was little sign of threat, and despite already having dined on fresh fish, she was overtaken by the dense earthy aroma of the stew and ate greedily. She even allowed the man to stroke her ears and when she had eaten she lay in front of the fire. This was just like old times, well, almost. A soft if threadbare rug on which to curl up, the soporific warmth of a radiant fire, and a full belly. The fatigue of the last few days caught up with her and she slept.

Loki too felt at ease, the discomfort in his shoulder was melting away and the atmosphere in the cottage was all calm. The thought of many miles ahead before they reached Willow Croft prickled like gorse in his head. *Why are we going back?* he wondered. *What is there for me? Anyway, I've yet to explore the kelp on this quiet seashore.*

So, when Clover awoke with a start, remembering the lurchers would be expecting to leave very soon, she found Loki reluctant to move.

"I'm not going," he declared. "I've never had a proper home with a human, not for any length of time anyway. This feels comfortable. I'm staying here."

"I can't leave you here," she insisted. "Not after what we've been through together. Suppose the grey men come and unmake this human, you'll be all alone."

"I don't believe they'll visit here," said Loki. "These lone men, I have a feeling they've been left deliberately. There's too much we don't understand to start worrying. Anyway, don't you like this place?" he asked, and she knew she did. It really was like old times, a quiet house with a gentle master. Even the cat didn't seem to be a problem.

"I'll be back very quickly," she said, and pulled open the door with her nose. She was true to her word, just minutes later running into the cottage and announcing to Loki that she'd told the lurchers, who were just preparing to leave, that she was staying. Her reason: to look after Loki.

"You're as much a storyteller as am I," he gurgled, pleased that she was going to remain with him.

Of course, the man had followed all their dialogue and, beaming, he went to rummage in the back room, returning with two wicker dog baskets and blankets. "My Suzie and Smudge found these very comfortable," he explained. "They've been gone a year now. You are welcome to sleep in them."

But Loki and Clover were already snoring, stretched out together in front of the fire.

24. Illumination

For the first time since escaping from Wickhurst, Garth felt the concussion of rock-bottom depression. Certainly the wolves had made him feel welcome, but their lives followed an established pattern, and the only fear they seemed to have was that someone would come and steal one of their cubs. They treated him like someone special, *But they don't need me,* he thought. *I'm no shaman. I'm just a damaged mastiff who seems destined always to be somebody else's poodle.*

He wished he'd gone with Bala to complete his mission, just for the hell of it. And he still had those voices in his head, the constant chattering in a tongue that was distinctly alien, sometimes in the language that he knew, and always seeming to be including him in their discussions, as if he had made a commitment to belong to their undertakings.

It's all because of this thing in my head, he raved. *It was put there to make me behave like a machine, and now that's exactly what the grey men expect of me.*

Once, when at a low point in his mood, he considered smashing the device, selecting a stout birch tree and taking a mad dash toward it, his head down like a charging bull's. But in the instant before he made a connection there came a sharp pain between his ears and a bright light appeared to flash between his eyes. When he got up from his swoon, he realised he had wandered into a part of the forest he had not visited before. Was it the headache that troubled him, or did the air smell different here? There was an old, musty odour floating about that he identified as human, a human stink unlike the sharp, nose smarting tang of those ultraclean men at Wickhurst. This was the smell of dirty clothes and unwashed skin.

He crept stealthily through the trees, the smell growing more powerful the further he went, his nose twitching quite uncontrollably. The ground beneath his feet was different, he noticed, compacted and scarred, the leaf mould thrown to the sides of what he realised was a path, a path made with the imprint of large boots worn by a heavy human.

Garth stopped, not in fear, for he feared little beyond his own mentality, but with surprise. *I understood they were all being taken,* he thought. *So who is this, and why?*

A man of middle years stood bent over a trestle table, skinning a deer. Behind him a crude shack made of fir branches, with a rusty iron roof, provided some degree of shelter.

He is on the run, decided Garth. *What should I do?*

His first inclination was to scare the man, to drive him away. He was thinking of the wolves, for whom this human's proximity in the forest could pose a threat. But upon reflection, the man looked weak and his skin had a sick quality to it. He might not be a threat at all, so long as he stayed where he was.

His next thought was to tell the grey men. After all, they had said they wanted to find humans who were secreted in the countryside, hadn't they? And as long as there were humans left the Canidae would not be free to exercise dominance over the world without competition.

Garth was just concentrating to attach his thoughts to the noise in his head when the man gave a cry and a rock came crashing down next to him.

"Get out of it, go on! Clear orf! Fucking wolf come after my dinner." The man held his knife above his head and jumped up and down, waving and shouting, "Woo! Woo! Woo!" hoping to scare away his uninvited dinner guest.

Garth simply turned and sauntered away through the trees. No, this man was no threat. Still...

He tried once more to reach the grey men when he'd returned to the wolf pack. The wolves had become used to what they regarded as his magical trances, when he would lay on his stomach, his forelegs crossed in front of him and his head erect, his mouth moving wordlessly as he mirrored the words spoken inside his head. But they could only guess what he would be saying, and watch his daft pink ears flap as they listened to words that did not arrive through the air.

"Thank you," came a grey man's voice, when Garth explained about the vagrant human. "There's nothing to be done. It is our will that he is there."

It was a further new element to Garth's frustration. What was going on, that the Derin had seemingly made an exception to their strategy? And what should Garth think if he ever discovered more humans lurking in the forest? He had found order with the wolves, and now this—disorder.

It was only a day later that his question was answered. That was the day the she-wolf described to Clover and Loki as when the 'grey men's ship from the stars' came down and took Garth away.

245

He was feeling fatalistic. It was how he had managed to survive all that time amongst the vivisectionists, and he was in control of his spirits again. At least, as much as the device in his skull would allow.

The two grey men who had come to meet him sat with him in a tubular compartment inside the frisbee, as the dogs were wont to call it. They perched on shiny benches that looked like metal but felt like warm skin, and Garth initially experienced spasms of nervousness when he believed his claws were at risk of doing damage to something organic and alive.

One of the Derin took his rod and held it against Garth's implant, twisting the rod as if it were a screw, and there came a feeling like the frequency of muffled voices being tuned to clarity, expanding through his brain.

The rod was withdrawn and the alien spoke without touching it to Garth's skull.

"We shall no longer have need of that," he said. "You will understand any words from the tongues of the seventeen nations without the need for intervention. Whatever words are spoken, you will hear them in the human tongue that you have come to know." He said something rapidly to the second Derin in a language that sounded harsher than his own and turned to Garth. "What did I say?" he demanded.

"You told him that, with his agreement, you would begin by explaining to me your true purpose here, on the planet below us, the world the humans called Earth."

"Good," said the first Derin, "and so we shall."

"Several thousand years ago we came to this planet. It is not necessary to tell you why in any detail, other than that we found it a natural place, unmodified by the creatures that dwelt here, a place where our science could be developed without contamination from established design. Do you understand my words?" The Derin paused.

Garth nodded. To his surprise he understood fully.

"Principally, our scientific interest at the time was akin to what the humans call genetics, including hereditary transmission through evolution. We studied, you will be interested to hear, the early canids, but our particular research involved the creation of a completely new life-form, one that we could conceive would have features that improved upon our own genetic model. That research and experimentation resulted in our creation of the species you have known as homo sapiens. We had hopes that it should be the basis of a life-form that would eventually replace us."

Garth found himself blinking to keep his concentration. The grey man's voice was without inflexion, and ran on like liquid. He heard the words but his understanding was always having to play catch up.

Seeing Garth's consternation, the grey man spoke in an aside to his companion and the Derin rose and walked away, returning swiftly with a deep bowl in his hands.

"You must refresh," said the first Derin. "Being in this atmosphere will dehydrate your brain. Please drink."

The bowl was placed next to Garth who sniffed it suspiciously. There had been many attempts to trick him during his time at Wickhurst, when all kinds of pernicious brews had been offered him. But no, this was water, and he lapped greedily on the cool liquid.

The Derin was keen to continue and thrust a hand in front of Garth's nose. "What do you see?" he asked.

Garth sniffed the hand, the three long fingers with yellowing fingernails, greyish skin over a bulge of dark blood vessels. And that's exactly what he described in his response.

"But does it not intrigue you?" asked the Derin. "It is not like a human hand, is it?"

Garth looked at the grey man expectantly.

"We studied the primates on your world. They had evolved in an advantageous form, their hands (or claws in some instances) bearing four fingers and a thumb. Yet they had reached an evolutionary terminus. We reasoned that with an opposing finger and thumb they should have been the progenitors of a supremely powerful and effective modern race of beings. For we, ourselves, have become powerful technologically even without that physical distinction."

"Our design of homo sapiens therefore incorporated the primate hand as an essential building block, while we went on to focus our attention on mental capacity. The result should have been a race of beings capable of imagining infinite technological development, and then realising those imaginings through application of their dexterous capabilities. A race which would in time supplant the Derin, for we have also reached our developmental terminus and will eventually step aside."

Garth wanted time to absorb all of this and took another long drink from the bowl. "So, you must have been pleased with the results of your science," he said. "For the humans built many machines, and cities, and they even spoke about travelling to the stars."

The second Derin spoke up at that point. "Psychology had never been the most enthusiastically studied science in our world. It is to our eternal regret that in only recent centuries has it been allowed to flourish. But we had insufficient knowledge—some say care—when we designed humanity, and we omitted a range of characteristics that we ourselves regard as standard and normal for our own people. The Derin are a peaceful people, without anger, cruelty or deceit. But here, our newly created species…" He stopped, his voice regretful, even in translation, then, in a determined tone, "We could not let humans entertain the thought of taking their uncontrollably aggressive natures out amongst the galaxies. Which is why we are here, to undo our work, to wipe the laboratory table clean, and to begin again."

At last, Garth felt he had a point to make. "But why us canids?" he asked. "Why not simply unmake the humans? There was no need to 'awaken' us as well."

"Look at your paws," said the first grey man. "You have four digits corresponding to fingers, and your dewclaw is the equivalent of a thumb. They are usable for holding a bone steady to gnaw, but useless for manipulation, yet they suggest to us a particular state of evolutionary authenticity. But it is your empathetic nature that particularly interests us, for it is not very far removed from our own. We want to see if, as dominant family of species with an already well-developed social awareness, you can do better than homo sapiens. The sheer multiplicity of canid types shows that your evolutionary path still has many lengths to travel. As for the humans, our work on their own replacement will be a long time coming."

"So, we are your experiment," replied Garth, his tone not at all one of content. "Well, this is one canid who has had enough of being an object in a laboratory."

"Are we not all subjects in a universal laboratory?" said the second grey man, leadingly.

"But let us not begin a discussion on the subject of free will." The first Derin was keen to deflect the conversation. "There are more urgent matters we must resolve, matters which threaten the development of the Canidae."

"Wait," barked Garth. "After all you have told me, you must explain the existence of the individual in the forest. You said it is your will that he is there."

"Certainly it is," was the reply. "There are many such individuals around the world. They pose no risk, for they are technologically primitive. They also have no opportunity to produce young, who may have grown to be a danger. These male humans represent a control mechanism. As the Canidae develop, we wish to see how much such individual humans, with thousands of years development behind them, can improve upon a new and primitive existence, without help from the kind of social bonds that sustain you."

"There are other humans living," added the second Derin. "We have gathered them into communities of human young. Without exception they have three fingers and no thumb, like us. Our intention is to see whether they can optimise themselves in a similar way to the Derin, but with an unmodified human brain. You see, as scientists, we are exploring each and every possible development path. Wiping the table clean has not meant a total destruction of our original materials and hypothesis."

Without warning, the two grey men rose and gathered their robes around their lean frames. Without their cowls Garth fancied they were made of wood, their skin cracked and furrowed, a coarse grey-brown membrane resembling the bark of an elm, and their noses long and thin, angling to a point. He was sure they had not made man in their own image;

then he remembered their mention of having studied the early primates. So that was their probable initial model.

"We shall leave you to relax for a while, while we assess the latest data regarding our present mission." The two grey men departed with a swish of their robes, leaving Garth feeling rather forsaken. Did he have anywhere to go from here? He felt as desolate as when he'd resolved to smash the device in his head. It was evident that, yet again, he was expected to be someone's agent to undertake some as yet unknown task. That's what he divined from the urgent matters that we—that is, he—would have to clear up.

But he was, for all intents and purposes, captive in a flying Derin craft from the stars, with no way of escaping back to the forest. And if he refused the task—for surely their urgent matters were the reason for him being brought here—what then? They claimed to be a peaceful and sympathetic race but—he remembered the vets at Wickhurst, who had stroked him and cosseted him with what felt like genuine empathy for animals, before strapping him up to be immobilised for the next experiment. He also thought of Tiny, whose voice was still in his head from time to time. Tiny seemed to have found his niche in their world; he sounded neither distressed nor jubilant, only very distant in time and place.

"We must now talk further," said the first grey man, returning silently on his own. "We must talk of difficult matters and a request I wish to put to you."

For all his bulk, Garth felt diminished. The words 'difficult matters' sounded like a threat. He just stared at the Derin and fixed him with a glassy stare.

"I shall continue," said the grey man, sitting down.

"As you agreed, the humans proved themselves capable of significant technological development. But they over-reached themselves because of an inherent condescension towards the powers they were harnessing. It was the same condescension they exercised towards yourselves and the other animals sharing this planet. That contempt for the world they dominated meant that their technologies began to destroy it. They spilled oil in its waters, they filled its sky with clouds of smoke, they even polluted their own bodies with the plastic they manufactured. They really were a vicious species, a species driven by envy in a world where there was plenty for all." There was no anger in the grey man's voice, only a shade of disappointment.

He leant towards Garth. "I talk now of the specific difficult matters. One of the technologies with which humans developed considerable capability involved the containment of the energy that keeps your sun burning. They needed its power to make their other inventions function. But they were clumsy in the use of their opposing thumb and finger. One such instance, which I will explain for your own understanding, and which will be important for you, was at a place the humans called Chernobyl.

"In that place, the energy they arrogantly believed they had contained, proved to be beyond their control, and all because of a design flaw that they should have known about but which was hidden beneath their sense of infallibility. During a test of their power installation at Chernobyl, a system shutdown was triggered, which led to explosions and the meltdown of the core in what they termed the reactor—the device that produced the energy for them. Consequently, the land for many miles around was contaminated by something that you won't understand but which we call radioactivity. Radioactivity lasts for millennia, it lives invisibly in the air, in water, the earth and in the bodies of those who encounter it. It poisons everything it touches, and the land poisoned by Chernobyl will be devastated for a long time yet to come."

He stopped and looked enquiringly at Garth. "have you understood what I have been telling you?"

"Some of the words are not familiar, but the essence of the tale is clear."

"Well, here is what we wish you to do for us; in fact, for your family of species." The grey man rapped his yellow fingernails on the empty water bowl to ensure Garth's attention.

"When Chernobyl exploded, the humans ran far away, but the birds and mammals generally remained. Naturally, a great many died from the radioactivity, or radiation, sometimes taking many years, but others remained and flourished in an environment devoid of humans. I say flourished, but at a cost, the radiation causing their metabolism to alter, sometimes quite extraordinarily, sometimes leading to their deaths, but at other times making them stronger and more formidable. We have recently witnessed such an effect of accidental radiation in your land, with one of your species."

"Now, listen to my every word. At Chernobyl, there is a pack of canids whose ancestors survived the explosion. They are chiefly derived from the breed you know as German shepherd, and their leader is a giant dog with three heads. Many of them have been modified by the radiation, but not disabled by it, for it has become their physiological norm. As influential beasts they terrorise the region and, since their awakening, they plot to extend their hegemony over neighbouring lands. It is as if they have inherited human traits rather than canine ones."

"We have repeatedly attempted to approach the leader with the intention of liquidating him, but he—and his lieutenants—are highly aggressive and adept at evading our lamps, hiding in the catacombs around Chernobyl. Several of my kin have been destroyed through the seizure of their wands. I am not exaggerating when I say these rogue canids are a threat to the dominion of the Canidae, for they will, if left unchecked, rule everywhere by force."

"And I know what next you are going to say," Garth interposed.

"Yes," said the grey man. "It will take a clever and forceful dog, one who knows our thoughts and our best intentions, to complete the task. You have only the pack leader to eliminate; he has a vast brain in those three heads, he is the motivator, the strategist and their source of ambition, and without him we believe the others should prove acquiescent and adaptable. History has shown us that it takes only one deviant to create mayhem."

"And me, what will become of me?" asked Garth, wearily. "I am waiting for you to tell me I must meet this three-headed monster face to face."

"We can offer you eternal freedom amongst the stars," replied the Derin. "Your friend Tiny already enjoys his release from the troubles of a physical existence."

"And this device in my head. Would it be gone?"

"It would be unnecessary."

"I have no time to consider, have I?" Garth felt that the conversation was coming to a precipice.

"We have been positioned high over the Chernobyl site for the whole time I have been speaking. You will be a hero amongst your species."

"As so often," said Garth in a small voice, "I feel I have no choice. I see now why you avoided a discussion of free will." He licked his nose, nervously. "But I will choose to do it, if you are sure it will preserve the ways of the Canidae."

Without hesitation, the Derin touched his wand to the device in Garth's head and that familiar warm feeling diffused through his skull. The warmth was red at first, like swirling blood, then it darkened until his head was filled with a great cloudy blackness, and he was aware of the grey man's bony fingers on his skull only for the last second before he blacked out. When he awoke, finding himself stretched out on the disconcerting bench, there was a sense of something new having been inserted in his skull, but no pain, not even a feeling that his head had gained more weight. A fresh bowl of water had been placed next to him and, taking a welcome drink, he noticed in its reflective surface that the device in his head seemed larger. *I really do look like Two-heads now,* he grimaced.

"I have enabled a light grenade," explained the grey man. "You have only to think it and it will explode. Detonation of the grenade will unmake the three-headed beast with the speed of light. But you must be close, as close as you and I sitting here, closer if possible. We will train you in managing your thoughts so that you can detonate it at will."

Strangely, Garth felt relief and a sense of elation. *What else was I going to do? Go back and chase rats at Willow Croft?*

"What do I call this three-headed tyrant?" he asked. But the grey man was already talking to another who had arrived with news of their imminent descent.

25. Cerberus

"But won't this radiation thing kill me as soon as I step onto land?" Garth was feeling that he'd not been sufficiently briefed.

"It doesn't work like that," said the grey man, who had been explaining to Garth how to control the thoughts in his head, particularly his passions and vices, in order not to accidentally detonate the grenade. "The initial explosion killed immediately, and the fire, but the residual radiation creeps into your body and eats away at your being. We have been down there and returned unscathed, for our visit was brief. You don't have to worry about being irradiated."

"Garth," he added, almost as an afterthought, "we're all depending upon your good canine instincts."

"My canine instincts?"

"Yes, when you're faced with something bad, what do you do—fight or flee?"

At that moment, still anxious about the radiation, Garth didn't feel terribly sure. "I just know I'm expendable," he shrugged. "But what does it matter?"

He sought for Tiny's presence in his head. He'd already told Tiny about his new mission, but all Tiny had said in words of great inscrutability was that he should take care to 'remember we're better than them', and that 'space has no envy'. Trying to understand, Garth assumed that the them to whom Tiny referred were the mutated dogs, or possibly humans, and as far as envy went, he could only make a connection with the grey man's tirade against humanity.

Frustratingly, the connection with Tiny could not be reinstated and he felt the alien craft had ceased to move. He'd be leaving without a further word from the great Dane.

Garth was unused to feeling nervous, he'd been through too many horrors to be anxious of what lay in store, but there was a palpable unease that seemed to travel through his whole body. His tail hung limply and his whiskers drooped. It was the prospect of meeting the challenge in a foreign land, with unfamiliar voices. "I will be able to understand them, won't I?" he pleaded.

"Did you not understand us?" replied the grey man.

It could be a useful tactic, thought Garth, *communication difficulties. Might solve that need to be close.*

He had a day's walk to the reactor site, although the grey man had said the dogs were on the move and he might run into them sooner. They had made their home in the exclusion zone and lived chiefly in its Red Forest, but occasionally they went on bloodthirsty forays into other canid territories.

Garth set off as soon as he was on the ground; it was easy going, the ground fairly even and covered only with thin grass and saplings. Occasional substantial blocks of grey stone were sprinkled over the land, looking as if they'd been scattered like dice by a giant hand. The air was full of birdsong and he saw deer watching him from amongst the trees. The day smelled good and he breathed the aroma of fresh grass and damp soil. He fell into following a narrow grassy track made

258

by some unknown denizens, maybe wolves or wild horses. He sniffed at likely places but there were no traces of other canines, and he left his own mark as a demonstration that he, Garth, had arrived.

The clear air seemed to clear his mind of the turmoil of anxiety and he became aware at last of Tiny's presence, which reassured him that he was not alone. "Am I being used?" he asked.

"We are all used in one way or another," came the distant voice. "If not by another being, then by the moment. To be not used would be to have no identity."

"I'm not entirely sure I would—" thought back Garth, only to be cut short.

"Use yourself well," bade Tiny. "You survived Wickhurst for this."

"It's all very well to send me pious approbations from somewhere in deep space," muttered Garth to himself. He peered cautiously around the side of a huge squarish boulder that hunched in the grass, "but it's me who has to do this deed, and I don't have a history of destroying my kin to make me feel comfortable with it."

"It's a talker," said a rough voice.

"Yes, another nutter from one of the eastern oblasts, no doubt."

Garth froze. He was still a long way from the reactor site. Was this a case of running into the dogs sooner that the grey man had spoken of?

"Come on," said the rough voice. "Let's take a look at you. We're not going to eat you, not today anyway."

A long nose followed by one large brown eye inched around the boulder's opposite side, then snapped back out of sight when it caught a glimpse of Garth's head.

"Hey!" Came the voice again, louder now. "You come out into the open, whatever you are. We're Red Forest dogs, on a scrutiny."

"My name is Garth," Garth announced himself, easing himself around the side of the rock, "Garth of the Derin."

"It is a nutter," said the second speaker, "like I said. It's talking gobbledegook."

The two canids stared at Garth from the shelter of the boulder. As he edged toward them, they retreated backwards around it, so that he could never see more than their snouts.

"What is it?" asked one of the dogs. "Funny-arsed ears and a bloody great globe in its head."

"I reckon its mother was a sow and its old man a horny lightbulb."

They both cackled stupidly at this.

By now, Garth had concluded that the grey man's translation device was working only one way, and that the dogs did not have whatever the grey man had to enable him to understand Garth. He walked out away from the cover of the boulder and went to a clump of grass, lifting his leg and ejecting a broad hot stream of yellow.

"It's a dog then, or something like," the rough voice sounded approving.

"Another muta then," said the second voice, "like us."

"Hey, muta, where you from?" the second creature called. "You're not from the forest are you; you from one of the Pripyat packs?"

"Better not be," muttered the rough voice in an aside.

From the animal's tone, it was clear to Garth that they were afraid of him.

Garth shook his head in denial.

"See, it can understand us, but we can't him. Must have scorched his brain. It's worse in the city, of course, everyone's brain gets fried there eventually."

One of the dogs emerged from behind the boulder and approached Garth tensely, ready to recoil if necessary. Having first examined where he'd left his mark, it then sniffed his piggy ears and wrinkled its nose, its one eye (the other being a cluster of pink sores) swivelled about, taking in Garth's size and evident strength, then it went and sniffed his anus.

"Well, it's all dog, and it ain't raised a lip at me, so I'm guessing it's safe, so long as it can't scorch us."

The other dog sniffed the air to see if there was any aroma from Garth that might offer a warning signal.

They were both of German shepherd descent, by way of a dash of grey wolf, and perhaps it was their benevolent wolfish side that saved Garth from aggression.

"We're on our way back to the forest. Make it a threesome for safety's sake?" the first dog suggested.

Garth nodded and shook himself from head to tail to indicate that he was relaxed with the proposal.

Once they started walking together, three abreast in the manner of wolves, Garth was able to take a better look at them. Neither seemed to offer any particular challenge to him; they were both about the same stature as him and their coats were full and glossy, but he had noted that one had lost an eye (or maybe only ever had one) and he now observed that the second dog walked with difficulty, its hind legs seeming to be missing a working joint at the rotula and, with the legs hinged at the hip, it walked as if strapped to stilts.

"Hey, we're stopping on the way, all right?" said the second dog after they'd walked several miles. "We're not supposed to be back before tomorrow morning. Boss's orders. Hey, what do I call you, pig-ears, I can't keep saying hey."

Garth tried again. "Garth," he said, in as clear a voice as he could.

"Arf?" repeated the dog. "Like in arf, arf, someone's coming!—is that right?" He laughed to his companion. "Looks like pig-ears here is stuck between barking and speaking. I ate a Pekingese once that talked like that. Arf, arf, arf, it went on like that all the way down until it hit the juices in my stomach."

"Since we're travelling companions," said the first dog, ignoring his chum, "I'm Grib, and he's Dote."

Garth nodded to show his appreciation, but inside he was feeling highly frustrated. *Why did the grey man make such a mistake?* he moaned. *Or was it my fault? I only asked if I'd understand them, assuming…Oh what an idiot.*

Abruptly, they reached the edge of the Red Forest, and the two dogs, Grib and Dote, immediately made for a hollow beneath a great heap of dead branches, emitting loud sighs and grunts of pleasure.

"Still here," croaked Grib, who had his head in the hollow first.

"Come on then, my share, and some for pig-ears." Dote stood with his head down and his jaws slavering, watching intently as Grib dragged the remains of a boar carcass out into the open.

They ate hungrily and completely focused on the meal and, only when sated did they turn to Garth and ask, "What you waiting for?" Evidently, the usual rules about pecking order did not apply and Garth took his turn, finding the meat tender and juicy. The possibility that it was radioactive was not an issue to trouble him, for he knew he must already have absorbed enough to kill him in due course.

What did trouble him was this matter of communication, and when the three of them had made nests in the sparse forest grass and curled up to sleep, he sent his thoughts out in search of Tiny.

The sun had gone down and owls were hooting in the forest before he found Tiny's presence, and Tiny did not sound terribly thrilled to hear Garth's request for help.

"What's become of you Garth?" he replied. "Have you forgotten everything? It was you who explained to me what went on in your own head, that it was like a library, a place where all knowledge is stored. So you are carrying your solution with you."

Garth gave an angry growl. *I've messed up again,* he thought, biting on his own tongue in frustration.

"You have two options," continued Tiny. "You either find a means of enabling two-way translation or you download their language—I suggest that Russian would work. Yes, that would do, look for Россия."

"But I can't just learn a language in a night," protested Garth, speaking his words out loud in frustration.

"You don't need to. You just download it. You just become it; you told me, how it happens quicker than a raindrop falling off a twig. Look, you didn't understand the word download until I used it just now, did you? But I can feel that now you do."

"Thank you Tiny," said Garth humbly. "Are you sure you will want me to join you, wherever you are?"

But Tiny had faded and there was no response.

When they were awakened by the sounds of dawn, Garth did not rush to try out his new linguistic capability on Grib and Dote. He had been practicing all night, terrified that the two dogs might hear him, but he had been left alone and believed he still had a secret when he awoke. He was wrong.

"Who you gabbing to last night?" demanded Grib. "Or was you dreaming?" By the look on his face it was obvious that the dog didn't expect Garth to furnish a reply, but when he did, Grib squealed and ran round three times in a circle. "You was teasing us all along was you?" he half laughed, half snarled with anger. "I'll have your whiskers for that."

"So, who was this Tiny you were talking to?" Dote had overheard their dialogue and Garth's pretence to cover up the fact that he'd been practicing Russian.

"Tiny's my friend," replied Garth.

The two dogs became suddenly anxious and rushed all around, sniffing at the ground and sampling the air. Then they stopped like statues and stood listening.

"Where is he then?" asked Dote. "We can't smell him and we can't hear him. You made this up or what? We don't take kindly to being taken for fools."

"Tiny is dead," said Garth. "He lives in space with the stars."

"He is a nutter, like I said," barked Dote.

"No" said Garth emphatically, "I speak the truth. I also talk with the grey men and they with me."

264

"The aliens?"

"You know them? Well, of course, I hear they have visited you in the past, hoping to catch your leader."

Both dogs cowered for a moment then they bounced back with a sneer.

"We saw them off," roared Grib. "They flung this huge net at Kryv, it was all made of a bright light, but he tore it apart with his mighty claws, and that left them in the dark with no captive and us lot ready to turn them into next week's dinner. They buggered off quickly then. I hope the radiation does for them."

"They mean no harm," said Garth. "They're just curious. I used to live with a wolf pack, where I was their means of discovering what the spirits from the sky required of them. They used to offer their cubs to the sky men as sacrifice," he lied. "It was down to me to parley the cubs' return."

Grib and Dote shuffled with affected disinterest away out from under the trees. "Going for water," explained Dote, but Garth heard them arguing worriedly, what was he, this creature with a pig's ears, and what was he doing here?

"Kryv your pack leader?" asked Garth the minute they returned.

"What's it to you?" snapped Grib.

"Well, it's just that you mentioned him a moment ago, and he sounded like a brave and powerful sort, the sort who might be a pack leader."

"He's not simply powerful," replied Grib, "he's mighty. It was Kryv who killed that boar we ate last night, with a single thrust of his massive claws."

"I'd like to meet him," confessed Garth. "I would regard it as an honour."

They journeyed on, the forest becoming more and more animated as they proceeded. Faces peered from bushes, trees and holes in the ground. A trio of horses whinnied and stamped when the three dogs neared.

"It's very lively here," remarked Garth, as two rabbits scooted across their path.

"That's because there ain't no humans." Grib trotted on for a bit before turning to Garth, "but they got us to look out for now!" He laughed maliciously and lunged with open jaws at a squirrel on a branch.

At one point, late morning, Grib and Dote suddenly crouched down, low warning growls in both their throats. "Pripyat dogs," muttered Dote. "What they doing out here?"

"Keep your muzzle tight," growled Grib to Garth. "They're likely looking for us. We sliced up a bunch of their young'uns on our way out, two days past. Kryv's going to chase them out of the forest for good very soon. He's expanding the Red Forest empire. We're going west into Belo, it's warmer there."

The group of Pripyat hounds moved away through the trees, fanning out and doubling back every so often, sniffing and peering around. When their movements could no longer be heard, Grib stood and led the other two down a track that became increasingly more hardpacked, and by the early afternoon Garth became aware of coarse voices in the near distance, with the air carrying a pungent aroma of dog.

"Not far now. When we get to our camp, you stay with the guards," instructed Grib. "Dote and me have to report to the guvnor. The guards'll find you a soft place to sit, and fresh water. Don't speak to their bitches or they'll kill you. They've had to fight hard for those girls."

In fact, the guards looked underweight, even scrawny, and they stepped back deferentially when Grib introduced Garth to them. His broad mastiff's physique was far more intimidating than theirs. They presented ears to be sniffed and rears to be examined, but declined to snuffle Garth's piggy flaps. One, a many-scarred lurcher, reminded Garth of Tak, and he found himself striking up a conversation with the dog.

The guards were spread around the camp in groups of three or four and Garth was curious as to what they were guarding against. "It's reprisals that we look out for," revealed the lurcher, whose name was Sviv. "They don't fight well when we go out to clear them, but they sneak back later and try to get a good bite at someone."

"What do you mean by clear them?" asked Garth.

"Well, clear them from the forest—or anywhere else that Kryv wants. Move them on, or if they won't move we finish them off. Most of them have the sickness anyway, and don't live much more than four years."

"But your pack, you are all mature dogs, it would seem." Garth had taken a good look at the many canines who roamed the space they had colonised in the wood.

"Kryv's family only picks sixth generation dogs for his pack, so we've all come from a line of radiation survivors." Sviv gave Garth a long studied look. "You seem to be in good health yourself," he remarked. "Apart from the unusual ears and that globe thing on your head. Come from a well-resourced territory, obviously."

Garth just nodded and sat on his haunches.

"Food's not so plentiful here just now," continued Sviv. "We have to travel a distance in search of good prey, and by the time we've dragged a deer back here, we're too exhausted to eat. I've been relying on scraps from humans still working at the reactor site, but they've recently disappeared."

"The grey men's doings?" Garth ventured.

"So they say...Hey, your companions are returning."

"Kryv wants to meet you," announced Grib. "It is a great privilege for an uninvited stranger."

"Yes," added Dote, "but we have told him all about you. About your having dwelt with our cousins, the wolves, about your relationship with the grey men, and especially how you speak with the dead."

"He was most impressed," panted Grib. "And not much impresses the mighty Kryv."

"And when shall I meet him?" enquired Garth, suddenly feeling that the moment the grey men had planned for him was about to be executed.

"After twilight barking."

"You do twilight barking here?" Garth was surprised.

"Of course," answered Grib. "It is our way of knowing who is on the rise and who is weakening. It feeds us with information that the mighty Kryv uses to plot our next move. For a week now, the word at twilight barking has been that the Belo packs close to the border of the radiated lands are half-starved and lacking strong leadership. We're expecting Kryv to give us the order to move west any day now."

"How far will that take you?" asked Garth, thinking that Dote for one didn't look up to pursuing a long march into battle.

"Long enough—for a start," growled Grib, unsettled by the question. "But we won't stop there. Kryv says the world is to be ours."

"Yes," quipped Dote. "Stay with us and one day you'll find yourself waking up back where you came from." He laughed like a hyena, his body seeming to rock precariously on his stiff legs.

Twilight barking came subtly through the shadows of the forest, like the dawn chorus beginning with just one or two voices exchanging their thoughts, then several, until the air was busy with a clamour of announcements and reports. Mostly speech was in the forest dogs' tongue, but Garth also heard others at a distance speaking in the language he had known since first being awakened.

"What are they saying, do you know?" asked Sviv, who had recognised something appealing in Garth, and stuck with him.

"For the most part, they are warning about the threat of a violent attack from the east."

"Mmm, so they've heard," remarked Sviv. "Inevitable, I suppose."

"It's not what the grey men want," Garth reminded him. "They hoped we would all live harmoniously after awakening."

"They hadn't met Kryv," Sviv scoffed, his words dry and without indication of his leaning one way or another.

As the evening's correspondence began to quieten, food was distributed. More wild boar, pieces of deer and what to Garth looked like a pile of lifeless dachshunds, their throats torn open by heavy claws.

He did not eat but, pretending fatigue, curled up next to Sviv, on the guard's blanket, and feigned sleep. He was hoping that he might speak with Tiny and tell him about the planned invasion of the western territories. The grey men might need to know.

Tiny's voice in his head was clear in reply to Garth's information. "Why do you tell me, Garth? You can stop it yourself. Or are you having second thoughts?"

Whether or not he was, Garth had no time to consider, for suddenly there was a wet nose prodding him and Grib's urgent voice telling him to come quickly, for mighty Kryv was waiting.

Garth was led across the home clearing of the Red Forest dogs to where the land rose over a hump of rubble and metal sheeting, left by one of the human clean-up squads. As he drew close the figure of a large German shepherd dog became visible atop a concrete platform that had once been the wall of a building. It stood on its hind legs, the forelegs being foreshortened and held out in front of it in the manner of a kangaroo, long black claws hanging menacingly at their end, with the position of the dewclaws making them visibly more thumblike than was usual. The dog stood well over a metre tall and was completely hairless except for the long, thick whiskers that protruded from its muzzle. Its skin was a patchwork of ochre and black that glistened poisonously, the belly a raw pink, and Garth noticed several ragged scars on the dog's flank that were worn with pride. But most remarkable was its three heads, and Garth breathed a sigh of relief that the grey man had forewarned him of this mutation, for indeed it was terrible to look upon.

Each of the three faces was turned his way, the dark eyes shining, although there was only the starlight to brighten them. The bizarre dog's erect tail did not wag and Garth felt the hackles on his neck stiffen as Kryv's six eyes stared malevolently, through all the time it took for Grib to accompany him from across the clearing. When the two of them reached the bottom of the mound together, the middle head signalled with a yawn for the emissary to depart.

Kryv's voice was not what Garth had expected; it was too high-pitched for a beast that size, but severely clear. He spoke from the head on the right, the mouths of the other two heads repeating the last few words of each sentence like a stereophonic echo. "Stranger, I will not ask what brings you here," he declared. "I am more interested in what will make you stay, for I am told that you are a creature of magic, a shaman who converses with the dead, an interpreter of the minds of alien beings; and it occurs to me that with those talents you could bring us a fresh element of supremacy in our fight to rule."

Garth said nothing in reply, but walked casually to a tangle of iron rods and relieved himself lazily, his eyes never leaving the huge beast above him.

Kryv laughed, a thin sound like the scraping of claws on glass. "Very good, I see also that you are brave to act so insolently, but I like it. Well," he paced the length of his platform, "you may have heard that I have remarkable plans for my pack, in fact I imagine that is what has drawn you like a pilgrim to our land, plans that will bring us power and such resources to sustain us as far exceed what any canid might dream of having. The Red Forest dogs are strong. We are feared for many distances around, and we will take those other lands for our own."

He stopped pacing and bent his central neck down towards Garth, the movement bringing closer the great curved black talons of his forelegs, like a bear's claws, which were splayed to maintain his balance. "Stranger, with your qualities I can offer you unrivalled standing in my community, for I am told you have access to a great well of knowledge, with its source somewhere in the stars, as well as the enviable touch of magic. As my lieutenant and seer, you would be second to none but myself. After me, you would have first bite of any fresh kill, and first choice of any new bitches we secure. All I would ask is your loyalty, and guidance when I demand it from the spirits with whom you speak." The head on the right ceased speaking and the middle head bent low on its sinuous neck before uttering, in the same strident tone, "But first I must know you better, know whether what has been spoken of is true. There have been false necromancers seeking preferment on more than one occasion that did not live to tell the tale. Now, tell me your name, for you have said nothing as yet."

"Garth is my name," said the mastiff. "I had heard of your greatness, how you vanquished the grey men who came to capture you. I can tell you that they still burn from the experience."

The head on the left, which had said nothing except to repeat the words from the head on the right, broke into a humourless cackle at that. Then, "Go speak with whom you wish amongst my pack, ask them to confirm their own commitment to me, think carefully of what I am promising you, and return here before cock crow with your decision. Bring also an expression of your magic that will validate your reputation."

Garth said no more in answer but turned and walked slowly across the central space of the clearing, aware that many eyes were upon him, many wet noses trying to catch a whiff of his scent and his mood, to know if he was bold or unnerved. Only a misplaced paw or too hurried a step would be enough for them to tell he was troubled.

He sat once more on Sviv's blanket, the guard having been sent on a tour of the clearing's perimeter, and to his unexpected consternation he found himself earnestly turning over the offer made by the three-headed dog. He knew that the lure of power appealed to him, he'd been aware of that when he led the Willow Croft dogs on their mission to the north, even though he had denied it after Bala's rebuke. For years, he'd been robbed of any kind of canine status, locked up in a cage in the laboratory, he'd enjoyed none of the usual stand-offs and skirmishes that were a joy to free running dogs. And now, he could be elevated way above even that hum-drum level of canine relations.

But what about the light grenade fixed in his skull? If he stayed, could it be detonated inadvertently at any time, on account of an accidental thought, or perhaps during a dream? He would have to tune his thoughts away from it if he was to stay. He recalled the brief episode of training the grey men had given him.

Remembering the light grenade reminded him of his objective, and he felt a flush of anger that he was being made to act as the grey men's instrument. Then again…

He became aware of Tiny's presence, a whisper in the dark edge of his mind. The old Dane had been listening to his thoughts. "I believe that is the key fact for you to consider," came Tiny's voice. "Will you be once again a slave or do you choose freedom?"

Garth felt chastened by that question. It also turned his thoughts back to Kryv's proposal. It would give him power, but on the monster's terms, and he would be owned once again, someone's tool, the creature of a force that demanded use of his, Garth's special capabilities. Worse than being a captive in a laboratory, he would be a lackey, and a highly conspicuous lackey at that. He imagined the sniggering and sneering of the other dogs in the pack, pretending to honour his status but whispering the nickname of piggy, even magic pig, or bulbhead. His imagination took off at that. But this proposal of Kryv's, it could not be rejected on the basis of a potentially wounded pride. Think of the strength the role of lieutenant would give him. A flush of conceit made his heart race.

"Don't overthink it," came Tiny's distant voice once more. "All I want you to think about is how you detonate that grenade. Remember, when you were freed from the laboratory, you escaped from being what you described as the slave of whoever owns the voice that commands. Remember."

Everyone had hushed and across the clearing Garth became aware that all he could hear was sporadic snoring and the scratching of claws on restless legs. He had thought enough and roused himself from the blanket. There was still the display of magic that the great beast had demanded, and Garth resolved to be spontaneous, for the best magic depends on surprise.

Walking back across the clearing he had to negotiate several sleeping dogs, and he took his time to avoid them, judiciously stepping around legs and careless tails. He did not seek to have any audience at his next meeting with Kryv.

The monstrous GSD saw him approaching and climbed down from the mound of junk, stepping on his two hind legs with ease, as if it was the most natural thing for a dog. The two heads at left and right had their eyes closed, for Kryv had been dozing, but the eyes of the head in the middle were wide and expectant. Still, there was no encouraging wag from his tail.

Garth stopped in front of the extraordinary mutant, his mind still working. If he refused Kryv's proposal, he knew that it was certain he'd be killed; he was a big dog himself, but unused to fighting, and confirming his fears he glanced at the long black wicked claws of the beast before him. The thought of a fight was an irrelevance, he was sure of that. Time instead to speak.

"It is a magnificent proposition that you have put to me," said Garth, and the other two sets of Kryv's eyes snapped open. "A truly magnanimous one." He looked across all three heads and saw the slavering jaws and eager eyes. The arrogance of wickedness in those eyes was beyond dispute, they seemed to burn right through his brain as they lusted for his answer. The look of malevolence came like an assault, the fire in his head which those eyes ignited feeling like the rage he had experienced that afternoon in the laboratory, when the grey men had kept him from despatching his tormentor; the fire that was quenched when Clover had calmed him by persuading him not to behave like a human. Tiny had been there too, he remembered, and later had reminded him that *we are better than them*. It had been said with great passion; it had been Tiny's pivotal thought.

"I have reached my decision," said Garth, in his strongest confirmatory voice.

"That is indeed welcome," replied two heads in unison, without waiting for further explanation. After all, whoever

275

had refused the mighty Kryv? While the third said, in a strangely unctuous tone of apology, "I am reminded that we have been negligent, dear Garth, in giving our welcome to you. It is canine tradition, of course, to touch noses with an opportune visitor upon arrival. And we understand you have chosen to be more than a mere visitor, for who could have rejected our offer? So, before your demonstration of magic, for which the whole pack will be awakened, in order publicly to seal your eminence, of course, please approach that we may make amends for our omission."

Which nose do I touch, wondered Garth, 'and do I really want to touch any of those vile snouts?' He studied the skeins of drool that hung from the dog's jaws and felt himself shudder. *But surely this would be a small price to pay to win the preferment of this powerful beast.* Garth decided that touching one nose would be sufficient and took a step forward.

Just that much closer, the sight of Kryv's slavering fangs sparked again that memory of himself at Wickhurst, the time when he'd boiled with rage at the grey man who kept him from his tormentor. *I'd been that close to tearing him limb from limb,* remembered Garth, *and then there was Clover facing me down with her quiet sensibility.* He experienced a precipitous storm of emotion as he passed from disgust at Kryv's abominable appearance, to remembered rage, and on through tenderness when he thought of the compassionate collie.

He was but a whisker away from the middle head's muzzle when he was hit by a blast of foetid breath. 'So foul!' screamed every nerve in his own acutely tuned nose. 'So close!' His canine instinct teetered on the fulcrum of fight or

276

flee, should he run from danger, submit cravenly to a new master, or make the first strike? Garth felt the fervid blood of confusion surge through his ruined skull.

"Garth, please, we are better than them." From far, far away, Tiny repeated his plea with a sense of despair. He had his eyes shut, attempting to focus his presence within Garth's whirl of thoughts. He neither heard nor felt a response from Garth but, without warning, a pure bright white light hit the back of his eyes like a hammer, and all his senses ached from the intensely delivered blow.

For what seemed ages, Tiny was blind and deaf, aware only of tumbling uncontrollably through silent space. When he recovered sight and hearing, there was no sense at all that he was still in Garth's head. The connection had gone, and he was left with just the emptiness of black space, punctuated by unfamiliar stars, which gradually resolved into the figure of a great mastiff.

Other fiction by Graham Pryor

Preferred Lies

Origins

Justice

Kaleidoscope

His Orgy of Crime

After Brexit

Salient

Feuilletage

Stranger Than Normal

Make Hay

Pig

To Be Frank

Alba Regained

Man With A Gun

Milton Keynes UK
Ingram Content Group UK Ltd.
UKHW022233081223
434043UK00012B/542

9 781035 835140